A RARER GIFT
THAN GOLD

LUCY BRANCH

ABL PRESS LONDON

Published by ABL Press 2016
Copyright © Lucy Branch 2014
Cover illustration by BookCoverZone
Logo illustration by Florence Boyd

Third edition

This book is a work of fiction. The characters, incidents and dialogue are
drawn from the author's imagination and not to be construed as real. Any
resemblance to actual events or persons, living or dead, is fictionalised or
coincidental.

The purest silence reigned in the small, private theology library. The blunt sound of a key being turned in a well-worn lock would have been lost within the chatter of students elsewhere in the university, but not here. The echo bounced across the monastic wooden floorboards and up to circle the beams of the low barrel-vault ceiling.

Damn! The porter must have forgotten I was in here.

Trying to swallow down the alarm I felt gathering in my throat, I rose, turned and walked quickly between the walls of shelves both sides of my desk. Slipping between the rows, I passed a further five corridors of books before making it to the foyer space which was marked out by several rows of mahogany filing cabinets, some card index boxes and a large coir mat in front of an arched wooden door.

I pulled at the door, but my ears hadn't deceived me: definitely locked.

'Hello!' I shouted, banging at its dense wood. Putting my lips to the iron keyhole, and feeling the breeze tease me with its easy access in and out, I shouted again.

'Hey! HEY! This is Abi. You've locked me in! Hello, Hello! HELLO!'

Nothing. I turned and sank down onto the mat cross-legged, leaning my head against the door. Maybe, he'd just gone for a break and would be back in ten minutes. I thought longingly of my ancient phone inside my bag in the student lockers. You weren't allowed anything but a clear plastic bag to carry items in and out of here. I suppose no study area was perfect. The lack of people was precisely why I'd begged for the privilege of using this space.

Three lectures into my chemistry degree, I'd realised the terrible mistake I'd made in taking such a complex subject. Mine was a degree where lack of brain-ache meant you were definitely missing something. After a top mark of 40% in my second year exams, I reconciled myself to drastic action. Swapping gossiping in the main university library for serious study, I begged Marco, a family friend, to wangle permission for me to use this sanctuary which he'd come across when doing his PhD.

Looking around, I remembered the narrow Gothic window at the opposite end to my desk and was on my feet in a trice. I climbed up on to the sill. The alcove was six inches too small for me to stand comfortably, but there was a tiny missing panel just wider than my mouth in the stained glass image of the Virgin Mary ascending to heaven. I couldn't see clearly through the thick stained glass, but there were the shapes of people and movement of traffic below.

I shouted. One figure stopped and looked up, but he dismissed the noise. I guessed my figure was shielded behind the stained glass. Two or three more shouts and I quit, realising that a plan based on me not being able to see those outside properly, and they being unable to see me, was not really a plan at all.

The raw skin on the palms of my hands stung from the moisture of anxiety. I pulled off the long black fingerless gloves – my self-imposed uniform to hide the messy rash sprawling across the underside of my hands and spilling on to my wrists – and blew gently on the irate skin. This was the price I paid for the work that I loved – I had inherited a profession at birth which I'd grabbed with both hands.

I'd been born into a family where the heart of the house was a foundry rather than a kitchen. If people think foundry workers are little more than manual labourers, they miss the significance of what we do. Ours is a skilled craft; an affinity with metal that has been shared through several generations. My own intimacy with metals, however, came at a higher price than that of my ancestors. I was diagnosed with severe contact dermatitis, complicated by psoriasis, soon after I began toddling around our family's foundry. While stress inflamed the psoriasis, it was contact with metal that really sent my skin into a frenzy.

The irony was not lost upon me.

I pressed my hands against the cool stone wall surrounding the alcove and exerted a lot of self-control not to allow myself to scratch them against the textured surface. To distract myself, I read the titles on the shelves a few feet in front of me: *The Trinity, Truth and The Word; Transubstantiation; Transmutation Principles.*

The last one caught my attention. *Transmutation* was a word we used often in the foundry.

I leaned forwards and eased the book from its close-knit brethren. It wasn't particularly old, published in 1963, but it looked like it had endured a hard life. It was leather-bound, the shade of green of tobacco. Its corners were worn and scuffed as if it had been carried in a pocket. Its pages had picked up the indents and prints of its owner and the paper was dappled. Probably since its arrival in the library, it had dried out and become brittle.

The symbols and old prints were the first things to attract my eye, but I skipped chapters on 'Miracles' and 'The Mass'. I was beginning to lose interest when I flicked past a chapter entitled 'Alchemy' and couldn't help retracing the route of my hasty fingers. I had a fondness for this theme, which in my early years had been a favourite myth. In the cramped space, I leaned against the wall at a diagonal as I read:

IN ITS SIMPLEST FORM, alchemy is an extremely intricate process which results in the transformation of base metal into gold.

The primary stage of the process involves the making of a substance known as the Philosopher's Stone. It is this substance, dubbed 'Stone', that has the property of transmuting base metal into gold.

Base metal cannot colour or change unless it has first itself been coloured and changed. The Philosopher's Stone teaches the base metal how to change by making it pass through a palette of hues from pale brown to blood red, from red to emerald green, from green to a dazzling white, and from white to royal blue. The term Peacock's Tail has been coined for this stage. It is then up to the power of the alchemist to make the final transformation.

'GIRL! WHAT ARE YOU DOING?'

My heart clenched in shock, and I moved my foot and missed the edge of the windowsill. The other leg buckled and I fell down the ledge, striking the stone sill hard with one knee then meeting the solid wooden floor. I cried out in pain, dropped the book and rolled over, clutching my knee. With eyes screwed up as tears burst from them, I tried to speak, but the pain seemed to have stolen my voice.

'Here is a place for the Guild and only for the Guild,' he shouted.

This was no gentleman. He didn't offer to help me up. When I did open my eyes, I realised he was looming over me. Dressed in black academic robes, he was in his sixties with short crops of silver hair sprouting above his ears. Anger rippled through him and I went rigid in anticipation that he was about to boot me with his neat brogues.

'Do you know who we are? Our Guild is the earliest ever recorded. All the others come from us.'

I started to scramble. This man was mad, and I was locked in with him.

Putting one hand on a bookshelf, I pulled myself up, and as I gained height, he stooped and pushed his beaky face almost into my own. He was so close I could see his skin's large pores.

'We are the Brotherhood of the Snake!' he yelled, shaking the book in my face. To stop him gouging my eye out, I grasped hold of the book and snatched it from him.

Turning away, I gathered up my gloves and half-ran, half-limped towards my desk where my bag stood. He tracked me like a shadow, talking all the time.

'You shouldn't be here,' he hissed.

By the time I made it to my desk, the pain was less acute and my brain seemed to be de-fogging. I threw everything from the table into the plastic bag, and dropped my gloves and the little book I was still clutching into it too.

'I *am* supposed to be here. I have permission,' I said, taking a deep breath and looking him in the eye. He seemed incapable of standing outside of my personal space and I had to put a hand against his chest to stop him walking into me.

He laughed, I think. It sounded like a laugh, but at the same time like a leer.

'Permission? Then you must be *very*...special to them.'

'No,' I said, pushing hard against him.

He did the same freaky laugh and I bobbed past him, getting myself as quickly as I could to the library door. I pulled at the handle – still locked. Not wanting to look back, I shouted at the top of my voice, kicking the door with my foot.

'Open the door! I'm locked in. Help! Help!'

My heart was hammering so hard, I was beginning to feel dizzy, so when he grabbed hold of my bag and I felt my feet paddle as I staggered backwards, I thought I might be about to black out. He shoved past me and slipped from his pocket a key which he inserted into the lock.

For a dreadful minute, I thought he was about to let himself out and lock me in, but instead he turned his back to the door, blocking my way out.

'Before I let you out, who are you?' he said in a more moderate voice.

'I'm Abigail Argent, studying chemistry at the university.'

I stepped forward, opened my hand out to gesture to him to open the door. He flinched as he caught sight of the enflamed skin on my hands.

'And, and, and?'

'And nothing,' I said, moving an inch further forward.

To my surprise, the library psycho stood to one side and opened the door, and I bounded out like a greyhound who'd seen his rabbit.

'You took a book!' he shouted after me. 'Come back!'
But there was no way I was going back.

THREE-QUARTERS OF AN HOUR LATER, I had a seat on the Tube going north and was feeling a bit stupid. I shouldn't have put myself in a position where I was studying alone, and I'd been lucky that he'd only given me a fright. I didn't feel too inclined to return to the library now, despite how quiet it usually was.

I knew Marco, who'd studied there on and off for four years, would laugh when I told him about the incident, though it was still too recent to seem funny to me. He'd probably say, 'I should have warned you about Crazy Bill, Bert or Harry.'

I checked the number of stops on the Tube map before my own: lots. I dug into my bag to pull out my chemistry text book, but my fingers grazed the slender book that I'd accidentally taken during all the drama. Lifting it out again, I sought the passage I'd been reading when I was interrupted.

BASE METAL CANNOT colour or change unless it has first itself been coloured or changed.

THESE WORDS HAD special significance to me because I am a *patineur*. In the foundry, I work with bronze – colouring statues. It's a craft – half science, half art – and most people never have heard of it.

According to this extract, the Philosopher's Stone could

not only change base metal, it could also colour it. The meaning beat in my mind; the way a patineur colours a statue is to apply chemicals in various ways to a metal's surface. If the Philosopher's Stone was able to colour base metal, it must be a patination compound, though no doubt a very special one.

Excitement prickled over my skin. I re-read the extract to make sure I hadn't misunderstood. It wasn't too great a leap of imagination to consider that the birth of patination might have come about through the pursuit of alchemy. After all, there must have been hundreds of wannabe alchemists who never struck gold, but did manage to turn their base metal some pretty colours.

Even the title, *Transmutation Principles,* seemed evidence in support of my theory. Transmutation was a word we used frequently in the foundry to describe the time lapse when a metal changes from one colour into another. The flaw in the theory was that alchemy was associated with lead, and chemically speaking, lead was poor at forming colours. You needed copper content as a main component of the metal to make a rainbow of colours.

I scanned the paragraphs again. It only said 'base metal'. It didn't specify lead was the sole component. Copper was also a base metal, and was often mixed with lead.

I read on:

Prior to the development of modern physics, the material world was believed to function according to Aristotelian principles. All matter was thought to be made up of a combination of the four elements: earth, air, water and fire. It strived towards perfection. According to this belief, alchemy was not only plausible, but possible.

Gold was seen as perfect, and lead would naturally tend towards perfection under the right conditions. In today's belief system, metals cannot, and never do, behave in this way under nature's hand, and as a consequence of this, alchemy has become a myth.

There is a vast oral tradition that has survived around this myth. Numerous written descriptions of objects that once existed prove that this feat has been undertaken. The credibility of these testimonies is denied because they occurred before the birth of the modern age. This is an arrogance of our time on a grand scale.

We know that transmutation of base metal is theoretically possible. Given a large enough power source, the atomic structure of an element can be changed. The question is not 'Can it be done?' but 'How could it have been done by people with less advanced technology than our own?'

Looking back to those slighted testimonies may be our only answer. Go (Ko) Hung, an ancient Chinese alchemist, wrote '... The art can only be learned by those who are specially blessed; people who are born under suitable or unsuitable stars. Above all, belief is necessary. Disbelief brings failure...'

If we consider this wise man's words, it seems that Go Hung believed that only certain gifted people had the ability to achieve these transformations. This sentiment has been echoed countless times in the writings of acclaimed alchemists.

JRB, a reputed alchemist whose true identity still eludes history, was quoted as saying, 'Pity the gift of the alchemist, for he is blessed and cursed in equal measures.'

Is alchemy a gift or curse? Few would argue the latter. However, the last quote still substantiates the idea that it is an individual with a gift who makes the impossible possible.

The human brain, perhaps the last uncharted province of our planet, may provide the key to this unfathomable mystery. The world's most immense power source might be within us all, *though access in its entirety is denied to most. Perhaps there is good evolutionary reason for this lack of development in the majority. The strain of such a mammoth endeavour must surely reduce life span considerably, or have other detrimental side effects as suggested by JRB.*

WE WERE past East Finchley now, and heading out towards Mill Hill. I knew my dad would love these little bits of trivia. The possibility of this thread connecting our own craft to one much mightier was like discovering an ancestor had once been the Queen: it wouldn't change our lives, but it would confirm our patriotism.

2

I came through the big arch into the foundry yard. All the doors of the old stables were closed and rubbish bags were stacked by the gate. These were familiar signs that everyone had finished for the evening. The house and foundry looked artistic in the amber sun which was readying itself to go down. Mum had refilled all the window boxes outside each stable with bright summer flowers, and the water troughs were deep in herbs.

Seeing it so tidy and tranquil, I couldn't help but reflect on the huge changes the place had undergone over the years. My parents had bought the old inn during the eighties when dilapidated old wrecks on the fringe of London were much less desirable than they are today. Photographs of the two of them standing in respective piles of rubble with tools in their hands and shell-shocked looks on their faces hung above the huge fireplace in the sitting room, a testimony to iron wills and no survey.

Their concept had been simple: they would rent work-space cheaply to other craftsmen. Larry, a patternmaker, and Richard, a mould-maker, who had both worked with my parents previously, had come first. Within two years, skilled friends of Larry's had moved in. One was a welder and wrought iron man, the other a sheet metal worker.

Twenty-five years later, every inch of the coach house and stables had been let. At his leisure, my father had cleared out and mended two big barns and three stone outbuildings which were now also all full. There was a stained-glass specialist, sign maker, gold leaf expert, a painting restorer, a toolmaker, a stonemason, a woodcarver, a carpenter, a glass caster and blower, sculptors, and painters to name just a few.

Several of the apprentices were chewing over their day beneath the mature horse chestnut tree which was the nucleus of the stable yard. I cut past the group and went inside to Dad's barn. As proprietor, he had taken one whole barn for himself. It had the luxury of a high ceiling and no-one else to hog his workspace.

My dad stood at the foot of a giant contemporary sculpture more than four metres high which looked like a hybrid between a woodland fungus and a tree. Its trunk was broad and bulbous. The higher it rose, the more billowing frill shapes in dramatic curves were layered one upon the other. Brushes, paste pots and rag were discarded about him, along with his blowtorch. There were half a dozen pots of chemicals on the floor and the scissor lift he used was parked at a tangent. He had his hands pressed against the surface of the statue and his head dropped down between them.

'What's up, Dad?' I said, taking in his weary stance.

He turned around in surprise and raised a hand in greeting. He pulled a black band from his wrist and tied back his longish salt-and-pepper hair which was a nod to his biker days. Exhaling heavily, he turned back to the bronze, stroking the surface.

'She doesn't like me. I've tried to be nice, but she just doesn't like me,' he said and shook his head. 'I know you are studying for finals, but I think I need a hand.'

'What about Ted?'

Dad pulled a face. 'If I can't get the colour, that daft sod won't manage it.' There was a chord of injured pride in his voice.

Although the application of substances to a metal surface sounds like basic chemistry, even the most educated chemists may not be able to form a simple green patina. The art of our craft is in the application, and two people do not necessarily produce the same colours, even out of the same chemicals. Some people can't produce any colour at all.

Being good at patination is like being good with animals: it's instinctual. Bronze can take as much petting, tickling, and sometimes bullying to produce a colour as any collie needs to make it behave. Unlike paint, a the colour arises out of a chemical reaction rather than existing as a shade in its own right. The precise hue achieved is not entirely in the hands of the patineur, but is also influenced by the environment, and the type of bronze which is being worked upon.

I walked over to the statue, dropped my bags and stripped off my gloves, and spread my hands over the skin of the sculpture. I loved my craft because it appealed to my sense of touch. To me, words were an impoverished way of understanding the world. The sensation of different materials under the fingertips was far richer. The first time I touched a piece of bronze, I felt like the ocean had washed right over me. The invigoration of cold salt water and the pulse of the waves were in that first meeting. I remember removing my hand, and smiling at the thought that I had found this whole world of wonderfulness.

'What colour are we aiming for?'

Dad passed me a photograph of another sculpture by the artist. The colour was autumnal – a warm brown in some places, lighter in others with an orangey undertone.

'What colour are you getting?' I enquired.

'Between mud and bog.' He raised his eyebrows in frustration.

'Go get a cup of coffee, talk to Mum. Let me make friends with her and see what I can do.'

I turned to pick up some copper wool that was on the floor, and with the speed of a snake, Dad caught my wrist. Firmly but gently, he turned my hand over, palm side up. We both stared at the mess where my skin should have been.

'Just as I thought, worse than usual,' he said, letting go. 'Do you even use that cream the doctor gives you?'

'Doesn't work.' I rubbed my hands hard on my jeans – I always needed to scratch more after I'd looked at them.

'You should let the air get to them more often,' he tutted.

'Do you want my help, or not?' I pointed to the door. 'Go!'

He shrugged and I watched him leave the barn. He slid his heavy steel toe-capped boots across the rutty floor with his hands deep in his pockets, shoulders round – the walk of a teenager going on fifty-five.

I realised I hadn't told him about what I'd read in the little green book. There would be time later. I cleaned off a large patch of surface, then began the repetition of warming the pink metal with a blowtorch using a low arc, and applying the chemicals mixed carefully by my dad. When I brush a piece of metal, my arm traces the same line as those of my ancestors: a ritual that that binds us.

As I worked, the tension of looming exams and equations that I didn't understand drained from me and I lost myself. All I could see was the colour I was trying to create; the warmth of the tone I wanted; the subtlety of its shade. When it came, the feeling was one of déjà-vu rather than surprise.

'Mum says dinner's ready.' I turned to see my dad standing in the barn doorway. 'You got it,' he said, voice ebbing with admiration which then morphed into irritation. 'How did you get it? I've messed around with it for two bloody days and...'

He swallowed the remainder of the sentence.

'And, you are better than me?' I finished.

He walked over to examine the colour more closely. 'Well, I used to be,' he said.

I WORKED LATE into the night to help Dad get the broad surfaces of the sculpture coloured. When I'd finally fallen into bed in the eaves of the farmhouse, I'd dropped into a dead sleep for a couple of hours, but by 2am, I was wide awake again.

My hands were throbbing, as they often did after intense work. First the irate skin became unbearably hot, before tiny white swellings formed like buried mines. When they were touched, terrible explosions of itching went off in tandem, driving me half-insane.

Every doctor I'd ever met asked me the same question: 'Why don't you wear gloves when working?' They didn't understand when I explained that the metal just wouldn't respond when I did. Secretly, I wondered if it could be my affliction that enabled me to feel the heartbeat in a piece of metal where others could not.

It was no good battling sleep; it would come when it was least convenient – it always did. I switched on the light and slathered the best part of a tube of steroid cream on to my skin, though my expectation of it soothing me back to sleep was almost nil. I thought about going down to the kitchen to find ice, but getting out of bed seemed too big an ask when my body was so tired.

Trying not to scratch, I retrieved the little theology book from my desk and delved back into the chapter on alchemy. There were three bizarre prints drawn by the same hand, their style flat and medieval: a bat-winged two-headed female; a crown clutching snakes and chalices; a naked couple having sex trapped in a glass bottle. The fourth image was entirely different in style and was initialled JRB. He had been quoted earlier as the most contemporary alchemist known to date.

I looked carefully at his drawing. It was the hand of a Renaissance artist, well-disciplined and trained in perspective. He had drawn a magnificent oak tree set in woodland with several exotic wild animals prowling around. The tree was shedding its leaves, and as they fell, words could clearly be seen written on their surfaces.

I read them in sequence:

...*GOLD IS the king with the common touch,*
　　Lead is the child that wants to be much,
　　Gold is the man that he may be,
　　The Philosopher's Stone is found in he...

USUALLY, the meaning of riddles hung tantalisingly outside of my understanding. They teased me towards insanity, but the substance of this one yielded straight away.

The Philosopher's Stone was made from lead. My assumption had been that the metal and the special properties of the Philosopher's Stone were quite separate. Here was an entirely different suggestion: the lead's own qualities were said to be the foundation of the Philosopher's Stone.

Sitting in the almost-dark, I arrived at the glorious conclusion that it was all coming back to patination. The Philosopher's Stone helped to transform base metal into gold via a process akin to patination, but I had assumed the Philosopher's Stone was a series of chemicals. Actually, this was saying that it was the resulting colours that were the Philosopher's Stone, because they were made out of the metal itself.

It might have been that under the strain of exams, my brain was desperate to find a distraction, and this little book served that need. Whatever it was, I was completely reeled in. All I knew was that making tenuous links in a trail that had gone cold thousands of years ago was infinitely more soothing than the steroid cream for my hands as it lulled me back to sleep much faster.

IT WAS impossible to sleep later than 7am in our house because, without fail, half the foundry trooped into our kitchen before work each day to have a cup of tea, and chew over whichever project currently had their attention. The kitchen rang with chatter and was better than any alarm clock.

Making my way downstairs, I eyed the horde with

hostile eyes. I couldn't comprehend how my mum could be so endlessly hospitable and never begrudge the mess or the noise. Our private space never seemed to be *private*. The shortened sleep and looming exams were making me more irritable than usual – I wanted to shout at everyone, '*Get out!*'

I needed to use Mum's computer, which she had shoe-horned into a corner at the far end of the kitchen. Kicking out from under the desk a dozen pairs of shoes, two rasps, and some AI-sized drawings for a job which had come and gone long ago, I wedged myself on to the stool and looked up warily at the bookshelves above my head. They were crammed with tattered cookbooks, old telephone directories, and romance novels. The shelves bowed under their weight, and I wondered *when* as opposed to *if* they would fall.

Behind me, I could hear someone telling a foundry-tale. 'So Nick's on his arse and there's all this sawdust floating about him in a cloud-like, and he turns to me and says...'

I tried to screen it out. Mum's PC was slow. As the emails downloaded one-by-one, I wished for the millionth time for my exams to be done with so that I could concentrate on getting some momentum behind the next stage of my life. I wanted to travel – circumnavigate a world that was outside of our claustrophobic foundry with its gossip, politics and people I'd known for ever. I would miss the work, though. In my dream-life, I travelled the world working as a freelance patineur for the best contemporary sculptors of our genera-tion. The idea of being a nomad with few possessions and nothing to tie me appealed immensely, probably because it was the precise opposite of the life I was living here.

We'd never travelled much as a family when I'd been younger. I hadn't really noticed at the time, but important projects at the foundry tethered us, and they always seemed to fall during the school holidays. As soon as I was old enough to go on holiday with friends, I loved it, but the short holiday hops were never enough. I wanted to go to places and stay there until we were done with each other.

I was so busy musing over my dreams that I nearly missed the email marked *Enquiry/Urgent*.

DEAR MISS ARGENT,

Recently, I met the sculptress Charlotte Taylor. We discussed your involvement in her recent project. She holds you in very high regard and spoke most enthusiastically of your skills. I would like to offer you a position on a project that is currently under my care in Venice. It will be for approximately three months, and you would be working on some bronze features in a chapel. It is a privately funded project and the remuneration will be generous.

I look forward to hearing from you,
Pierro Ricco

I READ it over three times to believe it. My heart started to pace. Had I willed it into existence? Had I fallen asleep and was having my favourite dream? I wanted to kiss Charlotte Taylor.

I jumped to my feet, bumping into my dad who had been reading over my shoulder. Privacy was something he claimed never to have heard of.

'Easy,' he said like he was talking to a horse. The top third of the mug of tea he was carrying slopped onto the floor. Passing me the remainder with a bacon sandwich, he gestured for me to sit. 'Who is this Pierro Ricco?'

'Never heard of him – sounds like my fairy godfather to me.'

Dad made a non-committal noise.

I took an excited slurp of tea, and balancing the plate on my knee, I bit into the sandwich.

'You're keen to go then?' I heard the hint of reproach in his voice. 'It might perk you up, I suppose. If you were a bronze, I'd say your colours were jaded.' He tilted his head.

I understood him perfectly: a jaded bronze produced colours with a slightly tired, greyish hue. The strain of studying such a complex subject had worn me out, along with working most weekends in the foundry. I'd been taking any extra shifts on top of my studies to build up my savings, which I planned on investing in plane tickets.

'You know, your real godfather, Terry, lives out there. He could keep an eye on you – might even put you up.'

I hadn't seen Terry in a long time, but he'd been my dad's great friend in his youth.

'Italy is grand. I was there with your mother for a few years after we got married. We could have stayed out there for ever. There was so much work; the whole country is dressed with sculpture. *You* will love it.'

'Perfect!' I sighed with satisfaction. My mind was already in a gondola, sailing down the Grand Canal.

'Sounds like the job is more restoration than patination, mind you,' Dad added.

My boat sank instantly.

'Will that matter? I'm not a restorer. Oh no! Do you think he doesn't know the difference? He'll withdraw the offer.'

Dad laughed at my horror. 'Go talk to Frank. He's a conservator.'

'Of marble!' I shouted, half-standing, making the plate clatter to the floor. Dad threw a look in my mother's direction. The hubbub in the kitchen had masked the noise and saved us both a sharp Irish rebuke.

'He'll give you some pointers – steer you in the right direction – stuff to read and the like. If it's bronze related, I'm sure you're up to the challenge, but I'd be clear about what you are and are not at this stage. It would be worse to get there and be disappointed.'

I nodded, taking in his sage words, and emailed back immediately.

WHEN I SHOULD HAVE BEEN FOCUSING on cramming, I found myself haunting markets – Portobello Road, Brick Lane, Roman Road and Camden – for second hand esoteric books.

The night before my final exam, I was sitting top to tail with my mum on the kind of sofa which threatens to swallow you between its flabby cushions. We had no overhead lights in the living room – it was all mismatched lamps. Its focal point was an inglenook fireplace with a lintel so skew that Dad always joked that he'd bought the house because it made him feel better about his own craftsmanship. A small fire burned in the grate.

Mum was reading a novel, and I was enjoying some grand escapism by perusing another little gem I'd found on a book stall that day. My excitement about my new find kept bubbling over and I couldn't stop fidgeting, much to my mother's annoyance. It was the diary of a priest called Father Stephen who had lived in Verona at the Church of St Joseph in the middle of the nineteenth century.

It read:

GOD WHO SEES all is witness to the miserable plight that I am suffering under. I am certain Father Francis is exploring the dark arts again. He has wrought such frightful havoc on myself and fellow brothers with his foul smelling smoke that seeps through our walls each night. He says he is doing nothing untoward, but I fear his abhorrent interest is slowly taking possession of him. He wears the smell of burning like a cloak.

When I challenged him about his attempts to learn the secret art of alchemy, he laughed. He dared to justify his abominable behaviour by using our own sacred doctrine, claiming it is the right of every Catholic priest to explore transfiguration.

I demanded he recant such a blasphemous statement, yet he replied with great audacity that I understood little of our faith. He continued to argue, citing the changing of our wine and bread into the blood and body of our Lord during the mass as a form of alchemy. He spoke of our Lord's Transfiguration from corporeal body to light upon the mountain as a form of alchemy.

As God tolerates all the different languages in the world, so also should I tolerate and trust my brother, and yet God, who knows our secret thoughts and the purity of our principles, will see that I believe his actions and words are those of Satan.

ANOTHER ENTRY a few weeks later continued:

FATHER FRANCIS EXITED his rooms as I was progressing to vespers this evening. His face was the colour of coal, his eyes red-rimmed and his pupils were wide. In that instant, I considered if he were a man possessed.

I demanded to be given admittance to his room, and seizing the advantage, pushed past him before he could deny me. Inside, there were earthenware pots clad with soot stacked up and toppled over on a gnarled table. His room appeared as the enclave of a whore rather than a priest. The air was very warm, but heavily tainted by the fumes of lime, which caught in my throat like they were trying to strangle me and made my eyes water.

I told him the time had come for our Abbot to know about his iniquitous work, but he laughed. It was his eyes, particularly, that scared me. I descended, in some haste, to seek the advice of Father Keeble whom I have shared my grievances with on occasion. He was hearing confession, but I felt this circumstance to be of such importance that disturbing him would be permissible.

He accompanied me to that sinful room. The fire was blazing like hell itself. Francis was nowhere to be seen, but upon the windowsill stood a large black crow, watching us. I swear before my divine creator that crow looked at us both with those terrifying eyes that minutes before I had witnessed.

'It is done,' I whispered to Father Keeble...

THE REMAINDER of the diary was filled with little details about Father Stephen's daily life: the insufferable heat in summer, the agony of kneeling in prayer, and the trials of fasting. Nowhere else did he mention Father Francis, and in no other extract was he so animated. I wondered if the loss of his nemesis had made life better for him, but something in the writing told me he had enjoyed being part of this little monastic drama.

I wrote out the two extracts about the suspected alchemist Father Francis along with other snippets of information I'd found, trying to put together a picture of the alchemical process, but I was coming to the conclusion that fog was more transparent. Father Stephen obviously hadn't any knowledge of the process himself, but for that reason, he was a more credible witness. Accounts by so-called alchemists seemed to speak in tongues: *'Mix three drops of dragon's blood with two tears of a virgin...'* or something equally cryptic. I had no illusions that I might break their codes; I was neither that clever nor that dedicated. Trying to understand the lyrical style of the symbolism would lead me to years of wading through deep words. A quagmire of metaphors was something I was going to have to try and work my way around.

This insight into the priest's world was a broader view of alchemy. It was not just about the transmutation of metal, but about the power to change matter from one thing to another. Father Francis saw it as the same power that was demonstrated in the transubstantiation of wine and bread during mass, or the changing of human form into light. He evidently believed that this power could be developed. The training a priest gained through his vocation must be an important part of it.

My mother stretched and closed the book, giving it a small hug. She turned her eyes upon me, reached forward and squeezed my hand. She was distinctive even now, and I admired her looks. Back in her youth, she had been Miss Ireland in the days when Miss World competitions were popular. She was almost stereotypically Irish in her look with shoulder length red hair which fell in gentle waves, her skin was slightly freckled. My brothers and I always joked that my parents had identical heights and hairstyles.

Unfortunately, I didn't take after her. I was medium height and my hair was dark, my skin tone creamier than hers. My father claimed to have Spanish heritage, though it wasn't apparent to look at him, and the consensus was that I hailed from that blood.

'Do you really want to go to Italy?' my mum asked.

I nodded.

'Don't you want to patch things up with Freddie?' Her voice wavered.

She hadn't asked me not to go to Venice, but now I knew she really didn't want me to. She despised my ex-boyfriend. In the year that Freddie and I had gone out, our relationship had been stormy, but his relationship with my mother had been like a series of tornadoes that rocked the house. It seemed Freddie, quite unintentionally, had opposing views on every subject my mother held dear, and neither could be wrong.

I smiled and squeezed her hand back. 'Love you too, Mum.'

'Your dad called Terry. He says, "Of course you can stay with him, and that if you don't, you're not to darken his door." Terry has reassured your dad that this Pierro Ricco isn't some maniac murderer. In fact, Terry knows him quite well – he's a patron of his, apparently. Oh, and the last thing I need to tell you is that Dan heard you were going away and left you a present. It's on the table in the hall.'

I was surprised. Dan had been training as a sculptor in the years before I'd gone to university. We had been good friends, even flirting with each other a little. I couldn't contain my curiosity so I slipped out to the hall as Mum switched off the lights for the night.

There was a small wrapped parcel in the shape of an egg. Inside was a greyish piece of stone, very smooth with a strange swirling pattern throughout it.

There was also a small note:

THIS IS *for your kit box. It's a piece of Greek limestone from a commission I have. It's very strange stuff. Your father tried using a piece, instead of the usual pumice, to prepare a bronze, and it did the most incredible job. It's a silly parting gift really, but I know how you like oddities.*

Good luck, Dan

PS I've crumbled more than I've carved so far!

THIS WAS SWEET OF DAN. My toolbox had become legend in the foundry. It was so enormous, it required its own wheels. I liked to be prepared and kept a little bit of everything in it.

I went to bed thinking about the Greek limestone instead of my exam, which was probably why I got a good night's sleep.

3

I stepped from the station and was kissed on the lips by Venice. I immediately felt befriended by the way the buildings along the water all faced one way, as if they were lined up to greet new visitors and welcome old friends.

As I travelled on the *traghetto* to reach my address, one of my first impressions was how feminine the city looked. The colours of the stones were soft, the bridges white and the water silvery. Never had I seen such dainty architecture.

I arrived at the Giudecca where I was to live with Terry, my godfather. He opened his door which had once been blue. This was only evident by the remainder of a few determined flakes.

'Abigail?' He seemed unsure. 'You have grown up. Last time I saw you, you were...rounder. We'll have to feed you up.'

I smiled. Terry was one of those rounder people, who believed anyone thinner than him was grossly undernourished. He would spend the next few months following me around the apartment with spoons full of delicious sauces –

he wasn't satisfied unless he tempted me to have a third bowl of pasta.

As he beckoned me in and took my bag, Terry reminded me of my father. He had the familiar rogue air of an East End boy, and spoke with a slight twang from his past. He had surprised all his friends in his youth by becoming an artist when a professional boxing career was on the horizon. His large frame still marked him out as a heavyweight, but his graceful movements hinted at the artist inside.

He had settled in Venice unexpectedly. Visiting the city on some skulduggery or other, he had never left. The closet artist in him had burst forth. Venice is such an inspiring city that I can imagine it prompts transformations of this variety all the time. Within a matter of months, he was selling his own paintings. Now, Mum referred to the two paintings of his that hung on my parents' walls as their pension.

Life was no struggle for Terry now. An exhibition in Rome, three years after he had arrived in Italy, had thrown him in the road of some wealthy patrons. Their loyalty and praise had ensured that Terry's unpretentious talent had become very popular. His flat on the Giudecca was Venice's premier social spot. Waves of interesting people seemed to be swept in and out with the tides.

The flat was as dichotomous as the man himself. The largest room looked on to the water with big, wide windows. This was his art studio. It was painted white, and had old wooden floorboards which had been sanded many moons ago. Over-enthusiastic plants were the only ornaments, apart from numerous art materials stacked up on tables and the odd shelf. There was a divan in the centre of the room, where the absence of a model made it look lonely.

The room that greeted me as I came up the steps was all sofas and coffee tables. The sofas were laid out in a circle which roughly echoed the shape of the room. The coffee tables were placed between each seat with enough space left for an entrance or exit. Although this arrangement originally struck me as odd, I soon understood it as I became accustomed to Terry's habits. This room made him Arthur in a modern day Camelot.

All around the walls were Terry's paintings. Many were studies of Thérèse, his wife; others were scenes of city life, particularly in London. There was a certain touch of Lowry in his works. He painted everyday events – a working man enjoying a cigarette; a newspaper seller yelling the headlines – and yet there was melancholia about these scenes which was detectable only in their compositions. The buildings were hunched over as if with fatigue. The skies were moody. There was a realism about the scenes which was so accurate, it amazed me that someone could be so articulate.

The room I liked most led from the studio and was called a library. There were bookcases on every wall, and more surprisingly, at least three single beds built into the bookcases. Turkish style silks were splashed over each bed inviting comfort and the promise of exotic dreams.

'You can take whichever bed you like, honey,' said a soft American voice from behind us.

I turned to see an African-American waif in the doorway whom I recognised from Terry's works. She was undoubtedly one of the most beautiful women I had ever seen. She moved forward with perfect deportment that whispered of her classical ballet training and introduced herself properly, kissing me on both cheeks.

Terry's eyes lit up when she looked at him, and he reached out to her as if to reassure himself that she was real and not some vision. He was such a big man that she looked fragile beside him.

'Terry and Thérèse – well, I'm not going to forget that.' I laughed at them.

'Aren't we too cute?' she said, slipping an arm round Terry's ample girth.

'She's my muse,' said Terry, giving her a squeeze.

'Must be nice to be someone's muse.' I smiled at her; she nodded and smiled back.

'Let me make you some coffee,' she said in her anglicised American accent. 'You must be exhausted from travelling overnight on those awful trains.' She said the word awful like waffle, and I couldn't resist running her version over my tongue.

'It was awful,' I said.

Thérèse beckoned me to follow her to the kitchen, and Terry left us alone to get acquainted. She was indeed Terry's muse; she was the key subject in most of his paintings, and I'm sure that Terry's success was much to do with Thérèse's exceptional look. Although the essence of beauty is very hard to define, part of her uniqueness was in the shades of her colouring. Her hair was long and just a few shades darker than her skin; her skin was glossy and just a few shades darker than her eyes; and her eyes were so rich they looked like they'd been mixed up with cocoa powder and a daub of thick clotted cream.

'You cannot have been to Venice before or you would have stopped by,' she said as she set coffee, creamy milk and fancy-looking almond biscuits on the table before us.

I took up my black coffee and slipped a biscuit from the plate.

'No, this is my first time, and already I love it.'

I lifted my eyes to heaven and noticed Thérèse refrained from tasting her biscuit.

'Terry says he hasn't seen you in years?' she said.

'Oh, ten years at least, feels like for ever. It'll be nice to get a chance to know him properly,' I said.

Thérèse had to be in her mid-thirties by my calculation, but really she looked much younger.

'Are you still modelling?' I enquired, nicking another biscuit. My faulty memory was working overtime to dredge up information about Thérèse which my parents had mentioned over the years.

'I do bits and pieces, but I write plays mainly.' A doorbell rang and Thérèse stood up. 'And model for him. That will be Terry's students – he teaches kids from the university a couple of afternoons each week. I usually sit for them. You don't mind if I go, do you? You could join them, if you want; Terry won't mind.'

I thanked her and shook my head. She left me to the company of the old kitchen. I finished my coffee and went to get my purse, desperate to see more of the city.

THE NEXT DAY, Terry took me to see the small church close to the Friary that was to be my project during the next few months. Although I'd insisted I could manage without a chaperone, he was sure that without him, I would be searching Venice's labyrinthine streets until Doomsday.

The walk there was full of wonder and frustration: the architecture along the route had me longing to stop and admire, but Terry was set on sustaining our pace. I satisfied myself with promises that on my return, I would enjoy the buildings at my leisure, but the further we went, the more I realised my stupidity in assuming I'd ever find the same path back again.

I enjoyed flitting up and down the steps of the twee

bridges and blushed at the young men chiming, '*Ciao, Bella,*' with admiring smiles.

Terry laughed. 'You'll get used to it, and probably not even allow yourself to enjoy the compliment in a few days' time. My advice is lap it up. Most women never know how beautiful they are. Italian men have their faults, but they do recognise beauty in its many guises.'

We entered a dark interior of a chapel known as The Church of Our Lady. Scaffold took up most of the floor space as the high ceiling was being restored, and I could just about make out a few people working high up on the ornate paintings.

Terry took me towards a group standing by the marble altar. They were speaking in rapid Italian. A balding man of medium build turned from the conversation and gripped Terry's hand like a brother as they kissed on both cheeks. He had the sun-ripened look that is common to both Mediterranean fruits and older Italian people.

Terry introduced me to Stefano who was to be my boss for the next three months. Stefano smiled at me, and his eyes fell to my hands, seeking the un-manicured nails of a real craftsman. My gloves seemed to disappoint him.

'Your father and I crossed paths when he worked on some statues in the Vatican many years ago. It was a strange experience, the Vatican – huge place, full of secrets.' He turned back to Terry. 'How is your beautiful wife, Thérèse?' he enquired.

Terry began to reply, but Stefano's mind worked quicker than Terry's mouth. He was already on to a new topic before returning his attention to me.

'I hope you are as good as your father was because you will be working alone. Marcello, the man who usually does my bronze, is so busy these days.'

Stefano raised his eyes and shoulders to heaven. He sighed deeply as if God was vexing him through Marcello.

'What you mean is you didn't want to pay two people, you miserly Italian.'

Terry gave Stefano an unexpected dig in his paunch. Stefano looked up again as if God was taking things too far this time.

Ducking in and around scaffold poles, I was taken on a tour of the church. It was very ornate and filled to the brim with sculptures, paintings and ornamental features. The result was a cluttered and eclectic feel to the place. The varnish on the paintings had discoloured, and the candles lit beneath them had sent up rockets of soot to shadow them.

The bronze sculptures were thick with dust and oily grime. Also, they were laden with thick layers of boot polish, and as a consequence their patina was not visible at all. I took a careful look at my first job, which was to be the restoration of the large bronze entrance doors. A fine series of religious friezes decorated the doors in the classical style. Unfortunately, their beauty was virtually undetectable due to the thick layer of corrosion and grime that smothered the images.

As I stared at them, seeing the stages that they would go through in my mind's eye, a man pushed the doors open. He was strikingly handsome: lean and fit. I took in his dark hair and defined features, as Stefano came hurrying over with Terry following.

'Ah, how fortunate we are to have a visit from the Head of Venice's Culture and Heritage Department,' Stefano said, smiling broadly and shaking the man's hand with gusto.

I was surprised. The newcomer wore the expensive clothes of a merchant banker. In England, at least, heritage roles tended to be taken by a less glamorous and more academic breed.

'Ciao, Terry, how nice to see you *here*,' he said with a slight question mark in his voice as he clasped Terry's hand.

'I am *here* with Abigail. She is my goddaughter and staying with me while working on your project.'

The man turned his eyes on me for the first time, and paused a beat while he took me in. 'Abigail, how nice to finally meet you. We are very fortunate to have secured your skills for the project,' he said, extending his hand.

I looked up into his intense blue eyes. 'Pierro Ricco?' I said, not entirely certain. He inclined his head in acknowledgment and gave a reserved smile.

Nerves sprouted from nowhere and seemed to lodge in my throat. Stefano, Terry and Pierro looked at me expectantly. Pierro even raised his eyebrows.

'I hope...I can...do justice to...this opportunity,' I panted.

This was not the impression I'd hoped I'd make. At home, it was true that I rarely dealt with clients – always leaving that to my dad. I was more the one behind-the-scenes, but I hadn't been nervous with Stefano.

Pierro's smile switched off, and he turned away to talk in Italian to Stefano. I could only presume he was asking whether they could secure the services of someone else with the power of speech.

I mouthed to Terry, 'Oh no!'

Terry rubbed his mouth to hide his smile. 'Pierro, we are going to move outside to look at the doors. Will you join us?' he said, presenting his arm towards the doors to encourage him.

I silently thanked Terry as our group moved outside. I had to be professional this time.

We all stared at the bronze friezes, trying to identify the

subject of the scenes. The corrosion was so disfiguring, we could hardly make out the delicately sculpted lines.

'They are, perhaps, the finest works belonging to the chapel,' Pierro observed.

He had a good eye. People seldom gave credit to the beauty of architectural features in the same way as more obvious beauties such as paintings or sculptures. Though caked in corrosion, these doors were particularly fine. I wondered what his expertise was – perhaps he was an architect?

'What would you suggest we do here?' Pierro asked.

I didn't dare to look at him, but stared hard at the doors instead, and they didn't steal my voice. I explained the cathartic process of restoration which I had been swatting up on since the job offer. It would involve the slow removal of the hard coat of corrosion that had been building on the doors while the lives of Venetians had been unfolding for generations. I would go on to repatinate the surface of the metal, returning it to the mature, dark colour of an antique coin.

Stefano let out a loud exhalation and looked relieved.

Pierro said, 'Yes, but aren't these green shades original?'

I shook my head. 'The doors were originally dark brown, bronze. You can see the original colour here.' I beckoned for them to come back inside and see the interior sides of the doors. These had been protected from the salty air and rain, and many areas were still a traditional bronze colour. 'I wouldn't remove the corrosion if we could still see the scenes, but the corrosion is preventing us understanding them.'

I met Pierro's eyes and I could see his mind ticking, although he allowed no clue of his conclusions to trespass over his expression. Then he gave me a curt nod that said *dismissed*.

He moved further inside the church with Stefano at his heels. My eyes followed him. In my head, he'd been different: warmer; less slick; less...sexy. I'd assumed he might take a particular interest in me as he'd brought me into the project, but that didn't seem likely.

Terry followed my gaze. 'That one ain't for you,' he said.

I blustered. 'I wasn't even thinking that.'

'He's too powerful by half,' he said, shaking his head.

4

I t was about my fourth weekend in Venice when I set out for fair Verona. I told Thérèse I intended to see as much of Italy as I could during my weekends off. She took great pains to go through my guidebook and highlight what was and wasn't worth seeing.

Sitting on the train at the beginning of the journey, rubbing the palms of my hands together to squash the itching, I tried to plan out my weekend. I would spend Saturday sightseeing, and then on Sunday I would call into The Church of Saint Joseph before I went home. This was where Father Francis had smoked out the residents of the monastery.

I hadn't had any time to give over to alchemy since I'd arrived in Venice. In retrospect, I acknowledged that the topic had become a minor obsession back in England, but I had it much more under control now. I read my guidebook dutifully on the train, keen to be organised about all I should see.

By the time I was out of the station, all thoughts of sightseeing had vanished. I found myself marching down streets, without a glance left or right at the charming city, desperate to find The Church of Saint Joseph.

The Church was an old and unassuming building. It was very unlike the chapel I was working on in Venice, which certainly had delusions of grandeur. I took a moment outside studying the grey-black walls of the church. They were mottled with dirt, and I was horrified that the bronze doors had been painted at some time.

My phone beeped just as I was about to go inside. It was a text from Dad:

TERRY SAYS you've settled well. Just spoke to Charlotte Taylor – was a bit blank when I thanked her for recommending you. Mum says ET, phone home.

I TEXTED a few promises back and hurried into the dark nave. It was hatched by tunnels of light streaming in from the windows. A priest, who was standing close to the altar, must have seen me squinting through the Caravaggio-esque light. He came to see if I needed help. I began a jumbled sentence in terrible Italian.

'I'm Irish,' he said. The relief written on my face made him laugh. He put out a hand to shake. 'I'm Father Christopher.' He was a tall, elderly gentleman with the purest of white hair. His face expressed a lifetime of goodness and giving; his reward seemed to be a lack of wrinkles. 'What can I do for you?'

He peered intently into my face, and I felt sure he was reading my sins.

'Well, I'm interested in the history of this church. In particular, I want to know about some internal affairs in the nineteenth century. I believe a priest called Father Francis who...'

I faltered, wondering how to phrase the next sentence.

'Who might have been an alchemist.'

Father Christopher smiled kindly, but I detected a shadow of disappointment in his face. He must have hoped I had more spiritual thoughts in my head.

'You mean the Crowman, don't you? It's just a local legend: a story about a priest becoming a crow. I wouldn't be surprised if it wasn't a ploy to get more people into mass. Nothing draws a crowd like a piece of gossip about the clergy, even these days. I don't believe a word of it myself. I wouldn't take it too seriously, young lady. I hope you haven't come all the way to Verona for an old crow.'

He patted my arm gently and half turned away as if to go back to his chores. I reached out to slow him.

'I'm quite interested in the story. Do you know anything more about it?' I asked.

He signalled me to walk with him.

'Well, supposedly, he sought the secrets of transmutation which was frowned upon by the church, of course. If you know anything about Catholicism, you might think that odd because transmutation is the act of changing form and is not so very different from the concept of transubstantiation. The latter is central to our faith and describes the transformation, during the mass, of wine into the blood of Christ and the wafer into the body. You would think that such studies might have been permissible, but even I must admit that Catholicism is full of contradictions. At one time or other, it probably was condoned, but after The Reformation, everything tightened up.' He shrugged. 'Anyhow, the way it was seen was that he was practising black magic, and in league with the devil.'

'Is there any record of his work?' I asked.

'Now, why would someone want to know that?' He stopped and tilted his head on one side. I could see the sides of his mouth turning up slightly in amusement. 'I think it might be time for confession. Are you Catholic?'

I nodded.

'Good, then you can tell me all about it. God can forgive you, and then we can go and look.'

FATHER CHRISTOPHER OPENED a door into what looked like a long tunnel. This had once been a narrow pantry with stone floors and a low arched ceiling. There were no windows so the light was poor, with only a single bulb, deathly pale, hanging from a strand in the ceiling.

I spent the rest of that day looking at all kinds of unpublished works, essays, examinations and dissertations written by those who had trained in the monastery. Chains of words rattled past my eyes until I began to find it difficult to focus, and the logical part of me ridiculed my fantastical optimism that something of Father Francis's might have survived. After several hours, I knew I wouldn't find it there. Although there was no index, there were consecutive numbers on most things and the dissertations were alphabetised. It seemed unlikely that someone would have stashed a random notebook or manuscript in among them.

Father Christopher was more optimistic and would not allow my weariness to crush my aspirations too early. He offered me a bed in the retreat quarters and an opportunity to look further the next day. The prospect of not having to find a hotel when I felt so tired was enough to encourage me to fight another day.

I SLEPT DEEPLY in the quiet room and woke early. My window looked out on to a pretty garden which was divided between flowers, vegetables and a large greenhouse. I was surprised to see two priests already hard at work in the garden; one was digging deep and turning the soil over, while the other was moving rapidly to and fro between small outbuildings.

A loud bell interrupted my nosey on-looking, and I watched as the men in the garden wiped their hands on aprons and walked in towards the church.

After breakfast, Father Christopher touched my arm.

'I've another idea where the books could be.'

I followed him through the vestry and out to the main altar. Father bowed as we passed before the altar, then made towards a set of stone steps that were closed off behind wrought iron railings. He opened them with a key of generous proportions, and we descended down into the vaults beneath the church.

A long corridor with a low stone ceiling was lit by torches. It was cold and a little too dim. I kept as close to Father Christopher as I could. Arched doorways left and right opened into dark vaults where the flickering torchlight skirted round the lines of stone tombs. Our footsteps echoed in the vaults like they were teasing the dead by knocking on their coffins.

Father Christopher looked over his shoulder and winked at me.

'You Okay?'

'Put it like this, Father, nothing on earth would make me come down here alone.' I laughed a little breathlessly. 'How come there is no electricity? And, who lit the torches?'

'You sound like you're afraid of the dark?' He raised his eyebrows.

'Well, if you live in London, you come to realise that you have to respect what the dark can hide. Otherwise, you'll pretty swiftly become acquainted with muggers, rapists, and other types of lowlife.'

'Wise words, though a little dramatic.' He chuckled. 'We never did get electricity run down here. You were lucky, though – on Sundays, we always bring wine up from down here for the masses. One of the other priests lit everything when he came down earlier.'

'I wouldn't want his job,' I said, but was cut off as Father Christopher took a torch off the wall. He turned into a vault clad in darkness and lit two other wall lanterns.

It was a large space full of old crates and pallets of grain, serving as a type of cellar. There were new torches leaning against one wall, candles in stacks, apples in crates, old robes hanging up, and more than enough mice.

'This is your plan?' I asked.

Father Christopher gestured at the crates. I was loath to think what I would find in them; mostly spiders and rats, I imagined with a shudder.

'There's stuff down here that hasn't seen the light of day in two hundred years, I'll wager,' he said with a cough.

'It just looks like everyday items,' I said, unable to keep the disappointment out of my voice.

'Well, where better to stash the belongings of a priest when no-one knew if he might return or not?'

The emphasis in his voice suggested he was offended at my lack of enthusiasm. I needed to use more tact.

'But wouldn't they have excommunicated him for his dabblings?'

'No, no, it would take much more than that to get thrown

out in those days. Priests could cause all sorts of bother and a blind eye was turned. If he'd returned, it would have been the prodigal son all over again. My guess is they kept his belongings.'

I began at one end of the vault and Father Christopher at the other. Soon, I'd become distracted by a box full of bronze church furniture. Some of it would have been very valuable after restoration.

I looked up at Father Christopher; in his hands were two leather-bound books, green with mould. He was turning the pages, and I could see that the words were hand written. I moved round to Father Christopher's elbow to see the sprawling writing better.

'This looks like a diary,' he commented. 'What a shame.'

He closed the book and handed it over to me. The light was so low, I had to move over to the torch. The mould had disfigured the jacket to such a degree, it was almost impossible to make out the marking on the front. I used my cuff to rub away some of the white and green growths.

'Anything?' he enquired.

'An oak tree, a snake and a chalice: alchemical symbols,' I whispered.

'Christopher.' Echoes of a faraway voice bounced into our vault. Father Christopher let out a sigh.

'It's as if they can't do without me for more than five minutes!' he said, his voice laden with irritation. He turned to me with an apologetic face. 'I'll have to go. By all means bring your spoils upstairs. Don't sit down here in this dank place.'

'If you don't mind, I'd like to look a little more and check there's nothing else down here.'

He shrugged. 'Spend as much time as you like, but I

wouldn't go wandering too much. Some of these vaults lead into other vaults, and even I have no clue where they go to.'

I smiled at his retreating back. The calling voice got closer and Father Christopher's footsteps grew further away, and I turned my attention back to the manuscript rather than continuing the search right away. Sitting down on a sturdy trunk, I flicked to the last page, and as the darkness crept closer to me, I began to read:

My mind diverges from my body and I know not how. I am able to take a journey without any fatigue with the full advantage of sleep and stretching of limb. Last night, I escaped the monastery. I walked the length of our neat garden, past the ordered rows of vegetables that mean so much to us, whose existence in so many other ways is barren.

Outside our walls, I faltered, for though I have lived in Verona for ten years, I have never been outside our monastery. The moonlight was bright and I was able to see about as if it were day. I decided upon a path leading uphill as I considered there would be a pleasant aspect from the summit.

There were fields on both sides of the path. Grass was sparse, but boulders were plenty and the terrain was rough. I had to take great care not to stumble. I came upon a little stream which wound its way this way and that as if it could not decide which route was best.

Eventually, I stopped to survey my position. The moon was unusually slender; I was quite distracted by its shape as if it were a silver sickle hanging in the sky. Thus unawares, I stumbled forward over a stone and somewhere between putting one foot down and the other up, I fell, reaching out my hands to mitigate the inevitable disaster.

The stones sliced through my skin unmercifully. My palms flowed red with blood. I let out a shout and looked around for some Samaritan figure to alight upon my path. Then it was that I noticed the intensifying colour of the landscape.

The fields became more verdant as if they were being picked out in malachite green by an unseen artist. The path became a chequerboard of brown and white stones. The night sky became a deep, dark blue. The stream was most disturbing of all: its water was no longer clear, but red and thick like the blood flowing down my forearms.

I had stood shakily and turned decidedly back towards the monastery when in front of my path stood the opening of a cave which was surrounded by a halo of light. Knowing that this cave had not been here moments before, I stepped forward to its mouth and asked by what power I was called hither. There was no response.

I seldom succumb to impulse, but by a compulsion that I cannot explain, I entered. Then all became darkness.

One step at a time, one foot after another in a slow but sure gait, I moved through the darkness. You may question my sanity at this decision, but I felt no fear. In fact, I felt sure that it was God leading me thus.

The darkness was with me for a long, long time, before I saw a twinkling far off in the distance. The brightness grew in size, and soon came towards me at high speed. The light was so bright, it burned me and enlightened me all in the same instant. I was bathed in a glorious, agonising gold which I could feel radiating through me and from me.

I stayed in that perfect, painful warmth without concept of time. It could have been a number of years, too numerous to count, or merely a second. Then, just as suddenly as it had come, the light faded again and the darkness returned. I woke as if I had just been born: shivering, disorientated, and crying out loud.

"Found something?"

The voice brought me out of the author's grip with a jolt.

I stared into the gloom to see a priest filling the doorway. The lamp flickered across his face. Maybe it was just the setting, but for a moment he looked more like a gargoyle than a priest.

I was gripped by the childish desire to run screaming from the room. Swallowing down my fear, I stood up and rubbed my side. I hadn't noticed the hinges of the trunk digging into my legs as I read.

"It's just an old notebook," my throat dried. "I should be getting back to Father Christopher," I said, taking a step towards the door. I took another, expecting him to give way, but though he stood to one side, he kept his arm in place, stretched across the doorway.

"Interesting, is it?" he hissed.

My own voice shrank down into my chest at the sound of his. I shook my head and swallowed, looking up into eyes that were dark.

Suddenly he dropped his arm. I didn't hesitate. I exited those vaults so fast, Usain Bolt wouldn't have caught me. Clutching the leather-bound notebook, I slammed into the relative light of the church, gasping from exertion and anxiety.

Father Christopher was talking to someone by the pews. He left them and hurried across to me.

"Everything alright?"

I was unable to speak.

His brows furrowed in concern and then they lifted, "Father Peter went down to fetch more votive candles. Did he scare you?"

I nodded.

"Hm, understandable. Ugly beyond reproach, that one," he said with a wink.

"Father!" I said, startled out of my silence.

"Well, you want to see him at Dawn Prayers." He screwed his face up, "He's got a face like a bulldog chewing a wasp."

I BEGAN to feel less flighty once I had a steaming coffee in one hand and a sizeable slice of almond cake in the other. The kitchen couldn't have been a better antidote to the catacombs; it was such a light and friendly place.

The passage in the book that had so entranced me was simply titled 'The Journey'. It didn't really fit with what I considered to be a typical diary entry. I wasn't sure if this made it more or less significant.

The colours mentioned in the dream were the very same as the stages spoken about in my little green book: brown, red, green, white, blue, collectively known as the Peacock's Tail. The river of blood, the moon, and some kind of religious experience were all key points in the story, too, but I had no idea how they fitted together.

I decided to look for Father Christopher to see if he could shed some light on any more of it. We sat together in a small chapel as he read through the pages.

He shook his head. 'Well, I won't pretend to understand the meaning of the passage, but have you considered the wider significance of it?'

I looked down and fingered the worn bench, unsure what he meant.

'You keep skirting around the issue. What about God?

Are you choosing to leave that part out? I mean, above being an alchemist, Father Francis was a priest. It seems to me God is the biggest part in this equation. It sounds like this is a meditation, which is an established route of getting in touch with God. Why would you need to bother, if the Almighty wasn't somehow a part of it all?'

I looked up and saw a serious expression on Father Christopher's face; his clear blue eyes were seeing right through me.

'If I knew the answer to all that, Father, then I'm sure I'd be too wise to be looking for answers in an alchemist's diary. There are very few people, I think, who know where God figures in anything.'

'Well, you'd better have a good think because it seems obvious to me. You'll be doing all this for nothing, if you can't see past the end of your own nose.'

His point was a valid one. Father Francis had had God in the equation, and this was something I had not properly considered up until now. With my science-based education and modern philosophy, I had not stopped to think that alchemy could be a miracle in the religious sense. I suppose it was as good a theory as any other, bearing in mind that the science didn't add up. I had come to Verona hoping to find some tip, or practical indication of the chemicals he had used. This was much harder to grasp.

God didn't really fit in with my plan. It wasn't that I didn't believe in God per se, but in common with many of my contemporaries, I had come to think of God more as a watcher than a doer.

Father Christopher broke into my thoughts.

'There's only one other thing, I think, I might be able to help you with. If this is a meditation then I can tell you a bit about the type of meditation we do here. Would that be helpful?'

I replied that it would. He explained to me about meditation in the Catholic faith, and how it was very closely related to prayer.

'There are two types of prayer: vocal and mental. The vocal variety is most likely familiar to most as it involves the petitioning of God or the saints for help. Mental prayer, however, is undertaken by means of meditation or contemplation.

'Meditation helps to make prayer a deeper experience; more from the heart. It involves the expulsion of conscious thought and awareness of the body. Finding the illumination that Father Francis described is a matter of clearing your mind from distraction. Only then is the blinding light able to fill the void. That source, which can be at once excruciating and fulfilling, is what the Catholics call Divine Grace of God. It is a gift. I assume Father Francis believed it could be used or harnessed.'

Harnessed: the word shimmied down my spine. This was the immense power source spoken about in the little green theology book which had begun my fantastical dream chasing. Reaching it via meditation seemed an odyssey, though. Meeting my maker was something I had hoped to do much later in my life, and preferably after it. I was pretty sure that after a person had any kind of religious experience, particularly of the awesome variety, they would never be the same.

Father Christopher gave me an exercise to help me understand. He pointed at a painting of St Sebastian, in which the saint had various arrows protruding from his flesh, and archers taking aim surrounding him. Father Christopher told me to look at every single detail of the picture, and think about how everything must feel. Concentrate on every dimension. See the sorrow in St Sebastian's eyes, and the pain pulsing through his flesh. He wanted me to think of the saint's youth and his fear. He told me to concentrate completely until my world was excluded.

Father Christopher went away for a while, and soon I became immersed in the murder scene before my eyes. I flinched at the wounds. I was amazed at how cruel and indifferent the faces of the archers looked as they took aim, wondering if they were even seeing their victim, or if he was merely a target for them. I studied the saint's frightened eyes as he endured his fate and waited in earnest for God's grace.

Then Father Christopher tapped me on the shoulder, which pulled me out of my reverie.

'Good,' he said. 'You were concentrating very hard. I stood behind you a full minute, and you didn't know I was there. This is how we teach meditative prayer to the novices. This is an excellent exercise because it focuses your mind; teaches you to concentrate so that you lose awareness of your corporal body. The final stage is to push away the images as well. As your mind becomes stronger, you create a void ready for God to enter. Practise as often as you can, your mind will strengthen.

'In the meantime, I want you to show me what's under those gloves of yours. I know a lot about herbs, maybe I can help.'

I smiled at the kind old gentleman. Many people had tried to help my hands over the years, or failing that, tried to talk me out of the work. Apart from not touching metal, no prescription, herb or therapy had ever improved their condition. These days I went along with people's suggestions to allow them to feel they might have helped, rather than for myself.

'Come on, then,' I stood up in a positive manner, 'but they say leprosy is catching. I hope you aren't squeamish.'

Father Christopher looked nervous just for a moment and his eyes widened. Then he laughed.

'Get away with ya.'

BEFORE I LEFT VERONA, I thanked Father Christopher profusely. He gave me herbs for my hands as a parting gift. His benevolent smile made me seek some reassurance that I hadn't even realised I needed.

'Is this a silly quest, Father?'

He reached forward and put a hand on my shoulder.

'Few people in this world have a grand passion. If something is telling you to pursue this – I would call it God – then there is a reason and an answer at the end of it all. It may not be the answer you want, mind you, but it will be an answer.'

5

The light patter of keys woke me. Thérèse had been working since dawn again, and I felt weary for her. I took her a pot of coffee and sat for a while at the small wooden table where she habitually worked, helping myself to a cup from the brown glazed pot which was her favourite. It was something more suited to the Yorkshire Dales than the elegance of Venetian life.

My find at Verona had surprised me, despite my intention to seek out just such a treasure. I had less faith in my own success than I'd realised.

'You do look tired, Abi. What did you do in Verona?'

Thérèse removed her slender rectangular glasses and stretched her long arms up towards the ceiling. She looked amazingly beautiful without any make-up. Her hair was pulled off her face and knotted on the top of her head in an rough bun. She was wearing one of Terry's white vests. It was miles too big for her.

'Thérèse, if I told you, you would think I was mad.'

She chewed on the ear pieces of her glasses and gestured to me to go on.

'I was looking for clues to support a theory I have about alchemy,' I said.

She inhaled deeply and stretched her legs. 'Oh well, I'm a little disappointed, then. I was imagining you were arm in arm with some handsome man, walking along the pastel-coloured streets. Isn't the alchemy trail a little cold?' she asked.

'Funny you should say that because I found something really interesting over the weekend.'

My eyes felt itchy, and I began to rub them. Thérèse put a hand gently on my arm to stop me making them sore.

I glanced at the great ship's clock that Terry had lashed to the wall and realised I was nearly late for work. I dressed hurriedly and pulled on my boots. Thérèse looked disappointed.

'You can't run out on me now. I want to hear about the alchemy.'

We arranged to meet for lunch later and I dashed out. The *traghetto* came quickly that morning, and gave me my daily short but refreshing ride. It was so different to the lengthy suffocating Tube system in London which made even the heartiest commuter bad tempered. I admired the beauty of the pale light which was Venice's own. The city's labyrinthine passageways were a tonic in themselves. They offered me a different route to work every day, and always took me past some new wonder or pretty place. I fleetingly remembered being spewed from the Tube, and feeling too numb to absorb any of London's abundant charm.

I really was proud of how well the bronze doors looked. Stefano had rigged a scaffold tower up for me so that I could get access to all areas. I had begun carefully, working the bronze to reveal the beautiful reliefs from under a thick shell of corrosion. They had been exposed to the elements without protection for so long that they had turned nature's favourite colour: green. Structurally they were fine, so my work consisted solely of returning them to their original brown lustre. Pierro Ricco, the Project Director, had been quite specific in his brief. He wanted everyone to see them as they were meant to be seen, which meant a full restoration.

It took me days to remove the corrosion. I made pot after pot of pumice paste with my very careworn pestle and mortar, and left work each day with arms that felt like lead and legs that felt like jelly. When every scrap of dirt and corrosion had been removed, I began to repatinate. I smiled with satisfaction at seeing the rich dark colour form so beautifully; the preparation was the key. The age of the metal had bestowed a maturity on the colour which I could never have imitated. Every time I passed the threshold, I silently thanked the doors for helping me to make my first project such a success.

I walked over to the three bronze saints on the altarpiece. These were to be the next phase of my work. Two wall painting conservators, Michel and Laya, were working on the murals in the eaves. They put down their brushes and waved.

Working alone had its drawbacks. Initially, there had been no-one in particular to befriend, and as a consequence, no-one to usher me into the bosom of Stefano's firm. Everyone had been polite, but it was up to me to push myself forward and make friends. I felt shy at first and came down off my platform infrequently, which meant I got a lot more work than usual done in one day, but it made work less of a pleasure. At the foundry, the camaraderie was thick in the air, oiling everyone's cogs and making the work run more smoothly.

My breakthrough came when I began to stop and admire the work being done by others. Whoever said flattery will get you nowhere hadn't a clue. These little bits of praise seemed to have the same result as offering to make someone a cup of tea in England. It made the others working in the church grateful and offered an opportunity to stop and chat.

'Laya, magnificent work! Tell me how you manage to mix those glazes? I've never seen their like. John the Baptist looks ten years younger.'

I was making use of the pride of a good craftsperson. I had never met one who, given a chance, wouldn't eulogise about their own work. A willing listener was a rarity, and I'd often seen an inquisitive client ask a simple question and receive the unabridged version in response. Their eyes would glaze over and a rhythmic nodding of the head would begin as they attempted to seem polite. Apparently, this was an international phenomenon.

'Does he really look good from down there?' Laya shouted down from her high scaffold. 'I'm so relieved; it's really hard to tell when you're up so close to these giants. Come up and see for yourself.'

Within moments, I was clambering up a ladder towards a new friendship.

Laya showed me how she had been delicately removing the varnish that had suffered from candle soot and ultraviolet light, which had made the surface go dark. The newly revealed figures mingled with us in exceptionally brightly coloured, classical robes. Being up there, close to those monumental people of the Bible, was like being up in heaven itself. They were the heroes of an older time: brave, handsome, wise, and kind, but above all, they were human with all the expressions of men enduring hard times.

I took a good look at the three bronze saints I was to tackle. They were about life size, dressed in classical drapery. Someone had smothered them in boot polish many years ago, so now their colour had become more akin to lead than bronze. After taking a small scraping with a wooden spatula, I was able to see that the original patina underneath was nearly perfectly intact. It was only a little dull and lifeless. My intervention would be minimal in their instance. I had to clean them thoroughly and then revive the jaded patina so that the colour was imbued with some new life.

The pose and expression of these figures was anything but saintly and serene. Two of them – John, whom Christ loved best, and St Peter – emanated anger from every fold of their robes to the tense stances of their bodies, hands and jaws clenched tight. The third was positioned slightly apart and was more pathetic. His robes were a little too large, shoulders rounded, head down, staring at his own large hands as if he could see Jesus's blood upon them. This, of course, was Judas. They were great works of art and worthy of a place in any art gallery in the world, where they would have been admired instead of forgotten.

I laid my tools out carefully on a dustsheet to the left of the first statue. My toolbox was as special to me as a jewellery box would be to most girls. I couldn't help but stroke the walnut surface before opening it. The first tray lifted out and, like a medicine chest, held small quantities of every patination chemical I was ever likely to need in little glass jars with tightly fitting lids. The glass on many of them was tinted to protect the chemicals that weren't light resistant. Alan, the glass-blower at the foundry, had made a fortune out of my whim for a rainbow of containers. I'd saved every penny I'd earned and done as many extra shifts and menial tasks as I could one summer, commissioning Alan to make something special for me at the end of each week. Kindly, Alan hadn't palmed me off with second-rate work. He had created many miniature masterpieces combining strength, colour and beauty which went far beyond the money I gave him.

Every item I had collected had sentimental value, as well as some functional use. I had designed many of the tools myself and had them made up by the toolmaker at the foundry, so they were unique. Some were made of special materials, like my squirrel-hair brush, or my semi-circular sable buffing brush which had a cast bronze handle made to fit an imprint of my own knuckles precisely.

I put on my battered leather apron, soft as parchment with so much oiling over the years, and a pouch belt. I filled the pockets with all I'd need, such as lint-free rags, brushes, spatulas of differing shapes and sizes – these were like wooden dentist's tools that wouldn't scratch the metal – and last of all, a small jar of pink neutral soap which was actually gentle enough to wash my face with. Then I picked up a bucket and went to get some warm water.

I covered the floor about me with large jute sheets, rolled up my sleeves and sat astride a stepladder. I gave the first of the three saints a gentle washing, taking care not to flood him or the floor.

'I could do with a shampoo and set, don't you think?' Stefano patted his bald head and chuckled at his own joke. He was working on the main altarpiece a few feet behind me and the saints.

'I doubt you'd want to be touched with these hands,' I said and lifted my palms so he could see how dirty they were. What I'd forgotten he'd also see was my monstrous rash, and I saw the horror on his face.

'My God, can't you wear gloves while you work?' he said.

'Well, I probably should for cleaning like this, but I can't for the patination. I don't know why, but it just doesn't work properly when I'm not actually touching the metal. The gloves sort of lift the colour, and I end up with patchy looking bronze. Some colours you have to massage into the metal, and they won't form at all with gloves on. Anyhow, I have three paying customers here – what would they say if I did you first?'

'They'd better not get dandruff, because Pierro is coming to inspect us today and that is all I need!' Stefano said, standing up from his cramped position to give his poor knees a rest. 'He doesn't miss a thing, you know.'

'How long have you known him?' I enquired.

'Since I was about your age. Only he wasn't Department of Culture then; he had just graduated from Harvard. He knows very little about art except its value.'

Stefano was obviously in a gossipy mood. He sat down on his platform facing me and gestured to one of the young gofers hanging around to make some coffee.

'But how did he get a position as head of Department of Culture with very little knowledge of art?' I enquired.

Stefano laughed and shook his head.

'My dear, you must be very young indeed if you think that people only get the jobs they are qualified for. In Italy, particularly, jobs are secured by those of us fortunate enough to have family and friends that are well connected. Don't look so sceptical, it is true. The Mafia run this country, as they always have, and Pierro is one of the wealthiest and best-connected men in Italy. I am quite sure that if he wanted a job as a neurosurgeon, he would get it.' Stefano received his coffee from the gofer without acknowledgment.

'Surely merit counts for something?' I argued.

'Merit helps but connections are much more persuasive,' he said, standing up.

I felt naïve. I wasn't sure if Stefano was being dramatic. Pierro was certainly a man who was aware of his own importance. He'd hardly done more than acknowledge me since the first day we'd met, but I didn't take it personally; he ignored the others in Stefano's crew, too. He addressed comments almost exclusively to Stefano about our work. It was clear he didn't care to prattle with tradespeople.

'And here he is. You are early and have caught me drinking coffee with my colleague.'

Stefano turned his attention away from me and stood up to greet his client.

'It's your colleague who I have come to congratulate,' Pierro said, completely knocking down my carefully observed theory of his snobbishness. 'The doors look magnificent.' He wasn't quite speaking to me, but his body was turned in my direction. 'They are a masterpiece, and the colour! It is rich and deep; I have never seen bronze look like this before.'

A proud smile spread across my face; I couldn't contain it. Rather than seem too affected by a word of praise, I turned my attention back to the statue. Stefano led Pierro away to look at a mural with problems on the other side of the church.

As they moved away, I could hear Pierro saying, 'They are so impressive now. The doors make you want to enter the church.'

My smile spread wider.

The statue I was working on was so dirty that I had become the same colour as it. I had had to lean into the statue and press really hard to loosen the dirt and boot polish. This layer seemed to have hardened into a shell-like concrete. When Thérèse arrived, she laughed as soon as she saw me and said we had better go home to eat.

As we were leaving, Thérèse met Pierro on the stairs of the chapel. His delight with the doors seemed to have waned because he ignored me once again, but he greeted Thérèse with kisses and compliments. He then linked arms with her and escorted us down the steps, leaving Stefano mid-sentence.

'What are you doing here, my dear friend? It is such a fortuitous meeting – why don't we go to lunch?'

Pierro's eyes flashed with charm, and the smile – which I had suspected he must have, but had not personally encountered – was bandied about without reserve.

'I am lunching with Abigail. She's staying with us,' said Thérèse, gesturing towards me.

Pierro ran his eyes over me.

'As you can see, I am not attired for dining out,' I laughed. I opened my arms so Pierro could fully appreciate the humour of my streaked top and dirty skin. It appeared he didn't.

'What a shame,' he complained.

'Come to dinner at the flat on Thursday evening. There will be several interesting people for you to meet, as well as Abigail, of course. You can be our guest of honour,' said Thérèse, touching his arm.

He accepted, and parted looking pleased.

6

It was such a glorious day that Thérèse and I chose to walk along the canal and enjoy the light dancing on the water before we took the traghetto lower down the island.

'He's completely different with you, Thérèse, he was flirting like mad,' I teased her.

'No, that's just the Italian way.' She shook her head.

'Italian, British, American, flirting is a universal language.' I laughed and nudged her arm affectionately.

'He's a very good client of Terry's. He buys a lot of his work.'

'I don't suppose you attach any significance to his buying works where you are the subject?'

'No,' she protested, but her eyes betrayed her. 'Actually, we've known each other a long time, way before I met Terry. His family visited my grandmother when I was growing up, and as I used to spend most afternoons helping her while my mamma was finishing work, I came to know them too.'

'I thought you grew up in the States?' I said. She nodded.

'Yes, they came to see her there. My grandmother was quite a revered lady. People travelled from much further than Europe to consult her.'

I was intrigued.

'Go on,' I pushed.

But Thérèse had spotted the *traghetto*, and we had to run so as not to miss it.

It was only when we were sitting inside the cool flat, away from Terry's class, with our peasant's lunch of bread, oil, and cheese that I could reignite the conversation.

'Tell me about your grandmother, what profession was she in? Law?'

'Well, not everyone would call it a profession in the conventional sense. She was what is known as a seer: someone with second sight. Some might have called her a witch, but she earned more money in a single visit than most men earned in a month, in those days, so she was no old hag.'

I sat back in my chair and looked at Thérèse to see if there was a glimmer of humour in her eyes.

'You have to be joking, aren't you?' I asked disbelievingly.

'No it's true.' She bent over her food, tearing it into little pieces rather than actually eating anything. 'She was so accurate. She could tell a person about their past or future. She could create or banish curses, bind ill will and sweet-talk the spirits. I witnessed gardens that died overnight, and would never grow a single seed again after my Nana whispered her special words to the soil. "People that sow ill will, reap it" was her only explanation to me as we walked past those hell-touched gardens after school.'

I stood up to make some coffee. Thérèse continued.

'She must have been good because she was successful by anyone's standards. You have to consider how hard it was for a black woman to get anything above manual labour in 1950, let alone earn enough money to buy an apartment in Park Avenue. She was old when she died, but she owned Rembrandts and Titians. You don't get that type of success without being exceptional.'

'Are you sure that wasn't just a front, and she was a drug baroness or something?'

Thérèse didn't laugh and I realised I'd been tactless; she was obviously very proud of her grandmother.

'How did she do it, by Tarot cards?' I asked.

'For readings or revelations, she used playing cards. She said numbers were the language of the universe. People would often leave with ashen faces or tears streaming down their cheeks at my Nana's words or advice. I would ask her why she told them things that made them unhappy. She would look at me with her grey eyebrows raised and say, "Why would they pay me to hide it? Besides, it's unlucky to withhold information from someone who has paid their penny." Mind you, she had a tendency to justify all her eccentric ways with threats of bad luck.'

'She sounds nice, lots of character.'

I passed the coffee over to her and sat down again.

'She was a rarity. Anyhow, Pierro's folks came a lot at one time. She did a lot of predictions for businessmen. In fact, I imagine they were her main source of wealth. Before mergers and big decisions, we'd get armies of suits filing in and out, often opposing parties meeting in our sitting room. It could be a trifle frosty, but they came nevertheless. I wasn't allowed to sit in with Pierro's lot, though Nana did often let me assist her with others. I remember playing with Pierro when I was quite small in her hallway as he waited for his parents to come out.'

'Have you ever asked him what they saw her for?'
I asked.

'No, it would have been rude. People didn't come to see
her for happy things. It was usually business, roving
husbands or wives, or illnesses. Nana wasn't exactly the
most ethical person in the world, and she had no Hippo-
cratic Oath to stop her discussing her clients with me. She
was usually discreet about their reason for coming to see
her, but she didn't mind filling me in on the extras which
she'd seen, but not spoken of. There was huge potential for
gossip, enough to set New York alight, but it was an unsaid
condition of my helping her that I must never let spill what
she'd seen and said. She would laugh about their lies,
bending over double with mirth sometimes.

'"As if I can't see the lies as clearly as I can see whatever
they're payin' me for. I ain't lookin' down a microscope. I is
looking at the whole picture," she would say. The whole
picture was the pregnancies, the affairs, the wife beaters, the
fraudsters – all the things they wanted to hide rather than
present. She was obviously professional enough to overlook
all these extras and deal with whatever matter was in hand,
otherwise she would have lost her livelihood in an instant.'

'Did you learn to read from her?' I asked.

'What you make of the patterns depends on the gift of
the reader. I don't have the clarity of my nana, but I do see
things in the cards – little messages, little meanings – and
some things are more glaringly obvious than others. It's true
that the mechanics can be learned, but not the subtle stuff.
That's where you need a true gift.'

She got up and fetched us some water.

'I'm also a little unsure about it all. I'm not sure if it's
better not to know, and not to prompt people into actions

that might be pivotal in their lives. I just think that you are stepping on God's toes there. I sometimes read the cards at parties for fun, but I only tell people the good stuff.'

'Is it really magic?' I asked as I ate an apple.

'I don't think so. It's like being able to hear better than someone else or see better. I think a clearer metaphor might be the idea of trying to describe music to a deaf person. It doesn't make music magic just because it isn't possible for them to experience it.'

'But music can be recorded as sound waves,' I said.

'True, but the events that my Nana could see were proven to be true over and over again. Isn't the accuracy of her readings a proof in itself?'

I had to agree with her.

I LEFT the flat in no mood to return to work. Lunches always stretched into two-hour affairs so I would be no later than anyone else. As I stood aboard the *traghetto* coming back towards the main island, I realised Thérèse and I had become so sidetracked, I'd quite forgotten to tell her about what I'd discovered in Verona.

Something she'd said reminded me about what I'd read in the little green theology book. Thérèse had spoken of her grandmother's gift as a developed sense rather than any magical power. The book had spoken in similar terms of the gift of the alchemist. Thérèse's story of her grandmother's ability actually sounded credible to me, and yet when I thought about plucking detailed information about a person's life from a set of playing cards, it sounded as likely as...alchemy.

I couldn't make up my mind whether Thérèse's grand-mother, or Father Francis the Crowman, were frauds or anomalies. It came down to whether I believed more in the people or the science. My opinion swung like a pendulum – neither felt like an answer I could be happy with.

7

I arrived back late from work on Thursday evening, despite having promised Thérèse that morning that I'd make it back in good time to help her prepare dinner. At least, I'd remembered the groceries on my way home. So thorough was my guilt at getting waylaid that as I let myself in the door and my ears were slapped by Terry's booming voice, I truly thought it was because of my tardiness.

I crept, head lowered, right into the no-man's-land of a domestic row. Words were hurtling back and forward over my head. Neither of them seemed to have registered that I was nearly an hour behind time, and that they had guests due in under half an hour. They were arguing in the library, which was also my bedroom. To get out of the firing range as rapidly as possible, I dropped the groceries on my bed, grabbed a handful of clothes and darted towards the bathroom. Here, I couldn't help but overhear, but at least I could distract myself by getting dressed.

'You just don't understand, do you?' Thérèse's voice

filtered through the wall. 'I don't want to go to bloody America. I left America, remember, and went to England.'

'I know, but it's not like you've got to emigrate there. It's six months tops. The money is terrific. You could become famous, for goodness's sake. I don't understand.'

I'd never heard Terry get angry about anything before, and I quailed at the power in his voice.

'Why didn't you tell me about the job at least?' he said.

'Because it was irrelevant. I didn't want to do it, so I didn't tell you.'

'Your agent says you've been turning down everything she offers you. She says that Gaultier was requesting you to do some huge ad campaign. Is she lying?'

'No, she's not, but it was the same as this film. I didn't want to take it, so it was irrelevant. I'd have had to spend months away doing promotional work.'

'How can something this huge be irrelevant? You are being offered work that people would kill for, and think of the money! How can you refuse it?' Terry yelled.

'I don't need the money, you know that,' Thérèse yelled back.

Terry quietened slightly.

'I know you don't, but it's your grandmother's money. This is success in your own right, and you get worshipped into the bargain.'

'Well, it's not worship as far as I'm concerned. I loathe standing in front of a mirror for hours while everyone pulls at my hair and plasters my face in make-up. I despise wearing the awful outfits, and being scrutinised under hot lights to catch every flaw, pound, wrinkle I have acquired since the last job. I hated it on my very first day when a make-up artist plucked out all of my eyebrows without asking me, and I hate it now. It's completely de-humanising.

Acting is just the same, but with a script: criticism, criticism, criticism. I've had enough. They hate me but they want me, and so they buy me and treat me terribly.'

A knock at the door interrupted them. Thérèse was obviously very highly charged, so thankfully Terry answered the door. He welcomed the first guest in a hearty way that made me think he was perhaps the better suited of the two to acting.

I looked down at the clothes I'd snatched. Mostly dirty washing – I'd have to go out and get something clean. I finished my make-up, ventured out and dressed hurriedly, then went to the kitchen to take Thérèse the fresh pasta and olives. Thérèse looked surprised to see me, but she couldn't stop her tears in time.

'Don't cry,' I said, hugging her.

She bent her head into my chest and sobbed. Her fragility and woe made me want to hug all the pain away. I couldn't imagine what it must be like being as beautiful as Thérèse, but I could imagine that the world she had described was as fickle and as mean as she'd said it was.

She looked up at me with eyes blood red with emotion.

'I didn't tell him that I can't bear to leave him. I should have told him. I don't want to go away.'

She shook with the pain of the sharp words exchanged between loved ones.

'You can tell him later, Thérèse, but he knows. He does know. It's just that he wants you to fulfil yourself. He doesn't want to think he's holding you back.'

'How could he?' she asked, drying her eyes on her apron. 'I desperately need to get published, and then he would be able to accept that I have a new career.'

In a heartbeat, she became practical, her emotions

evidently spent. She pulled off the headscarf she'd been wearing while cooking and shook out her long, dark hair.

'Come on, it should be fun tonight,' she said, giving me a small hug.

The majority of the guests had arrived by the time Thérèse and I crept from the kitchen. We left Terry to be batted between them while we gathered ourselves together.

This evening, we were to have the first sit-down dinner at the flat since I'd arrived. I'd begun to imagine that perhaps Terry and Thérèse didn't go in for this type of bour-geois entertainment. Guests who came round were not specially attended to. They helped themselves to wine, chopped salads, or made everyone coffee, behaving as extended family, and consequently were no chore. The whole system was a wonder to me.

Pierro arrived last. I was helping Thérèse bring herb-laden salads in from the kitchen when he made his entrance with three bottles of Cristal champagne.

'From my cellar,' he told Terry loudly.

Thérèse immediately went to greet him with two kisses. I was unsure whether it was the done thing to embrace your boss when you didn't exchange so much as a good morning most of the time. I chose to hover about and nod Englishly instead, but he made his way over to me and I noticed his eyes upon me.

'You look very beautiful tonight, Abigail. What a colour. It's perfect for you.'

I was wearing a rustic red halter neck bodice that shim-mered in the light and a short dark skirt that kept to the line of my figure. I had left my hair down so that it grazed my collarbone. I was grateful for his compliment.

Terry brought us both over a glass of wine.

'Where are you from, *carina?* You look, not Italian

exactly, but Portuguese. Your dark hair, volcanic eyes and satin skin cannot be English,' said Pierro.

'Well, you are close. My parents are British, mother Irish. My father's mother was French and her mother was Portuguese. My father tells me I do look very much like my great grandmother,' I said, blushing.

'Ah, how interesting. What a cocktail of blood you have,' he replied.

Our conversation was interrupted as we were called to table. I was intrigued at the mixture of guests. We were twelve in all: the local baker and his wife; two of Terry's students; a priest; Pierro; an English lady of advanced years who was a client of Terry's; a tall young man with blond hair to his collarbone who was Terry's nephew; and a petite girl with chic short hair who was with him. Thérèse beckoned for everyone to sit and begin the first course of antipasti and artisan breads brought by the baker. There was a sumptuous range: sundried tomatoes in peppery olive oil; marinated sweet peppers; almond and raisin bread; bruschetta with spiced tomatoes; goat's cheese; rye plaits; grilled aubergine and roasted garlic. I sat next to Thérèse and had the elderly lady, who kept topping up her glass with a quick hand, on the other side. Pierro sat opposite.

The lights were low, but there were many candles. The conversation had begun on art, as it always did at Terry's. The girl, whose name was Ellen, was sitting next to Terry. She worked at Sotheby's in the Contemporary Art department. This revelation had sent Terry off into an explosive eulogy on the disgraceful state of the art market, and all the fraudsters masquerading as artists. He pointed a knife at Ellen.

'Whatever happened to the artist knowing one end of a paintbrush from his elbow?' He appealed to one of the students. 'How long has it taken you to master a pencil, Federico? Two years at least, and it'll be another two before he's allowed to start coming up with his own ideas. A child has to learn grammar and vocabulary before they can speak with any coherence; it's the same with art.'

Federico was taking great gulps of wine. He was obviously crushed at the idea that he would have to put in another two years before he was allowed to create anything at all. Ellen tried to answer Terry's question, obviously not realising that he wanted to answer it himself.

'Last week, my agent told me that I might have to start looking for a market in America because figurative work won't sell in Europe. He says they have the best taste these days. It's a sorry state when the nation that brought us Ken and Barbie have better taste than we do. You go to any art school. A student that wants to paint figurative work won't get the time of day from his tutor. I see kids all the time, brimming with talent, with their confidence quashed because they've got poor degrees. The tutors will only assist you if you build installations, or shit on your canvas.'

There was a slight silence. Thérèse laughed.

'Hear, hear,' the old lady bellowed, which made me like her. She wasn't holding back.

Ellen bravely defended her own corner, giving a valiant speech about changing values in art. She justified installations as expressions of thought in the same way as figurative pieces, but Terry was shaking his head and making heaven-help-us eyes at Mrs Heath on my right.

'The top and bottom of it,' Ellen concluded, trying to pacify her host a little, 'is that fashions change. Figurative work will come back, just the way that mini-skirts and flared trousers have. It's just that at the moment, we've had enough of The Virgin Mary painted exactly the same way by 150 different artists.'

Poor Ellen was not having a good night. Her comment prodded the priest to sermonise on the actual differences between the Renaissance Madonnas. Fortunately, I escaped by helping to clear away the starter plates and deliver the main course, which was exquisite clam pasta.

When I sat down again, the conversation was slightly more segmented. The upper half of the table were discussing modern music in comparison to modern art, and the priest was telling Mrs Heath about his recent trip to Athens. Pierro sat silently, choosing not to involve himself in either party until Thérèse engaged him.

'Pierro, where did you get that incredible ring from? It's so unusual.'

He looked pleased that she had noticed.

'What an excellent eye you have, Thérèse. It was my grandfather's. It is an alchemist's signet ring. In fact, it has been a hobby of my family for generations to collect alchemist's possessions.'

I looked at the ring for the first time, and was amazed I hadn't been dazzled by it sooner. It was, in fact, so bright it actually pierced the darkness around us. Two initials intertwined each other in the gold centrepiece. The ends of the letters were beautifully detailed, one with the head of a serpent, and the other tapering to support a crown. It was magnificent.

'What an unusual hobby – you must be interested in alchemy yourself?' Thérèse enquired.

'Yes, as much as my ancestors were,' he answered.

'That's so funny, now I know two people who are interested in alchemy. You must chat to Abi about it. She was just telling me the other day how she'd found something interesting about alchemy during a trip to Verona.'

I couldn't swallow my mouthful of pasta. I was horrified that Thérèse had mentioned my interest and kicked myself for not asking her to keep it to herself.

'Really?' said Pierro, and he looked up at me with interest in his chestnut eyes, which I noted, for the first time, were bound by an unusually dark ring encircling the irises.

'Well, it's really just an academic interest. Of course, what else could it be?' I was aware my laugh sounded too high pitched. 'It's mainly because I came across some references to similarities between alchemy and my own craft some time ago, and it got me hooked.'

Pierro was really listening now. He'd put down his fork for a moment.

'Remarkable, I have never come across any such references myself. You would be very welcome to look at my family's collection, if it would be of interest to you. It's at my house in Florence. Maybe if you are visiting there some time, we could trade hypotheses?'

He lifted his glass to me as if we'd struck a deal.

'Thank you,' I said, and clumsily tried to change the subject by asking the priest an inane question.

At the end of the meal, while many of us were savouring coconut ice cream with dark chocolate sauce, a speciality of Thérèse's which she never ate herself, Terry stood up.

'Now, I don't know if you are all acquainted with my nephew David, but he is a very talented musician who will be off to New York to make his fame and fortune in a week or two. He has donated his delicious dessert to me so that he isn't too full to play, and so if you'll all give him a clap, I'm sure he might offer up a tune.'

I'd noticed David disappear a few minutes before, and

now he re-entered the dining room with a sleek saxophone. He looked relaxed and unselfconscious. I admired this; I couldn't imagine standing confidently in front of people. David seemed to soak up his audience's mood and his presence grew.

Thérèse stood up, going to the other end of the table to fetch the wine. As she leant over the table, Terry's large hand covered her tiny one and held it there, silently saying sorry.

The music was rich and sweet, not flamboyant as some modern jazz can be. It entered minds opened by wine and danced with our memories. All of us sat entranced in the darkness, meditating on the melody looping backwards and forwards. The clear notes brushed the hairs on the back of my neck sensually. I looked up at David and studied him properly for the first time.

His face was quite symmetrical, the quirks of his features repeated on both sides. He had strong brows, which cut the corner to his nose before straightening up again. His jaw was the same as Terry's: a shallow loop to his sweeping chin. It was hard to see his eyes in the dim light, but he must have sensed he was being surveyed because his body shifted a degree towards me so that I could better see him.

I concentrated on his eyes – green or grey? I wasn't sure as the shadows made them change continually.

Everyone was clapping energetically. I was suddenly aware that I'd been staring, and David was holding my gaze, entirely aware of my scrutiny. I felt myself flush, threw a hasty glance at Ellen to ensure she hadn't clocked my ogling, and belatedly joined in the applause.

Chatter filled the space the music had left, and people began to stand and move seats to chat with other people at the table. Terry was offering around cigars. I was content to remain inside my own head with the last fragments of the music.

I filled my glass up with wine.

'Do you mind?' I looked up to see David holding his glass out towards me. He sat down opposite and I offered him the bottle, not wanting my wine-woozy hand to give my state away.

'Terry tells me you're staying here?' He lifted his glass forward to meet my own. '*Sláinte.*'

His eyes were definitely green, and forceful in their contact.

'I've been here for a month now. Where are you staying?' I enquired.

'Here. In fact, I imagine we're sharing. Rooms, that is.'

He smiled. I felt a roar of attraction run up into my chest, but immediately tried to smother it. I didn't want Ellen to see me flirting.

'Ellen is very nice,' I said, mostly to remind myself of that fact. My voice cracked as he leaned in across the table.

'Yes, she is wonderful. You'd like her a lot.'

I nodded and tried to sit further back in my chair. My throat felt dry.

'So you're away to the States soon. Will Ellen be going with you?'

He shook his head.

'No, she'll be returning to London. Sadly she has a lot to do before the next auction. Have you ever been to America yourself?' he asked, his skin luminescent in the candlelight. I shook my head. 'Maybe you should come visit me. In a week or two, I'll have somewhere to stay.'

His words weren't laced with any heavy innuendoes, but I felt a strong need to bolt. The invitation seemed highly inappropriate for someone sitting about three feet from his girlfriend. I stood up and picked up some dishes.

'Well, thank you for the offer, but my plans only extend to Europe at the moment.'

I gave a curt smile and moved with some speed towards the kitchen where I could let my racing heart slow in peace. As I sloshed water into the deep sink, I felt sick with double disappointment. In the first place, he was already taken, but in the second, how could he flirt in such an open, unfazed way?

Thérèse came through the door with more plates.

'I'm hiding out,' I volunteered, but she didn't hear me. Immediately, she rushed over and hugged me – awkwardly, as my hands were still bathed in soapy suds.

'Pierro says he knows a publisher who might be interested in my work. He says they are very close friends and that he owes him a favour.' Her eyes were dancing with excitement. I couldn't help thinking that any man looking into her eyes would promise her the moon and the stars. 'He says that he'll arrange lunch next Tuesday. Isn't it terrific?'

She was seeking my approval, and who was I not to give it to her? Pierro did seem to be a different person with her, and they had known each other a long time.

'Good for you, Thérèse, you deserve it. Have you told Terry?'

Thérèse hesitated for a second.

'Well, no, I haven't had a chance, but I'm not sure I should until I have had this first meeting. Perhaps the guy won't have any interest in my work. At the very least, I hope he'll put me in touch with someone else. Terry isn't crazed about Pierro, you know, despite the fact he is a good client. I think I'll wait until after Tuesday.'

I didn't want to deflate her excitement by pointing out

that Terry was a good judge of character, but Terry spared me the opportunity to do so by hitting the kitchen door with a knockout jab, making it smash dramatically into the kitchen dresser.

'Our guests are leaving,' he announced, filling the entire doorway with his bulk.

Thérèse moved towards the music that was now spilling in through the opened door. She danced into his arms, and as the door swung backwards and forwards on its hinges with every other beat, I caught a glimpse of the two of them waltzing towards their guests.

8

The next morning, I woke to find David standing by the side of my bed. He was holding out a cup of tea with a shaky hand.

'Thérèse told me to wake you for work,' he said in a gravelly voice.

'Thanks. Can you put it down on the side table?' I asked, not wanting to pull my hands out from under the covers in case he saw the split and aggravated skin.

He sat down on the edge of my bed.

'I'd like to see the chapel you're working on.'

I shrugged. 'If you like, but I'm pretty busy.'

'Well, how about I meet you for lunch?' he persisted.

I hesitated, not wanting to cause offence.

'Tonight then.' He smiled as if I was being demanding.

'Why don't you bring Ellen? I could show you both around, and we could all go for lunch together.'

I hoped my meaning was clear.

'OK.' He shrugged before standing and moving back towards his own bed where he slid under the covers, shuffling into comfort with his back towards me.

I got dressed mechanically, and not having any appetite for breakfast, I picked up my bag from the floor ready to go. I was about to say something to David, but his back ignited my anger. Why was he lying there acting all hurt and self-righteous when he was the one flirting, and not with his girlfriend? I left in high dudgeon, banging the door with unusual force.

The *traghetto* was a less pleasurable experience than usual as it swayed around in an exaggerated manner. Hanging on to an iron post, I tried to focus on the land, but my mind swam back to David.

I had been rude. It was possible that he was just trying to be nice. I began to doubt last night's liquor-laced impressions that he had been flirting. With a girlfriend as attractive as Ellen, why would he bother?

I was beginning to feel decidedly feverish. A chill was rippling up and down my skin, and at the same time, I could feel myself flush hot with the embarrassment of misinterpretation. If I had misread the signs, how foolish did that make me seem? I bowed my head in shame while waves of humiliation washed over me.

AT ABOUT A QUARTER TO TWELVE, David, Terry and Ellen arrived at the chapel. Terry waved at Stefano, who was yelling at one of the masons for cutting marble dry inside the chapel. This produced a hurricane of fine dust which then settled on every available surface.

'Hello, darling,' said Terry, giving me a bumptious hug and two delicate continental kisses. 'I haven't seen how you are gettin' on for a while, so I thought I'd come an' check up on ya. Give you some pointers. You've missed a bit.' He laughed, pointing at the cloak of the saint that I'd finished cleaning down.

David and Ellen stood marvelling at the variety of works going on in the chapel. I noticed David didn't meet my eye. Stefano scurried over and shook everyone's hand.

'Bloody idiots, some of these people,' he huffed. 'I guarantee that tonight when you wash your hair, you'll find a kilo of marble dust blocking the plughole.'

'It's lookin' good,' Terry waved at the ceiling and altarpiece. 'A vast improvement since I was last here.'

Stefano dropped his frown.

'Glad you think so. The ceiling is marvellous!' he enthused. 'Would you like to take a look?'

Stefano gestured to the tall tower scaffold rising 50ft from the floor.

'That would be great,' said Ellen. David nodded too.

'I'll take you up there. Follow me,' said Stefano, beckoning Terry to follow.

'I think I'll stay safely down on the floor, Pete. That ceilin' looks bloody high, and that scaffold is awful skinny to take a big chap like me.'

Stefano shrugged. 'It's quite safe.' He didn't wait.

I watched the little group climbing higher and higher up the tower. 'Well, Ellen's brave, isn't she, Terry? I mean, most people would shudder at going up anything that high,' I said.

Terry looked like he was shuddering just watching her.

'How long have she and David been going out?' I enquired casually.

'Going out?' Terry was still following their ascent. 'Did David tell you they were going out? I thought they were just friends; it's news to me.'

I felt like I'd had a bucket of cold water thrown over me

at the same time as someone had given me a huge bunch of roses.

'Oh God.' I covered my face with my hands. 'Oh no, Terry, why couldn't you have filled me in last night?'

Terry looked at me in surprise.

'I didn't have a chance, why?' he asked.

I pulled my hands part way down my face, revealing only my eyes.

'Oh, I've behaved like a moron in front of David. Last night, he was trying to befriend me and flirting a little bit. I thought he was seeing Ellen and behaved like he was an adulterer. Not to mention this morning, when I slammed the front door at him just because he'd asked to come and see the chapel. Oh no!'

I hid my head again, my blushes likely colouring my hands as well.

'What does it matter? David's an easy-going guy. He'll think it's funny,' said Terry, laughing.

'Oh God, he must think I'm a freak,' I lamented. Terry put a beefy arm round me.

'You are a freak,' he comforted.

I buried more blushes in his bicep.

'What's going on here?' said David who had come down from the scaffold, leaving Ellen with the other restorers. 'She's having an incredible time up there.' He gestured up to Ellen. 'What's going on?'

David looked at my suddenly shy eyes, and glanced enquiringly at Terry.

'Abigail thinks she's made a fool of herself. She thought you were seeing Ellen and feels she might have misinterpreted your attempts at friendship last night.'

I hadn't reckoned on Terry's attempt to help me out, and wished he had kindly left it to me to sort. I was now so red that I had to take off my jumper, and I wanted to run out of David's sight and never see him again.

Terry's boom of laugher made me lift my head. David was smirking while leaning against one of my saints for support.

Stefano and Ellen joined us a few minutes later.

'Shall I take you on a ground level tour?' Stefano offered, adding sarcastically to Terry, 'For those of us without their balls with them today.'.

Ellen laughed and Terry followed him. David stayed behind, still smirking. I picked up my wooden scalpel and knelt down to carry on working.

'OK, you can stop feeling so superior now. I've suffered enough,' I said. Looking up at his amused green-grey eyes, I heard my voice jump slightly, though I was trying to sound unfazed.

'I'm just weighing you up,' he offered in explanation. 'I seem to have glimpsed an awful lot about you in a very short time – far more than if we hadn't had that little misunderstanding.'

I tried to concentrate on my work, not trusting myself to hide the smitten grin which I could already feel stretching my cheeks. The intricate engraved pattern on the hem of the cloak, which I had been trying to reveal, suddenly started to blur.

'So, you think you know me pretty well, do you? Go ahead.'

He moved to the third saint so he could see better what I was doing.

'Well, you jump to conclusions pretty quickly, so I'd say concerning people, you are not very thorough; you skip details. However, as I see you exhuming a delicate lacework pattern with great precision, I can tell that concerning your work, you are quite the reverse. You're not the to-hell-with-the-consequences kind of girl, otherwise you'd have taken me up on my advances last night, whether or not you thought I was with Ellen. You seem to like jazz, which always shows good taste. Terry and Thérèse are very fond of you so you can't be all bad. Living with them isn't easy; I've done it. Their apartment is an open house, people coming and going at all hours, so you have to be quite laid back. Last of all, you are quite the most gorgeous girl I've ever seen, and seeing as you obviously care what I think about you, I might have a pretty good chance of taking you out to dinner tonight.'

He said this all in an infuriatingly teasing tone, then bent down to my level and ceased my work by holding on to my hand.

'We can start over at dinner, if I have it all wrong.'

Shots of attraction flew through my body towards his own.

'I think we'd better have lunch before dinner,' I said, gently breaking the intimacy between us. 'Come on, let's find Terry. He knows all the best restaurants.'

A COUPLE OF EVENINGS LATER, David took me to the Friary to see a production of the opera *Rigoletto*. In the last couple of days, we had spent a lot of time together. We had swapped stories about our families and even celebrated my degree result together with Terry and Thérèse. I'd gained a respectable 2:1, and we had enjoyed a fun evening of Skyping my family while drinking seemingly unending bottles of champagne.

We weren't entirely alike. He told me of his desperation

to leave Venice behind and get to New York. He felt Venice was like a museum; a city with a heart that had stopped beating long ago, leaving a shell haunted by tourists and eccentrics like his Uncle Terry. I felt such overwhelming affection for the city that his opinion upset me more than it should have. Venice had become much more than a place to work for me. I loved the lack of cars; the musical water; the sunlight; the bridges. To me, it was the nearest thing to living in an idyllic painting. I could identify with the soul of the city and it saddened me that David did not.

David said he'd meet me at the Friary as he'd been shopping with Ellen. I was glad when he arrived early. We reached our seats with plenty of time to enjoy the ambiance of the unique church by candlelight.

David wanted to know what I'd thought of Verona when I visited.

'Did you go to the amphitheatre?' he enquired. 'Now that's another place we should go to sample the opera.'

'No, to tell you the truth, I didn't see a whole lot of Verona while I was there. I was...' I stopped, unsure how best to proceed, '...visiting a church.'

He looked up at me for a second, and I could tell he was contemplating how best to escape if I confessed to being extremely religious.

'I was visiting the church because it had a link to some research I was doing, and I was hunting for additional material in the archives of the chapel.'

David exhaled, looking a little relieved. 'I suddenly thought I might have to convert.'

His cheeks coloured slightly.

'Bit premature for that,' I said, blushing too.

'Is that your research into alchemy? I overheard the discussion at dinner.'

I inhaled and nodded, having no idea what his reaction would be.

'That sounds incredible. What did you find in Verona?'

I wondered if I should tell him, but he looked genuinely interested, and I suddenly felt the need to share my discovery with someone.

'Well, I did find an account by a priest who was supposed to be an alchemist. He spoke of a journey he'd had, but it sounded more like a dream. It was in a landscape of many colours – many of the shades he described are associated with stages in the process of alchemy. He went on to describe a fall he had, injuring himself. He then entered a dark cave where he walked, deprived of sight and sound. Suddenly, he found himself surrounded by a golden light so intense, it was almost tangible.'

'Sounds like he was abducted by aliens,' David commented dryly.

'Hardly. I'm not sure what the last part is all about, but I'm sure it's significant to my research.'

'I won't try to be an expert, but it does sound like he's describing the dark night of the soul,' he said in earnest.

'The what?' I stared at him blankly. 'I didn't know you knew anything about theology?'

'I studied music at university, and in my final year, I had to take a course on religious music in the seventeenth century – a complication involving flunking something else, and having to make up extra points in order to pass my degree. Anyway, it was actually quite interesting. All about how music was influenced by the transcendental movement based on writings about a religious experience. The dark night of the soul was usually experienced after intense meditation, and was described as coming into the presence of God, often in terms of bright light.'

I sat back in amazement. Not only was this man attractive and forgiving, he was helping me with my research. What more could I want in life?

It was becoming clearer that the meditation was the key to the transformation.

Suddenly, the music began, cutting off further discussion. Music was not really a passion for me as it was for David; mostly, I preferred silence. Opera, like jazz, sometimes felt like a foreign language. The sounds were familiar, but their meaning elusive. If I was in certain moods, a sensuous solo could feel like purposeful torture – a noise jarring on tender nerves.

That night, the music penetrated me as it had never done before. Perhaps the dramatic setting, the cold night, and my budding feelings for David came together with such force that they punched their way through, allowing the music to float in.

AT THE END of the performance, the crowds began to clear. David and I remained, letting people flood past us. We were too stirred up to descend out into the real world. We chose to sit for a while, cocooned in our operatic experience, and talk to one another in a place filled to the brim with atmosphere.

'Did you enjoy it?' he asked, watching me.

'It was beautiful.' I looked past him, hypnotised by the candlelight all around. 'There was so much colour in the sounds, I feel like I've spent my life listening in black and white. Some sections were like shades of each other, close colours, gently tumbling in on one another, while others were like shocking pink against blood red – arising from the same shades, but clashing and argumentative. Did you feel that?'

When David didn't answer right away, I was suddenly aware that I had probably said too much in response to a simple question. I looked to his eyes for reassurance.

'I've spent my entire life listening to music and studying it. Never once, even at university, surrounded by hundreds of musicians, have I met anyone who has described music in terms of a palette. It's like you are translating what you've heard into another language to understand it, rather than enjoying it in the mother tongue.'

A shout made us both look up; a man was indicating we had outstayed our welcome. We got up to move outside.

'How do you see music, then?' I asked, slightly breathlessly.

'I don't see music at all. The experience is totally aural. It's like my other senses are stilled, and my hearing envelops all of them,' he explained.

We were outside now and walking.

'I think I find music hard because I can't touch it. At least when I visualise the music, it becomes a little more tangible, because I know what the colours feel like.'

David chuckled and put an arm round me.

'You are crackers, do you know that? You are absolutely mad. How can anyone know what a colour feels like?' he said, squeezing me affectionately.

The feel of colour was hard to describe to someone who had never felt it form beneath their fingers. How could the graininess of salt and the astringent suck of vinegar equate to green for anyone other than a patineur? There was no explanation as to why the sting of ammonia mixed with the damp clamminess of humidity should shoot a volley of blue through my mind's eye. If I hadn't known what colour felt like, my world would have been entirely two-dimensional.

David steered me through some doors into the small bar. My fingers rippled with memories of unique colours, as if in a belligerent response to David's comments that such feelings might not exist. A delightfully shy mauve, which I had coaxed from a conceited bronze high in silver content many months before, danced on the tip of my thumb. I tried to ignore it as David ordered wine. Deciding not to explain what he may interpret as my eccentricity, I let the subject be exchanged for another.

A carafe of house wine was brought to our table. The waiter's hand brushed mine, just for an instant, as he filled my glass. I reacted badly, pulling my hand away like I'd been stung, knocking the jug out of his hand in the process. The wine fell in a fan shape across the tablecloth. There was a fuss with the waiter and David both trying to assist me.

I sat still as stone, feeling utterly foolish while the waiter whisked the tablecloths away. I couldn't possibly explain to David the mortification I felt about people touching my hands. The awful rash, which spread all over my hands, wrists, and even up my arms at times, kept my relationships with people on a long leash. I never shook hands, never went anywhere without gloves, and very rarely touched people's skin with my hands.

The reaction people might have was not all imagined. My first boyfriend had retched when I'd finally shown him. People on the Tube would stare at me if I wore a short sleeved t-shirt, and my gloves didn't quite cover the inflamed skin. They would push themselves up against the furthest possible point in case it was catching. Even the most under-standing friends would flinch when my hands were uncovered.

When we were settled again, I apologised for being so clumsy. David was sweet.

'No matter.' He laughed, but his eyes were serious. I could tell he was running over my behaviour in his mind, wondering why such an innocent act had caused such panic. 'Let me show you what I've bought today.' He lifted the shopping bag he'd been carrying. 'It's for Thérèse,' he explained, releasing wafer thin tissue from its tape.

Inside was a dress as delicate as the paper it was wrapped in. It had a fleeting resemblance to a medieval gown, though much sexier. Made in black chiffon, full-length, it was designed to show every curve of the female body. It would have been slightly too transparent to be worn in public, but for the addition by some ingenious designer of a white chiffon layer over the black. Cut into a V from the shoulders, plunging to just below the bust, it was gathered in like an A-line dress, but instead of dropping to the floor in the demure way an A-line was designed to do, it parted like a curtain to reveal the comely black shape of the wearer. The white framed the black on its descent to the ground. It was a work of art and utterly perfect for Thérèse.

I couldn't immediately give David the praise such a choice deserved, because I was so thrown by his insight into what Thérèse would like, and his good taste. When the words did spill out, I could see the relief fall into him.

'Thank goodness,' he breathed.

'It must have cost you a fortune.' I touched the label, not daring to turn it over.

'Well, I've blown my deposit for the flat in NY, but I've got friends that will let me crash while I get some more money together. This is for you,' he said, smiling as he passed me a very slender parcel, disproportionately heavy, wrapped in Venetian marble paper. As I uncurled it gently, a sheer satin gold burst upon my eyes. It was a fountain pen no wider than reed; even the nib was gold. In its unpolished state, gold has a spectrum of colours akin to those seen by the setting sun on the horizon. It is far deeper in hue than the polished finish of flashy jewellery.

'It's for your research,' he said gently. 'It's to inspire you.'

I fell in love with him at that moment, sitting on a chair in a café. I should have told him then.

'I've been thinking how close America and Venice actually are,' he said. 'We could commute.'

'I can't tell you how much I'd love to do that,' I said, looking into his chameleon eyes. I leaned forward and kissed him gently on the lips.

We took the *traghetto* back to the flat. Our kisses were soft and sweet, the drizzle of wine in our bloodstreams enriching our feelings. We walked arm-in-arm towards the front door, and just as we were about to enter, he tried to take my hand. I anticipated his move and stepped away.

'Why do you do that?' he asked me.

'What?' I tilted my head on one side, mocking his seriousness.

'You'll kiss me, but...' He stopped, searching for the right word. 'I feel like you're lying to me.'

I took a deep breath and shivered a little.

'Lying about what?' I shrugged.

'OK, then why do you wear gloves all the time?' he said, a note of anger rippling in his voice.

'It's a habit...my hands are always cold,' I stammered.

'Fine!' he said, turning and walking into the flat in front of me without a backward glance.

9

A couple of days afterwards, I was rather unenthusiastically giving the saints a final wax and buff. My mind was on David, who had arrived safely in New York. I hadn't tried to give him an explanation before he left. One thing I had learned from having so many brothers was not to tackle men when they were angry. Things got sorted out with less drama when everyone had calmed down. The morning after the opera had been too hectic for meaningful conversations, but we'd parted on good terms with promises to speak as often as possible.

Stefano shouted down from his scaffold.

'Their colour's so rich it looks as if they've a holy aura emanating from their cloaks.'

I smiled at the appreciation. I cast the rag over my shoulder and had begun to walk backwards to get a better view of the overall finish when I trod on Pierro Ricco's soft suede shoe. A silence bursting with my surprise and his suppressed yell held precariously between us for just a moment, before I remembered my manners.

'Pierro, I am so sorry, I had no idea you were there.'

'No, no, it is my fault; I was in your way. I was just watching you work.They look marvellous. Superb,' he purred reassuringly. 'I wonder, are you available for lunch?'

His request was entirely unexpected. I looked down at my working clothes self-consciously.

'I'm not really dressed for it.'

He shrugged. 'No matter. There is a lovely little restaurant where I know the owner very well. He would not dream of making a fuss,' he said.

I agreed and went to wash my hands. Pierro's exchanges always left me with a bitter taste in my mouth. Perhaps it was my own paranoia suffocating my common sense, but I couldn't help but wonder why he had been watching me. Had he been trying to catch me using some unorthodox method?

We sat in a busy little restaurant on Piazza Margherita with several other hungry couples. The rain was relentless, and sporadically people sprinted through the doorway and shook like dogs to get dry.

A plate of antipasto was served, and we began to get to the purpose of this impromptu lunch.

'Are you going to stay with Stefano after this project?' Pierro enquired.

'He has asked me to join him on his next project, yes.'

'Have you agreed?' His voice was velvety, laced with the delicate wine.

'Not yet. I probably will though.'

'It's just that I know of a job you might be interested in, but it's in Florence. It is private work, but very lucrative. I am a patron of a very good young sculptor called Sergio Rudolpho; he is looking for a patineur. He has been dissatisfied with all of the finest foundries in Florence. He says they have no feel for the modern. I was telling him that you specialise in patination, and as you were young, I was sure you would understand his concept.'

'Can you tell me a little more about what he wants?'

'Well, this collection is mostly abstract – lots of unusual smooth shapes, large ones and small. He is very into colour as a mode of expressing his ideas, but says that he is hindered by a lack of vocabulary.'

I had come across a lot of artists at the foundry who had grand ideas, and little appreciation of the complexity of realising them. They were usually very hard clients to work for because they wouldn't take any advice. They had a tendency to speak down to me as if I couldn't possibly appreciate their brilliance.

'He is hoping for a wide ranging palette. He has a wonderful studio – his family is very rich and has invested substantially in his career. He will offer you workshop space in his own studio. It's not like those dingy holes you see in Europe: old shacks converted and the like. It is all glass and wooden beams, purpose built for maximum light and creative flow.'

Obviously, Pierro had no idea that he had perfectly described my family's foundry with his allusion to dingy holes, but his description was so apt that it almost brought tears to my eyes. I felt the emotional rope that bound me to our foundry tug hard at the pit of my stomach, reminding me that though I was loosely tethered, I wouldn't be allowed to get away.

I tried to make my voice sound steady.

'It is the work that goes on in a studio, rather than the design of the building, that I would place most emphasis on.'

'Of course, but everyone likes to be in a fine working

environment.' He smiled in a placating way and changed tack. 'But of course, there is also work with Stefano to consider, if you prefer other chapels.' He waved his fork to indicate that they were all around us. 'Less challenging work, though; less well paid.'

I tried to swallow my pasta, but my stomach was buzzing, making it hard for my food to go down. This was exactly the kind of work I dreamed of doing: patination for a cutting-edge contemporary artist. Also, until David left, money hadn't been an issue, but if we did want our relationship to work, then expensive trips over to the States and back would have to become the norm.

Florence was tempting for other reasons, too: I would get to hang out with Marco, whom I had grown up with, and he would provide an instant introduction into Florence's social life. Also, he worked at the History of Science Museum, and there was every chance he might be able to help me take my research further.

I put down my fork. 'I would have to meet the sculptor before deciding anything,' I said.

Pierro inclined his head. 'But, of course. I'll make the arrangements.' He picked up his phone and made the call instantly.

With a meeting arranged, we seemed to have run out of conversation. The butterflies in my stomach wouldn't settle enough to allow me to finish the pasta, so I made my excuses and walked back towards the chapel, thinking over the exciting proposition.

When I arrived back at my saints, I was annoyed to find that somebody had moved my kit. It was nowhere to be seen. I walked around, shouting up to the others, asking them if they'd moved it or seen anyone who had. Everyone's response was negative.

After a half hour of searching, I started to grow concerned. It wasn't that I couldn't complete my work without it; I had very little remaining to do, but my tool kit held such sentimental value to me, and it contained the notebooks I had on my research.

Stefano and the rest of the team, noticing my increasing distress, began to help me search. An hour later, we were no closer to finding it, and I went back to the flat brimming with tears.

I found Terry and Thérèse reading together on one of their leather sofas.

'What's wrong, honey?' Thérèse asked, looking up. I blubbed incoherently and walked over to my bed to sit down. Thérèse hurried over to put an arm around me.

'Sweetheart, it'll be okay,' she soothed.

I shifted position as I was sitting on something and was amazed to see quite a lot of my stuff emptied out on the bed.

'Did you do this?' I asked Thérèse. She shook her head.

'Of course not.'

I looked down at my suitcase which I usually kept under my bed, and it was protruding slightly. I bent down and looked inside. Everything was a mess, and there were other bits and pieces on the floor under the bed.

'This is definitely not how I left it,' I said in confusion.

Thérèse looked at me with surprise in her eyes.

'Don't be crazy, honey, no-one's been in the flat. Any thief would have definitely taken stuff. You're just upset.'

I started to feel more alarmed. I definitely hadn't left everything out like this – I was very aware that the bed, being in the living room space, should look as tidy as possible when I wasn't there.

'Have you been out today?' I asked. She nodded.

'We both have, but no-one has keys and nothing else is

out of place.'

She clearly thought I was mistaken, and I wasn't sure what to think. It did seem unlikely. Thérèse went to make a cup of tea for me, and I bundled together my clothes, make-up and other clutter. I felt nervous, which made me scratch at my hands more than usual. Was someone trying to scare me? Why would they bother?

Terry came over and patted my shoulder.

'What's up?' he asked.

I told him about the kit. 'I really don't understand. Apart from anything, it's so huge. You couldn't just walk out of there with it.'

'We can replace your kit, but I know it won't be the same. We had a break in about six years ago and they took all of my best brushes along with jewellery I'd given Thérèse. I was much more upset about my brushes. Didn't anyone see someone hanging around? It was probably one of the crew.'

I shook my head. 'I can't believe that. It had so many things in it that I can't replace.'

'It's amazing how we can get on without the things we thought we needed.'

He gave me a hug. Thérèse returned, and I told them about my job offer.

'It does sound as if the sculptor is a bit of a prima donna, but I would be doing avant-garde stuff, which is just what I love,' I enthused.

'We'll miss you,' said Thérèse, and her kind eyes told me she meant it. 'I'll be coming up to Florence soon to meet Pierro's friend, the publisher, and I have lots of friends there. I'm sure I will be up and down a lot.'

Excitement rippled in her voice. Terry raised his eyebrows but said nothing.

'It sounds awful, but I wish it wasn't Pierro that had

offered me it. It's completely unfair as he's been nothing but complimentary and businesslike with me. I just find him cold.'

'I agree with you,' said Terry, 'but don't confuse business with your social life. He's an upstanding member of Venetian and Florentine society, very rich, educated, connected. He's been a patron of mine for a long time, and though I don't choose to spend time with him, we both benefit from the arrangement.'

Thérèse had her own point of view.

'You two misunderstand him. It's cultural differences, that's all. He is a bit of a snob, and you English hate snobs I think he has a great fire inside of him. I get the feeling that he is controlling it all the time. It might be the reason he is such a successful businessman, and why he doesn't have a steady partner. He changes his girlfriends like he does his suits. He always has some gorgeous girl on his arm, but rarely the same one.'

After a moment's pause, she added, 'How long before your current contract ends? I've already started planning our New Year's Eve party and you must be here for that. We are going to dress the flat up and invite everyone. Terry has arranged some excellent musicians and everyone is coming in costume.'

'My work here isn't due to end until Christmas so I promise to be around for New Year's.' I moved across to a fat looking sofa with some serious love handles. 'I hope my kit turns up by then. Much as I loved it, it was losing the notebooks I regretted most. Why hadn't I kept them somewhere safer? It occurred to me that this loss might be the end of the alchemy trail for me. With that thought, my desire to go to Florence lessened fractionally, whereas my inclination to go to New York picked up.

10

My plane set down at Heathrow on 24 December. Baggage reclaim was doubly busy with extra bags full of presents for loved ones. Like a mule, I strode sure-footedly but with little speed towards the arrivals lounge. My heart was heavier than my bags. Mum had told me on the phone the night before that there was no way they'd be able to pick me up, and I'd have to make my own way back. Apparently, a commission had been received two days ago and the whole family was trying to push it out before Christmas Eve. Even my brother Tim, who worked in A&E, had to take double shifts just to get Christmas Day off.

There is no emptier feeling in the world than having no-one to meet you at an airport. I felt the prickle of absentees in my throat and the back of my eyes as I put my head down and moved through into the arrivals lounge.

There is no more euphoric feeling in the world than being greeted by a group 'Oehi!' when you're least expecting it. Mum, Dad, two brothers and Larry were leaning over the barrier like a family of grinning gorillas, and they'd never looked more wonderful to me.

I felt slightly less charmed when I realised they'd all come in one fairly large car. It was like we were all eight years old again. We had developed a seating pattern some time ago when family outings were regular. A dozen years later, we adopted our pre-allotted positions, but now two pigeon chested squirts had turned into great hulking lads, plus we had Larry. By the time we got home I was about ready to fly back to Venice.

WE SAT down around our kitchen table at 7pm the following evening for Christmas dinner. We never ate at the traditional time as Mum preferred the entire day to prepare. Larry joined us for what proved to be a very European turkey. I'd brought a huge hamper from Italy which was intended to be a joint present for everyone. It contained dozens of Venetian delicacies, including fragrant cheeses, olives and smoky prosciutto, fine wines, coffee, and biscuits of every variety.

Mum went out to carry some presents in. It was our custom to open a present at the table, and then the rest afterwards in the sitting room. Rue, my eldest brother, was helping himself to wine and forcing some more on Sally, who was my youngest brother, Kael's, girlfriend. Mum handed out the gifts she'd picked up from under the tree. Dad got an enormous one passed over, which seemed to please him, whereas I was handed a tiny, perfectly wrapped box.

Everyone around the table grew quieter. This was such a rarity in our house that I knew something very important must be inside. I opened it quickly and gaped at it with the eyes of a disbeliever. It was at least a five carat colourless diamond cut into a heart shape on a gold shank.

'It was your grandmother's. It's very valuable,' my mum explained. 'We thought it was time to hand it on. You may as well enjoy it while you are young and beautiful.'

I slipped it on and admired the kaleidoscopic colours which were only ever visible for an instant at a time. I had never owned a ring as it was the kind of ornament that would draw attention to my hands, but it was so beautiful. I hugged my parents.

'Wow, you've definitely set the bar very high for any future presents,' I laughed.

Larry popped a bottle of champagne; Rue turned some music on; Mum served the vegetables; Kael kissed Sally; Dad laid out spicy mashed swede on the table; and then the telephone rang.

Dad went to answer it.

'Abi, it's for you. A David?' he bellowed. I flushed.

'I'll be back in a minute. Get started,' I said, gesturing for them all to carry on.

David was drunk.

'I know it's late. I'm sorry. I really wanted to say Merry Christmas.'

There was a lot of noise going on behind him.

'It's not late for me,' I tried to tell him, but he wasn't listening.

'I miss you, Abi. This long distance relationship stuff is stupid. I'm actually thinking of coming back to Venice for you, and you know I hate...Well, I don't hate Venice, but...'

'David, I'm going to Florence.'

'Terry won't mind if I stay with him, and maybe, when

we know each other a bit more, we could find a flat. I really like you, Abi, really.' His voice was dense.

'David, can you hear me? I've got a job in Florence.'

'I really miss you,' he said.

My mum came into the study with a scowl.

'Get off the phone!' she mouthed.

'I'm coming, I'm coming.' I waved her away. 'David, I've got to go. I miss you too. Can you call me tomorrow?' I begged.

The noise grew louder behind him.

'Abi,' he yelled in a strangled sob. 'Abi, I love you.'

It's an amazing thing when the right man says, 'I love you.' I felt the words kindle something inside me, and within seconds it was like a fire was raging in my chest. I struggled a moment to get any words through.

'Abi!' shouted my dad from next door.

'I have to go, David. I'm crazy about you too. Promise to call me tomorrow. I don't know where you're staying...' but he'd gone before I could be sure he'd heard.

I needed to tell him about my hands before I told him I loved him.

Boxing Day was really quiet. Most of the boys had made arrangements to see their girlfriends' relatives, except Tim who had to go back to work at the hospital. Mum and Dad had arranged to see Larry and some other old friends in a pub nearby. I spent nearly the entire morning on the phone, making arrangements to see people whom I hadn't been in contact with since I'd gone away. A long line of coffees and excited news-swapping stretched out across the rest of my holiday. Hearing so many of my friends' voices made me feel homesick. Despite the fact I was actually home, I knew I'd be leaving again soon.

After I put down the phone, I thought about what I could do to keep my mind off David. I had two ideas: I wanted to play with some spelter, and I wanted to make Terry an unusual gift. The foundry whispered conspiratorially to me.

I made my way to the kitchen for a cup of tea. I had been starved of good tea in Venice. It might have been the water, or the actual tea itself, but somehow the flavour was insipid and slightly salty. This had forced me to embrace the coffee culture. Since I'd been back in England, I hadn't been able to get enough of the real thing.

I slipped on a pair of my brother's boots and took my tea into the workshop with me. I was dying to see if anything had changed round the old place since I'd gone away. At first glance, all was just as I'd left it: a platoon of benches standing to attention, awaiting inspection.

I walked up and down the rows, which were divided at regular intervals. Many of the benches were neater than usual with works finished and tools tidied away. There were a few new shelves, a bench empty that had not been when I left, but all in all, I felt comforted that change hadn't muscled in while I was absent.

I stopped at my father's bench which I had shared with him over the years and rubbed its stubbly surface. Jam jars of chemicals, all in need of refilling, were gathered in groups on his shelf. There was a basket of dirty brushes next to them and quite a bit of clutter stuffed underneath the worktop. The upkeep of the bench had always been one of my chores. I ensured that our supplies didn't run low and our brushes were always cleaned after every job. I felt pleased at this small indication that I wasn't easily replaceable, and whoever was assisting him these days wasn't really up to the job.

I sat on my stool and finished my tea quietly. Between sips, I could feel a drum beat in the tips of my fingers – the spelter was calling to me. No-one would bother me from the house; the workshop would be the last place they'd want to be during the Christmas break, and I'd have all the tools, chemicals and facilities I'd need here.

I slipped over to the three industrial barrels next to the furnace, which we dubbed Lucifer. The containers held scrap metal ready to be melted down again. I stared into the barrel of non-ferrous misfits. Standing on a chair, I leant in and plucked out a legless ballerina. I ran my hands over the bronze, reading it like Braille, and discarded it. The metal was too pure. I was looking for spelter, which was a cheap bronze alloy containing a proportion of lead.

This barrel could have been in a post-modern gallery; every freak that I pulled out showed a failure in an artwork's production. There were gaping holes in the centre of a horse head where a huge air bubble had lodged itself, and a paper-thin bust of Henry VIII was almost transparent as the core had been made too thin. I dug past all of these pieces which had been made with fine alloy, pushing my arm deeper into unseen objects.

When I first touched the soldier, I immediately moved on as his slightly warm temperature was so unfamiliar. When I stroked him again while moving past a neighbouring piece, the difference was less pronounced. I pulled at his feet, and he came away with a scratch up his back from the end of some other piece.

I looked at him: a bugler in uniform. He looked like other bronzes, but he felt different. I pulled a coin from my jeans and scratched his surface. Instead of the pink shiny skin of a good bronze, this one had a murkier colour. I had found my spelter.

I took the statue over to my workbench and secured it in the jaws of a clamp. The cushions of my hands burned with excitement, and I rubbed the insatiable itch distractedly while I focused on my statue. Unmercifully, I cut it into largish chunks with a sharp saw.

My intention was to explore the nature of spelter, which I was entirely unfamiliar with. It would be a process of trial and error. The green theology book had described the colours of the Peacock's Tail and my ambition was to form them.

I cleaned the spelter up quickly, not bothering with a full preparation; I just wanted to get an understanding of the nature of this metal, and what it could do. In its naked form, the metal had a slightly depressed hue. There was just a suggestion of darkness below the surface.

I decided to try to form a simple colour to start with: a medium brown. I mixed up a liver of sulphur solution and got out my dad's burning brushes. I heated the metal and began to burn into its pores, allowing the chemical plenty of time to form. It seemed to form with a greyish hue, but I gave it the benefit of the doubt. Often you couldn't tell the precise colour until after the object had been waxed.

However, even with wax, the colour was somewhere between rat and mule – a horrible non-descript mud.

I cleaned off the colour and began again, this time with a stronger solution. There was a moment when I thought it might open up, but then it was gone and the muddy colour appeared again. I was undeterred and in an indulgent mood for about the first three-quarters of an hour, but as time ran on, I began to get fractious, knowing that I should be at least seeing a hint of progress.

After a good hour, my conclusion was that the metal was frigid. It responded very little to touch, unlike better pedigree bronzes, and seemed to produce mute and sulky colours. I needed a break so I rinsed my hands and went back to the house to make a toasted sandwich.

The Aga was warm; I leaned against it while the kettle boiled and turned the toast rack over to heat the other side. What was I doing wrong? It was a pig of a metal!

I sat with my back to the Aga and our Jack Russell, called Dug, at my feet, staring out of a large rectangular window. I could see mile upon mile of green farmland; the scene hypnotised me. When I finally stood, an idea had seeded without me noticing.

I went to Dan's bench to look for some more of the strange Greek limestone he'd given me as a going away present back in July. Everything was tidy and swept away, but in the same way the foundry had an off-cut barrel, the masons had a scraps box, and here I found what I was looking for.

I stared at the soldier's leg. 'Please don't mess me around any more,' I told it in an authoritative tone.

I began again, but this time I took a little more time with the preparation. Instead of using pumice powder as was our custom, I substituted it for the little block Dan had given me, which he'd once mentioned was softer than pumice.

I moved back and forth with the stone, keeping the metal's grain in one direction, and then changing and moving perpendicular to it. After ten minutes, I began again with the burning. There was a glimmer; it made my heart jump up and do a back flip. The colour formed, and then instead of instantaneously greying, as it had been doing for the last hour, it teetered but stayed. I sat anxiously, letting it cool. Almost reluctantly, I picked up the wax and a brush, and tenderly tickled it.

The colour wasn't spectacular, but it was a medium brown. It was a start. I'd never felt so relieved in my life. I had only been a hair's breadth from fetching a piece of good bronze and checking I hadn't lost my touch. It was by no means a huge success, but I had learned something, and I decided to quit while I was ahead.

I dutifully washed out my father's brushes, restocked his shelves and tidied beneath his bench. I took the remaining pieces of the soldier with me; I intended to play around with them a little more in Italy. When I switched off the lights, I felt sick with nostalgia and dizzy from so many choices: David, Florence, and home.

THE MEDITATION HAD NOT BEEN GOING WELL; Terry's flat had not been an ideal place to practise. The public nature of my own space in the library meant I was almost never alone. I felt far too exposed when I did try, and my mind bounced between the exercise and the possibility that I would be interrupted at any second.

Home, on the other hand, offered security. I'd begun to appreciate doors in a way I'd never done before; open plan living isn't all it's cracked up to be. Our small rooms had walls close enough to each other that you actually got a hug as you came in. When I began meditation in this environment, I was two steps closer to Nirvana without even closing my eyes.

At no other time of the year was the foundry at peace like it was at Christmas. Works always slowed in the days before the holiday, and this year was no different. Everyone took a holiday of at least two weeks and our house exhaled with relief.

I took cautious steps at the beginning. Meditation was a hazy concept to me, something like my notion of heaven. I began by calling to mind St Sebastian as soon as I shut my eyes, and achieving this was the first fairy-size step forward. It began blurrily at first, but my concentration strengthened, and details would come shyly into focus.

One night, a troop of brothers, followed by Mum and Dad, came to say goodnight. Affection was dense in the air; it was the most tangible that love had ever seemed to me. When I commenced my meditation that night, the colours in the scene appeared bolder as if some artist in my head was adding pigment. By the end of the session, I was forced to open my eyes because the intensity of the hues was too vibrant to contain.

I thought carefully over what I had done differently that night. It was clear that though my actions were the same, my state of mind had been different. From then on, I began every meditation by evoking feelings of love. I used my family, my home, my friends – every good thing that could cloak me in love – as a source. As a result, the success of my meditation was proportional to my state of mind every time.

Apart from the colours, I began to be able to manipulate the viewpoint so that I was no longer a viewer of a scene, but rather a participant in it. The last night that I practised this exercise was the most disturbing. I felt a sadness so profound that weeping was no relief at all. Deep, deep emotion, and pain for the saint, racked my body. When I opened my eyes that night, I was exhausted with grief. I felt that empathy with a dead saint seemed qualification enough to move on to the next phase.

It was easier to clear my mind than it ever had been

before. I let things go, and I had the strength to hold them out. The Sebastian exercises had given me good foundations. Now, at each sitting, I pushed my thoughts further and further from a point in my mind where my presence seemed to reside, as if my mind was holding things at a distance, and again I made headway each day. It was like holding a circular force-field up; the strength needed to push away became easier to bear, and in some moments (or were they minutes?), it took no effort at all. There was just an equilibrium.

THE DAY BEFORE I LEFT, I slipped into the foundry to make Terry his gift. I'd spotted an old pair of iron knuckledusters on the mantelpiece of his art studio. They were leaning up against one side of a carriage clock as if waiting for an assailant to come around the corner. These were tools from Terry's violent past; now they gathered dust. I think it was the simplicity of the concept that appealed to me so much. I found myself looking at them several times.

They were very basic: four circles for the fingers to slide inside and a thick iron bar to clasp in the palm of the hand. Anyone hit by these would certainly remember the punch.

The more I studied them, the more I wanted to improve them. It wouldn't be difficult to make bespoke knuckledusters. I had asked Terry to squeeze some clay for me, but didn't tell him why. Wrapping the impression in a damp cloth, I housed it in a Tupperware box to take back home. I then took some dimensions of his fingers, and explained merely that it had something to do with his Christmas present.

I meant to make him a set of bronze knuckledusters so

comfortable, they'd feel like a glove. Of course, they were to be for the purposes of fine art rather than function. I couldn't see any reason why he would need to use them, but if he did, they would certainly serve their purpose diligently.

I took the clay impression of the clasp of his hand, and added to it four finger arches according to the measurements of his fingers. To make the knuckledusters even more dangerous, I added angular notches on top of each arch. I then set about making the mould with silicone rubber, and strengthened it with fibreglass.

I filled the knuckleduster-shaped cavity inside the mould with an emerald-coloured casting wax which had been heated to liquify. This wax was specially designed. It was easy to carve when solid, easy to shape with a little warmth, and quite strong.

Once the wax was cool and solid, I tugged it from its mould, and attached three lengths of long wax-like worms, which we called sprues. I then mixed up the grog, a coating that would be packed around the wax form. It would eventually become the vessel that the molten metal would be poured into. It was quite an old-fashioned method of casting, but we still used it for architectural objects like lanterns and railings – objects that didn't need fine surface detail of high quality.

I covered my wax template and sprues in the porridge-like grog. When I had built up sufficient layers, it went into our small furnace so the wax could run out – the sprues were its escape route. What was left was a shell with a knuckleduster shaped space where the wax had once been. After I'd strengthened the grog shell by baking it in the furnace for some hours, the mould was ready for the metal.

I melted a crucible of bronze in the furnace and poured it into its little mould. Once it had cooled, I chipped and sandblasted away the grog from the surface to reveal the most regal looking knuckledusters an ex-gangster could ever wish for. I rasped out the sides of the finger holes to make them super-smooth, then polished the tips of the arches to make them gleam nastily, and I made the surfaces satiny before patinating them a rich dark bronze. I knew the colour would wear gently with handling, revealing highlights and low lights and several shades in between.

I tried them on before packing them away. The grooves of Terry's hand, taken directly from his grip, made them feel very personal. Though I had only just made them, they reminded me of ancient weapons housed in the British Museum where the imprints of the owners could be seen etched into the handles: person and object fused together.

I was as sure he'd like them as I was that Thérèse would hate them.

11

I returned to Venice early on New Year's Eve. Thérèse was organising their annual party which was to be a bigger hoopla than usual, due to my imminent departure for Florence. When I arrived at the friendly flaking door, I had to stride up the stairs four at a time to avoid knocking over the hoard of supplies stacked up the steps, and continued on into the living room.

Thérèse was wearing faded jeans and a jogging top, and was perched on top of a set of ladders, tacking some lantern lights to the bookcases.

'Glad you're back, honey, you can take that brushwood and acorns into the studio. Terry's going to spray them silver,' she said. I took a deep breath, but before I could say a word, Thérèse cut in. 'Actually, before that, can you just hold up that chiffon on the sofa while I drape it around the lights?'

Thérèse was frighteningly focused; I could hardly get her to talk about anything but the party, let alone stop for a break. I was still standing in my long winter coat and sheepskin-lined boots a half hour later when Terry came home with more booze than I'd ever seen outside of a public house. Terry, in a somewhat more relaxed mood, got us a coffee and plied me with Christmas questions.

Thérèse wasn't having any of it.

'Can't you two chat and spray at the same time?' she commented while whipping past us, carrying a huge box of bread.

Terry raised his eyebrows and signalled for me to follow. We lifted armfuls of brushwood on to newspaper-lined tables, I opened the windows wide, and Terry shook a can of spray paint lazily.

'I spoke to David today. He's left a number for you to reach him on. Sounds a bit smitten to me, but what do I know? Try him in another hour – best time to get him is the morning, so he said.' He nudged my arm knowingly.

I managed to give Terry his gift without Thérèse noticing. I'd wrapped it in a little cardboard box tied with string. He was overwhelmed when he saw it. It did fit perfectly, better than I'd hoped. He hugged me.

'You are clever. I forget how skilled you are. I hope David isn't the first recipient of my new killer left hook. He better treat you right or watch out.' He did a little shadowboxing then slipped the knuckledusters inside his pocket.

I tried David on the hour, every hour, for the rest of the day with no success. I'd spoken to him on Boxing Day when he'd seemed a little subdued, and I couldn't get much out of him. After seven tries on the telephone, I felt sure that he was avoiding me. By five o'clock, we were all irritable and jaded. Thérèse was nearly in tears over a huge cake that mysteriously hadn't risen.

Terry entered the kitchen calmly; I expected him to help himself to more coffee. Instead, he swept Thérèse up like she weighed no more than a pillow and carried her out of the kitchen. She kicked and twisted her body in protest.

'You need a rest, Thérèse. You're driving us all mad,' he told her.

After that, the flat was very quiet. I slept too deeply and was woken by my alarm at seven o'clock. I met Thérèse coming out of the bathroom with rollers in her hair. She apologised for being so uptight and gave me a hug.

About eight o'clock, I looked round the flat and everything was ready. Vases and bowls were filled with acorns and brushwood, giving the flat a mystical woodland feel. Fairy lights were hung along the cornices around the ceilings. The cables were painted in silver and bunches of wild berries hung from them. Poinsettia had been ordered by the dozen and set out on tables. Terry had asked me to make a few basic candle racks with angle iron which I had done before I went home to the foundry. We stacked thick church candles in rows on them, and lined them up by the windows so that people arriving could see them glowing from outside.

Terry exited his room wearing a robe of shimmering blue and a detachable long white beard. His only other prop was a tall staff.

'I am Gandalf the Grey,' he announced with a bow when he saw me.

'Well, we are a fine pair. You should recognise me, Gandalf, I am Galadriel of Lothlórien.'

'And very magical you look too,' he complimented. I was wearing a long dress of shimmering silver green. I had put my hair up and sprayed it with glitter, putting some silk flowers in as a final touch.

'Wow, and look at that ring; that's really something,' he said, 'May I?'

Even though I was wearing a thin pair of lace gloves, I hesitated just a beat before giving over my hand so that he could look at the ring properly.

'It is beautiful,' I agreed. 'I feel like I never want to take it off, though it's hardly practical for every day.'

Terry was distracted by his musician friends, who were setting up when the first knock at the door signalled the start of the party. I went to open it, but it was so dark, I couldn't quite see who was coming up the stairs. I hardly recognised David in his tuxedo when he stepped out of the shadows and into the flat.

I rushed into his arms and he swung me round.

'So you're only crazy about me.' He pecked me on the lips. 'Not madly in love with me or anything?'

I didn't want to let go.

'You were drunk; I thought you...didn't mean it.'

He laughed at me. 'Well, as you can see, I'm here to claim you,' and he kissed me properly for the first time.

Thérèse came out of her room in the dress David had bought her. All of us were mesmerised. Her hair was in ringlets and sprayed white, dotted with diamanté.

'We weren't expecting you,' she said, kissing David on both cheeks.

'Well, I was,' Terry owned up.

'But you let me ring him all day,' I pointed out.

'Yes. Cruel of me, wasn't it?'

His laugh rumbled round the room. More guests were now filling the stairs and hallway and pushing in past David. Thérèse was slipping between people, getting them drinks and sparkling more than her diamantés. There wasn't a man in the room who didn't envy Terry his wife that night.

David and I went to sit on my bed. 'I'm leaving for Florence in just a couple of days. I've got a new job,' I began.

'Yes, I do remember something about that. So do I have to move to Florence?' he said and took my hand, which I snatched away. He looked hurt.

'Tell me first, how is New York?' I said.

'It's ideal for the music. I don't think it will be a problem to get jobs; I've already got some leads which I'll follow up when I get home. I've found a flat – a friend of a friend is leaving to work in Italy, of all places, and so I can sublet from him.'

'That makes it worse,' I said. 'I can't ask you to leave when you're only just getting started.' I scuffed the cushions of my palms against my dress.

'Why don't you forget this new job and come back with me to New York, then?' he asked, with eyes twinkling flirtatiously.

I shook my head. 'It's such a good project for me, and I can't let them down.'

'But you can let me down.' His eyes had stilled now.

'Don't do that,' I said. 'It's not as straightforward as you make it sound. There's something I want to finish up in Italy which I can't do in New York.'

'What's wrong with your hands, Abi?' he asked me so directly there was no way I could avoid the question.

'You're right, there is something wrong with my hands, but please don't make me show you tonight. It will spoil the whole evening for me. Please let me answer you properly tomorrow.'

He nodded. 'You haven't told me how you feel yet.'

When I turned my face to him, I saw the relief before I even spoke a word.

'Good,' he said. 'At least we feel the same way, the rest is just details.'

David put his arm out to stop Thérèse zooming past and clinked her glass. '*Sláinte*,' he toasted.

'Oh, glad I've found you. Seeing as it's your going away party, Abigail, I'm want to read your cards. I'll tell you how many rugrats you'll have, and whether you'll marry in New York or Florence,' Thérèse joked.

David nudged me.

'Would you like me to?' she asked, a little timidly. I shrugged.

'Sure.'

She dashed away to get the cards. When she returned, she hung her arms around my shoulders and hugged me.

'Are you ready for me to read all your secrets?'

I allowed her to lead me into the library and over to the sofas and coffee table, which were thick with people.

'Come on, up, up.' She shooed people out of their deep comfy seats. They graciously made room for us and then nestled in close so they could hear her read. David and Terry entered just as I was shuffling the cards, and sat on the arm rests. 'Now, take the cards and shuffle them thoroughly, then cut them three times.'

I nodded and passed them over to her after they were thoroughly mixed. She laid them out in four rows and four columns, and then three out to one side. She looked at them carefully and remained quiet. The whole room seemed to have sensed something exciting was going on because the few settee dwellers were now flanked by bodies standing side by side.

All of us looked at the familiar playing cards, but they just seemed like a mix of colours and numbers to me. I glanced at Thérèse who was staring hard, and wondered what on earth she could be concentrating on so deeply.

After a couple of minutes of silence, in which a few people began to whisper and squirm, she slapped her hands on the cards and gathered them up roughly as if in anger.

'Shuffle them again,' she said in a sharp voice.

'Is there anything wrong?' I asked, a little concerned.

'No, there's just nothing there – that's all.'

The vibrant glow that had emanated from her smile the whole evening was gone and, if it was possible, she looked even more like a snow queen. She took the cards from me and laid them out again, staring at them closely. She then looked up at me intently. The colour was visibly draining from her face. I had never seen anything so eloquent; it sent a shard of ice into my chest. Her eyes were suddenly full of tears and her hand, which was resting on the coffee table, was shaking.

'What is it?' I asked in a scared whisper, putting my hand on her own. She pulled away and handed me the cards again.

'Do it again, one last time,' she said in a halting voice. Just as she'd asked, I shuffled and laid them out. She slumped backwards against the sofa, and continued to stare at them fixedly with tears now escaping down her cheeks. Then in a rapid movement, she swept the cards off the table and on to the floor. She stood up, pushed herself through the crowd of onlookers and ran towards her room.

Everyone was shaken. After a moment of hush, whispering and high pitched giggles began. We were all left looking at each other in shock. David put a hand on my shoulder. Terry had already gone after Thérèse. People were looking at the cards on the floor.

'What happened?' I asked David, as if he'd seen something I had not.

'I don't know; she definitely saw something.'

'Well, from her reaction, I'm thinking it wasn't good news.' I stood up. 'God, I feel sick. I want to ring home.'

Within moments I was on the telephone, asking my mum if everyone was alright. When she reassured me they were, I told her not to let anyone drive tonight. She didn't understand my concern, but my insistence made her agree.

I turned from the phone. People were eyeing me strangely. I began to walk towards Terry and Thérèse's bedroom. David intercepted.

'What are you doing?'

'I need to know what she saw.' I met his eyes pleadingly.

'No, don't.' David put his arms round me and turned me away. 'Let her calm down. She has had a lot to drink, and she really isn't used to it. Let her work it all out of her system before jumping to any conclusions.'

We walked towards the dancing. I dug my nails into my hands, needing the momentary relief this always provided. I glanced at the coffee table as we walked past, but no-one had dared touch the scattered cards on the floor, as if whatever Thérèse had seen might rub off on them.

David and I danced slowly for a while, my head resting on his chest. He tried to talk of cheerful things like how perfect the next couple of days together would be, but I couldn't concentrate. Various awful scenarios that Thérèse might have seen kept playing in my head.

'Are you listening to me?' David interrupted my thoughts. 'I said Thérèse has reappeared.'

She looked ashen as if she had been physically sick. I felt terribly guilty, though I had no idea why. I wanted to rush over to her, but felt shy.

She and Terry were making their way over to us. She wouldn't meet my eyes.

'I'll get you a brandy. It'll steady your nerves,' David offered. Terry stroked her hair affectionately.

'I'm sorry I frightened you,' she said, and her voice shook, but not with tears. 'I did see something, but I am not going to speak of it, in case it is I who calls it forward.'

My heart leapt with fear. 'Thérèse, please.'

She glanced up at me then, but only fleetingly, as if meeting my eyes somehow burned her own. She tried a half smile.

'I'll be fine. You know I'm a bit dramatic sometimes,' she said as David brought her drink over. 'Dance with me, David?' she asked, taking his hand and pulling him off to an already heated dance floor where people were jiving and jigging all over the place. Her movements looked overly energetic.

Terry put his hand on my shoulder. 'Don't worry; enjoy your night with David. Her crazy old grandmother made a lot of money conning gullible people. Thérèse loved her nan, who died before Thérèse was old enough to see through the pseudo magic. She's sensitive, especially after a few gin and tonics.'

He laughed and hugged me.

'Come on, let's dance.'

12

I had forgotten how noisy traffic could be. Going from Venice's serenity to Florence's hubbub was a shock to the ears. My flat was behind the Piazza della Signoria, close to the Uffizi Gallery. My new boss owned the flat and would allow me to live there rent-free for the duration of the job.

I opened the front door to find a relaxed and manly abode. It was open plan apart from the bedroom. Well selected modern Italian art hung on every wall, and there were soft leather sofas with a tortoiseshell patina. It also had a bonus feature of a huge roof terrace laid out with candles set into small terracotta walls and plants growing in pots on different levels. There was a rustic table and a frayed hammock. Though I hadn't met Sergio yet, his taste suited my own. The whole flat was full of traditional features like wooden work surfaces in the kitchen, an old fireplace, and a wrought iron bed.

I made myself a cup of coffee and took it out on to the terrace to enjoy the last of the day's sun. Suddenly, I felt overwhelmingly depressed; tears were lining up behind my eyes. David and I had had an awful row on our last day together.

We had decided to eat a late breakfast at a local café on the island of Murano. I knew trouble was brewing; we didn't speak much as we ate, and even less as we walked around the little island. David had tried to take my hand, and this time when I pulled away, he freaked. Turning to face me, he shouted so loudly that other tourists inside the little shops peered out through the windows at us.

'What the hell is going on, Abi? I'm sick of this.'

I grabbed his coat and tried to steer him towards a churchyard where it would be more private, but this time he pulled away. 'No, I won't let you just apologise for this. I want to know why two adults can't even hold hands, let alone do anything more intimate. You promised that you would tell me, and I haven't pushed you.'

'Please, David, let's do this somewhere quieter.'

'No. Let's settle things here.' He got out a coin from his pocket. His hand was shaking. 'Heads you come to New York, tails I stay in Italy.' David flicked the coin high in the air and it fell on the stone paving. 'Heads!' He laughed without humour.

Although my own anger was rising, I closed my eyes. I had lived with five boys for most of my life, and I knew I could never out-shout them. I looked David straight in the eyes and spoke calmly.

'Fine, let's do it here, then, with all Venice looking on.'

I couldn't control the tears. They were hateful ones stinging my eyes.

David stood in front of me. 'You don't seem to understand. I'm serious about you; whatever it is won't change the way I feel about you.'

His eyes were as transparent as his feelings. What I said, I wish I could have taken back. It came out spitefully.

'Of course it will.'

The shock invaded his eyes as I peeled off my gloves. Slowly, I turned my hands over, but I kept my eyes down. My skin was at its worst: blistered, chaffed, a volcanic rash. 'I have psoriasis, and it's made worse because I'm allergic to metal. My skin is always like this. How do you feel about me touching you now?'

There was silence between us. I put on my gloves. The crying had stopped, but now I felt immense anger rising up inside me: anger at my hands; anger at him; anger at the humiliation I felt showing him. I didn't give him a chance to respond; I just went back to the boat, leaving him standing by the shops in Murano.

I let David leave for the airport without making up the fight. There seemed nothing more to say.

My mobile phone rang, pulling me away from thoughts of David. It was Marco. We arranged to meet at Santa Croce. I got ready quickly in order to have a chance to look at the beautiful church before Marco arrived. As I wandered there, I thought about my last days in Venice.

Thérèse didn't leave her room for a couple of days after the party. Her behaviour scared me. I called home a couple of times to check if all was well. There had been no accidents or misfortunes to speak of, but still I worried.

When Thérèse did come out, she seemed relaxed, and gave me a huge hug. She said firmly, 'I don't want to talk about it. I thought I saw something, but now I'm sure I was wrong. I'd had a lot to drink and was excited. You have to be focused to read people's cards otherwise your scattered energy can make you interpret all sorts of normal things entirely wrong. I don't want to upset you by telling you some ridiculous mistake of mine. It wouldn't be fair.'

It made perfect sense, of course. After all, Thérèse wouldn't let me walk into my own doom if she could prevent it.

I did arrive at the church early. The power of the enormous hanging crucifix was such that it made even a heathen like me feel the need to drop to my knees and pray. However, before I got a chance, Marco tapped me on the shoulder. We hugged affectionately.

He was a foot taller than me with the fine bone structure that spoke of his aristocratic lineage. His eyes were unmistakably Irish, blue with grey flecks like choppy waters, identical to his mother's. His skin was definitely Mediterranean like his father's.

Marco did have, perhaps, the most unusual family anyone is likely to come across. His father was a genuine European prince. He was a mild-mannered, kind man and had met his wife during his university education at Cambridge. She was a relatively penniless Irish girl with an incredible academic gift. They were a good match for each other, although her father never thought he was good enough.

Marco's mother was my mother's closest friend, and our two families had spent much time together since we'd been babies.

'How's your mama?' he enquired.

'I imagine you know more than me. Dad had to put in an extra phone line last year. He said if there was an emergency, no-one would be able to get through, what with our mothers gabbing night and day. He blames the nuns at their boarding school. He thinks they should have been separated early on for the good of their future husbands.'

Marco laughed. 'It's true. Speaking of my mother, ever since she found out you were coming to work in Florence, she's been giving me hell that I didn't invite you to stay with her.'

'Fortunately, I have a flat in with the job, and it's not half bad. Anyhow, I couldn't stay at your parents' place; it's like Buckingham Palace. I'd be too scared of waking the suits of armour up if I came in late.'

'It isn't very homely, even I have to admit that, though it is my family home. But, Italian princes do have certain standards of discomfort that they must put up with to maintain their rank in society. Being a prince isn't all it's cracked up to be.'

'Poor you, I do pity your lot in life,' I said sarcastically. He grinned.

'No need to pity me yet. I might never inherit the incredible burden of unlimited wealth and a title that will open any door.'

Cattrine, Marco's French wife, was waiting for us on the steps outside the church. She embraced me warmly. She was willowy with faintly bronzed skin and foxy red hair. I felt like a dumpling beside her.

We all linked arms and walked towards the restaurant, which was very plain – whitewashed walls and clean tablecloths with no effort at ornamentation. The food was all the decoration the place needed. There was a feast on every table, and delicious smells were winding in and out of each other and colouring the room.

A waiter came to our table, placing down bottles of red, white, and water. He told us the menu.

'We love this place,' said Cattrine, squeezing Marco's hand as the waiter departed. I was reminded of the David-size hole in my heart.

We were served bowls of steaming pasta.

'What have you been up to, then?' I asked.

'Well, looks like we're going to be working with Leonardo da Vinci for quite some time,' said Marco. 'I think the museum is more excited than we are. They are actually funding us fully, which is a first. We are putting Leonardo's original notebooks on the internet. They will no longer be available only to the privileged few.'

'Very noble,' I said, and he dropped his eyes to his pasta, a little embarrassed.

'Anyone looking them up will be able to see every hand-written page, and with a single click on any particular section, they can have it explained, or translated, or even pull up other articles written by contemporary authors on the same subject. It's a project that could go on and on. So many of his ideas have touched such a broad spectrum of inventions that the related areas could extend on indefinitely.'

'Can I come and visit you at the museum? I'd love to know if Leonardo was interested in alchemy. He's someone I would peg as a dabbler. I've been doing some research into alchemy; it's a pet interest of mine.'

Marco turned to Cattrine and let her answer.

'Well, I'd say he was more a chemist than an alchemist. He was interested in revealing the hidden properties that materials contained, but I haven't come across anything that would convince me he had put any real time into it.'

'That's annoying,' I said. 'I'm particularly trying to solve the origins of a tool: a sickle-shaped knife.'

This time, Marco spoke. 'There's nothing like that in Leonardo's artefacts, but I have seen a bullion which was a kind of witch's tool shaped like a sickle. It is on display in the museum. Could it be that?'

'I'll check it out. It sounds promising.' I smiled.

'And we'll set you up with a library card for the museum library. We have the most incredible collection,' Cattrine added.

Our second course was as delicious as the first. A fish stew, the like of which I have never tasted: dark broth, rich with tomatoes, and chunks of white fish meat between tangy vegetables.

'Enough about science, our biggest news is that Cattrine is pregnant.' Marco beamed. 'We've been trying for a while, but it seems that this project has been lucky for us in lots of ways.'

'Congratulations!' I hugged Cattrine and Marco together across the table. 'I am so happy for you. May this be the first of many.'

13

T he next morning, I walked past terraces of forthright Renaissance buildings, all with solid personalities like a troop of men you can count on. The Basilica and Duomo surprised me as they didn't seem to fit in at all with their surroundings. Their flirtatiousness and frivolity was a nice intermission, and I felt they gave the city a bit of humour.

Florence was like a fanfare of bronze. Everywhere, there were signs of remarkable craftsmanship and experience in my field. I had the sense that I had arrived at a magnificent party, but was several hours too late. What I would have given to see the thriving foundries and art studios in the Renaissance era. Some of the work was better than anything I had laid eyes on in my lifetime, and I longed to have a chance to know the secrets that doubtless had long been lost.

My first impression of Sergio Rudolpho was one of utter dislike. Almost the instant I sat on his PVC chair in his ultra-trendy flat, he threw down a large wad of cash beside me to establish the hierarchy. He was a young man of around twenty-eight who I suspected had never done a real day's work in his life. He had the stature of an Italian model: tall and lean with a chiselled face. His well-cut clothes and beautifully manicured hands made him quite an artwork himself.

Another man dressed all in black with heavy framed glasses was reading a French novel on a cube-shaped sofa. He lifted his eyes at the disturbance, but made no attempt to remove himself from my interview.

Sergio didn't indulge in any pleasantries and got straight to business.

'My work was more figurative prior to now, but as abstract art is selling so well, I thought I'd cut myself some slack and make some easy money.'

His attitude rankled. I wasn't naïve enough to imagine that finances had nothing to do with art, but he didn't display the least suggestion of genuine interest in the capabilities of the style.

'What is your theme for this collection?' I asked.

The man curled up on the sofa said, 'Dreams. Each artwork is a dream in itself to be expanded upon by the language of colour.'

It sounded pretentious and a bit hackneyed to me, but I didn't say so.

'Have you heard of the Surrealists?' asked Sergio.

'Yes.' I lengthened the word, mimicking his patronising drawl.

'Good. It would benefit you to review some of the colour combinations used in their paintings.'

I bit my tongue, but really wanted to say it would benefit him to learn some manners. I had gone against my instincts in the first place by accepting the job before meeting the client, so I only had myself to blame for this situation. But

Pierro had sung Sergio's praises, and at the time his terms
had seemed more than fair. Now, though, I had decided not
to take the job. Sergio struck me as the type who would be
very hard to please.

I stood up and was about to say I didn't think the job
would suit me, but he misinterpreted my movement and
presumed I wanted to see the studio. Before I could say a
word, he had turned towards an opaque glass door
behind him.

'Yes, yes, it is through here.'

As he clearly wasn't listening to me, I thought it better to
look him in the face and make sure he understood my
meaning. I sighed and followed his lead.

As I entered his magnificent studio, my desire to leave
quite so swiftly dissipated. The ambience of the room
instantly wrapped around me like a protective force field.
There was natural light cascading in at different angles from
a ceiling created from a series of simple shapes that were
juxtaposed. These shapes were outlined in roughly hewn
wood with glass in their centres. It was as if they were
floating in zero gravity; each one was located at a different
angle and held by clear panes of glass. The floor was amber
in shade and was made from teak. Our foundry was the
antithesis of this sculptural haven.

It only took one look at his art works and all my doubts
vanished. His sculptures were large abstract pieces, all in
good quality bronze. They had flowing planes, curved
surfaces and dynamic ripples. Some surfaces had been
highly polished, others had been textured with different
tools. They were like heavy clouds where some shapes were
pushing their faces out, and others were withdrawing back
into the main mass.

The suggestion of four horses' heads pushed their way

forward. Their ears were back and fear ran through their eyes, making the viewer wonder what they were being chased by. What might come out after them?

I had not expected this talent from Sergio. His furniture suggested a man deeply seduced by a commercial world, whereas his art spoke of a much more profound person. I wondered if this was the influence of the man in black.

I walked towards the shapes as if under hypnosis, and could only distantly hear Sergio's voice talking about his concept. I tried to listen more closely as Sergio explained his ideas to me, but I could already see the cacophony of colours that they would become. The more I took time to look at them, even in their naked state, the more they said to me. My excitement at the prospect of advancing them further overpowered any feelings of doubt that I had.

SERGIO and I sat down at a table at about midday. I'd requested he sketch out his ideas for each piece of sculpture before I commenced the work, but Luca, his friend, informed me they would rather discuss it than be too rigid with the aesthetics. This put me in a precarious position: if they didn't like what I did, I would have little proof that it was what they had asked of me.

We had an intense discussion about each piece, beginning with its name and how they envisioned it, and I took notes. Luca poked his opinion into every gap in the conversation. To my immense surprise, I was actually on a wavelength with Sergio's own vision of his work. Luca's ideas always stemmed from depression and angst, and his concept of colour was equally dark, whereas Sergio was a little lighter hearted, and I could potentially enjoy his suggestions much more. If I had to reproduce Luca's visions all day long, I might be in danger of suicide.

We sat for nearly three hours in total. When our meeting broke up, I managed to take Sergio on one side and suggest he did some sketches for me in his own time, which he agreed to do. He and Luca made no pretence that they had any time for me other than on a professional level, and couldn't leave the studio quickly enough. I was happy to be left to the more courteous handyman Michael who had been hovering around the studio all day.

IT WASN'T LONG before I left, too. It was a beautiful day, and I wanted to walk over to the Galileo Museum to meet Marco and Cattrine at work. I could feel my hands beginning to erupt at the anticipation of the work I would do, so I removed my gloves and pressed one hand against the rough brick walls of the buildings I was passing, letting the friction ease the tingling.

It took me ten minutes and lots of asking for directions to find Marco and Cattrine's minuscule study deep in the museum complex. The door was ajar, and I slid inside to find the room empty.

Their desks were pressed together in the centre of the room. On top of them were tall turrets of books, each using the one below as a bookmark. I was wandering over to the window to look out at the pretty courtyard below when I heard frantic giggling echoing along the corridor. I turned to see a petite blonde girl burst into the office, cheeks flushed with high spirits. Marco was two steps behind her, wearing his glasses and looking terribly handsome in a bookish, academic way. He was carrying a couple of dusty volumes in his arms.

'How lovely.' He smiled broadly when he saw me. 'Have you been waiting long?'

He dropped the two books expertly on top of the already leaning piles without causing a landslide and kissed me twice on the cheek.

'No, I've only just arrived. Where's Cattrine? I was hoping we could get a coffee together,' I said, studying the blonde girl whose spirits had sobered up instantly. She gathered together her coat and bag self-consciously.

Marco followed my gaze. 'I was just being a lion,' he said in explanation.

'Really? I don't remember my professors playing games like that with me. I thought yours was supposed to be a serious profession.' I looked deep into Marco's eyes for signs of guilt, but found none.

'Cattrine is at the dentist, but she did leave you two things.'

First, he passed me a reading card for the museum library, and then a book that had been sitting alone on his chair. It was called *Alchemical Prints*, and was published just about the time Father Francis had been dabbling in alchemy in Verona. Every print was religious in nature – etchings or engravings of gruesome New Testament scenes. Christ was on the cross, gushing with blood from his wounds; Christ carrying the cross and bleeding profusely from the gashes made by the crown of thorns; saints receiving the stigmata. The gory nature was all that the scenes had in common with each other, but there was no reference to alchemy as far as I could see.

'Where did you get this book from?' I asked.

'It's a text mentioned by Leonardo in one of his notebooks. He calls it a fundamental alchemical text. Cattrine found it for you.'

'Well, it might have been fundamental to him, but I can't see anything in it that connects it to my theory.' I closed the book and replaced it on the desk. 'Thanks, though.'

Marco looked at his watch and pulled on his blazer, which was slung over the back of a chair.

'We had better head off. I got a bit sidetracked with Serena, and I must pop to the market to pick up some stuff for dinner tonight. You are coming, aren't you? Cattrine says she could do with some help making the pesto, and I will certainly be no use, because I am making the pasta.'

'Haven't you got servants to do that kind of thing?' I teased. 'Yes, I'll be there, but I did want to take a quick look at that tool we were talking about yesterday.'

He nodded and escorted me to the room it was in before leaving. I found the knife in a small display cabinet with a label simply naming it as a witch's tool; I had been hoping it would give me an indication as to what the knife was used for. Taking solace in the fact that at least I had found it, I reasoned that I might come across something more about it in the library, at which point I would be able to come back and re-examine it.

14

During the next six weeks, my life settled into a pleasant routine of work, study and friends. I emailed Thérèse a lot, trying to get her to come up and stay with me, but she seemed evasive, which made me fret about what had happened at the party.

Most days, I went to work by 8am, and put my heart and soul into the sculptures. Despite my reservations about working with such a prima donna, Sergio was fairly hands-off. Periodically, I suspected when he was bored, he would come in and complain that he didn't like what I was doing. I made a fairly good show of listening and then carried on precisely as before. Usually when he returned, he was delighted with the improvement his suggestions had made.

I worked steadily using a mixture of cold patination methods and torch techniques. Cold patinas were so named as the colours formed by chemical means alone, without the aid of heat. This method was good for covering large surface areas, though lacked the drama and the precision of using a torch to heat the surface before applying a chemical.

The latter method enabled the creation of a much more painterly finish to the statue's surface. Precision and texture could be worked up by the use of differing brushes to apply the chemical. A bold palette could also be achieved when heat was involved in the reaction with the surface.

I was in my element. I had the capability to play out all manner of finishes that I had stored up in my head, blending one into another to create drama and mystery on one surface. I loved working with the cold colours as it was vigorous, and invigorating. I felt the same kind of buzz that only dancing to loud music could usually induce.

One sculpture, I created entirely in brown, though I dared Sergio or Luca to call it such. It was a poem: five hundred shades all described by one impoverished noun. Though it wasn't as loud or as brilliant as some of the torch pieces, it was my favourite; the one I would have taken home if I could.

Although Sergio had given me a starting point of the Surrealists, when he saw what I could do, he didn't restrict me, and I drew inspiration from all my favourite artists. We had a homage to Pollock with patinated drips and splendid splashes; the perfection of pointillism with a unique twist arising from the character of patina rather than paint. One piece was completely inspired by the drapery of a dress by Titian. Sergio thought he knew art, but I doubted he'd recognise even half of my references. As I was growing up, when most of my friends were hanging out, going shopping and meeting boys, I'd distract myself during my weekends with details like these.

There was one piece that unfolded without intention. I was working with black and white, and quite unexpectedly, I found myself patinating blurry rectangles. I hadn't let myself dwell much on what had happened at the New Year's

Eve party. It seemed a fruitless pursuit, but as I moved the blowtorch over and back, and flicked and pressed my brushes to the surface, the pattern of the cards spilling on to the floor that night began to take shape.

The pattern continued all over the bronze's bulk so that the misshapen rectangles seemed to be in motion. The background was a swirl of colours that spoke of what I had witnessed: pearly grey for sadness and tears; deep reds for anger; a prevailing indigo for fear. This was Sergio's favourite piece and the design he took most credit for.

Some days, Sergio would have visitors and would tour them around me as if I was quite invisible. Pierro Ricco visited often to plot my progress and give his vociferous opinions. The visitors didn't choose to stay long when I was working as the smell of the chemicals hung around the statues like a cloud. This disturbed the visitors even though the room was well ventilated.

The fumes didn't trouble me as I had what we jokingly referred to in the foundry as a nuclear mask. It was a sealed unit going over my head and covering my face with a transparent shield. At the mouth point a many layered filter was fitted, said to halt the ingress of all organic or inorganic vapours and dust. The filter canister was long and hooked downwards, which made me look like Gonzo from *The Muppets*.

Each day, I finished up about four o'clock and immediately headed to the museum library. It was a beautiful place: vaulted rooms with frescoes; people reading huge medieval manuscripts, or looking at illuminated atlases. At first, I felt a bit intimidated as everyone else seemed to know precisely what they were doing and be familiar with the etiquette of this grand place. As I had no idea of what book I wished to request, I had to look in the catalogue, which in itself was as wide as five bricks. I asked the librarian for some help, and after the scariest response ever, I decided not to do that again.

Fortunately, there seemed to be an inexhaustible list of titles containing the word alchemy. My selection of texts was narrowed by my inability to read other languages, but there was still plenty on offer as many of the more contemporary texts had been translated.

Eventually, I was handed the first book I had requested, and I found myself a little space at a large desk. I was looking for the answers as to what to do with the sickle-shaped knife, or whether the blood of Christ had a purely religious or practical meaning. It was written around 1903 by an Englishman who had made it his life's work to study the history of the subject. Though full of promises in the introduction, the book was absolutely incomprehensible to anyone not fluent in alchemy. I looked through page by page, hoping for even the slightest clue, but everything of potential significance was locked up in some hybrid animal metaphor.

I went back to the museum library almost every day for an hour or two, thumbing through pages and finding nothing meatier than vague recipes for colours, but they weren't even specific enough to confirm what I already knew. In the evenings, quite often, I returned to Sergio's studio to work on the spelter. He was never there at night, so I had the place to myself.

I really disliked the spelter; the delicate cocktail of copper and tin which usually makes up a bronze was completely soured by the addition of the lead. It felt like adding ink to Buck's Fizz.

I continued to try to achieve the colours listed as the Peacock's Tail. Usually, true colours were harder to achieve in patination than a half colour like a pastel. The metaphors used in the little book that I had found in the library months ago had been clear in their description: red like blood, emerald green, dazzling white, royal blue. After my initial experiences back at Christmas, I knew this was going to be no easy task. Trial and error had been the way my father had taught me my trade, and once again it was the only way of finding these colours on this hostile metal. It took me ten days to get a really robust brown.

First, I worked merely with altering chemical formulas, sewing in a little of something new each time, or increasing or decreasing the concentration or alkalinity of the solution. It seemed that spelter's hide was tougher than bronze and didn't respond to weak chemicals. Strong chemicals that would have burned bronze seemed to work the best, but I knew that they were not the whole answer.

I nearly always noticed that the first colour I formed at the beginning of each session was the best one, and this struck me as strange. What was different about the start of my sessions rather than the middle or the end? I was in the museum library, reading some text that described a long, laborious process of preparing the metal when the answer came to me. I wasn't really concentrating, just reading mechanically – something which had become a habit. It must have been my subconscious that made me stop and turn back.

It wasn't what the text said that rang a bell; it was the amount of pages dedicated to the preparation. At the end of a session, I always cleaned the metal particularly thoroughly for the following day's work, and re-cleaned it the next day as well, whereas when I was repeatedly trying to achieve a colour, I was more slapdash about removing every trace of it. The more time I spent prepping, the better the result.

After this realisation, patination moved forward in leaps and bounds. I achieved the second colour on the list three evenings afterwards, and watched in amazement as a deep emerald green was born beneath my hands. I felt a familiar euphoria sweep over me; spelter and I had accepted each other, and I understood its needs now.

DURING THAT INTENSE FORTNIGHT, I also came up with a theory about the blood of Christ. Walking back to my flat after leaving the library, I stopped at a particularly pretty church along the river. As I entered, I could hear that mass was being said, and I slipped into the nearest pew and sat down. Waiting until the congregation rose to go forward to receive the Eucharist, I watched an old man sip from a bejewelled goblet, and considered how to approach the priest for some sacramental wine. I found it hard to believe that sacramental wine was involved in alchemy from a scientific standpoint, but it seemed the only obvious option. Surely nothing else could go by the name of the blood of Christ.

When mass was over and the congregation was beginning to clear, I decided to brave the priest. He was a small man with a crumpled face which smoothed slightly as he showed signs of surprise to see me. I blurted out my request for some sacramental wine, unable to think of any way of putting it that would sound sane. He frowned, crumpling the bottom half of his face so that it perfectly matched the top half.

'Why?' he asked, understandably.

I had known he would ask, but I had not prepared myself properly for how it would feel to lie to a priest. I don't find lying easy, but lying to a priest is in a different league. I made up some awful story about being a foreigner living alone in Florence, and feeling safer with some sacramental wine and holy water in my apartment to protect me. The priest was kind; I saw it in the way he smiled. He'd taken pity on me. I felt like a worm.

Before he went to get my supplies, I stopped him.

'Father, is wine that was blessed in the mass still the blood of Christ after the mass has ended?'

He said it was, and he would get me a container for what had been left over during this mass. While he was away, I looked at a huge sculpture of Christ on the cross. Signs of his sorrow and agony were everywhere in Italy as constant reminders of his sacrifice for all of our sins. I tried not to think about mine.

BY THE END OF APRIL, I began to feel that many of the texts I was looking at in the museum had been written by people who couldn't make their living at alchemy, and subsequently wrote about it instead. I still hadn't found anything relating to how or when the sacramental wine was used, or the purpose of the sickle-shaped knife. I had an inkling that the wine might have been used to produce the final transmutation, but nothing to back up that theory.

On the last Friday of the month, my day started off as usual. I went to the museum about four o'clock and settled down to read. The librarian handed over the text I had been reading the day before, but when I opened it, someone had slipped a note inside:

THEY KNOW. LEAVE!

I couldn't believe my eyes. Scratching at my hands distractedly, I read it over twice more and looked around me to see if anyone was watching. There was no-one around who wasn't deeply involved with the work in front of them. I smiled at the note, but the hand that was holding it shook a little. This couldn't possibly be taken seriously. I didn't know anything, and besides, who could be in the slightest bit put out that I was reading these books, apart from the humpy librarian?

I carried on with the book for about half an hour, but felt too distracted to do any more. The note hadn't frightened me exactly; it just struck me as strange. I immediately went to find Marco in his office. He was still there, though Cattrine had left.

'How is your little project going?' he enquired in a slightly patronising tone. When I told him about the note, I thought he would laugh, but he actually looked quite shocked.

'You are kidding? That sounds serious,' he said.

'Really? But I don't know anything,' I contradicted.

'It seems that someone thinks you do and that could be just as bad.'

'Marco, you're freaking me out. I thought it was funny.'

'Listen, Abi, I've heard about societies that protect the secrets of all sorts of things: alchemy; magic; occult stuff. These people might be fanatical and think that you are moving too close to their territory.' Marco's tone was stern. 'I think you should lay off your little hobby. Go to New York.'

'Marco, this is madness. I'm just interested in the history of alchemy. What harm can I do?'

'I don't know. It could be that you are requesting texts that they hold dear and they don't like it. Some texts are believed to hold curses, and all sorts of odd things happen to people who read them.'

'Marco, you can't believe all that? You read physics at university.'

He started to look irritated.

'Look, Abi, if you want my advice, don't go back. Take it or leave it.'

Marco's words did filter in. I stopped going to the museum after work and did some overdue visiting instead. I went to see Marco's parents several times, and some of the sights in Florence. During this time, I thought more and more about David and how unfair I'd been to him. I realised I hadn't even given him an opportunity to respond when I showed him my hands. I had made an assumption about him which was hardly fair, and I needed to apologise for that.

I tried calling him several times without success; he never seemed to be in. I texted Thérèse and asked her if she could get me David's email address, and in the meantime, I wrote out what I wanted to say to him using the elegant gold pen he had given me.

By now, I had achieved the five colours of the Peacock's Tail, but was still no closer to the answers to the other crucial questions. It seemed like a good time to get some distance from the whole project; New York was the perfect amount of distance. I had made a lot of money in the last few months – Pierro Ricco had been right about the work being lucrative, even if he had omitted to mention the brat factor in his protégé. I was aware that after the exhibition, I might be in the luxurious position of not having to get a job for a while.

Several days later, Thérèse texted back with David's address and email. By this stage, work was becoming frantic.

The exhibition was due to open in five days. I was working late almost every night, and felt sure I wouldn't get to an internet café to type up and send my long speech off to David. Instead, I put my rambling apology into an envelope and posted it that day.

15

The day before Sergio's exhibition, I was supervising the sculptures being wrapped and transported to the gallery. I had a throbbing headache, and my hands felt like I'd had a hundred lashes of the cane. It hadn't helped that the last twenty-four hours had been one continuous argument with Sergio. The prospect of the exhibition was bringing out the worst in him, and I'd had just about as much as I could take.

When the last statue was finally on the transport truck, I followed the van in a little VW Beetle that Sergio had loaned me. Literally yards from Sergio's front door, we came to a standstill. Two cars had hit each other and the drivers were in a full-scale war. The driver of the transport truck had got out, not to ask them to move out of the way, but to join in the argument.

I leaned my head against the steering wheel. It was really hot and the sun was cooking me through the windows of the car. I closed my eyes; I hadn't been sleeping well. Despite my protestations to Marco about how ridiculous the warning note had been at the museum, my subconscious was rattled. I was finding it harder and harder to fall asleep. My eyes watering with fatigue, I would keep doggedly going over the same equation in my mind: tools and notebook stolen + my possessions searched at Terry's flat + Thérèse's reaction to reading my cards + warning note = DANGER.

In the daytime, it was easier to look at these occurrences differently. After all, my tools did have a financial value, and their box was unusual. It might have caught the attention of an eagle-eyed visitor. They weren't to know that I'd stored my alchemy notes in it too.

I had to keep reminding myself that Thérèse was not her grandmother, and as far as I knew, second sight wasn't a hereditary trait. Also, she had been drunk! I was sure someone had been through my things at Terry's, but Thérèse was convinced no-one could have accessed the flat. It was plausible that there was an innocent explanation; I just couldn't think of one.

I looked up from the wheel, but the argument continued unabated. The noise was actually escalating. I wanted to shut out the braying horns and angry shouting, so I drew up the windows and turned on the air conditioning full blast.

Lowering my head again, I let my thoughts drift over to David. Handsome, tall, slightly rugged David; was he even my boyfriend any more? I hadn't told him any of my current worries. I wondered if he'd got my letter.

Finally, the truck jerked forward and we were moving, though it came to a halt again not five minutes later. The driver got out, seemingly oblivious to the fact he was blocking most of the road. This time, I jumped out of my car, ready to unleash some British road rage into the mix.

I ran over to him. 'What the hell are you doing?' I said. He shrugged.

'We are here.'

I looked at the traffic backed-up, squeezing between our truck and the wall on the opposite side of the road. The curator of the gallery, an elegant female Florentine, came out to have something signed. I greeted her and introduced myself.

'Surely, it would have been simpler to carry the sculptures from Sergio's studio to here?' I laughed, but she didn't find it amusing and went inside with one of the porters.

I looked up at the building. It was a grand Renaissance palazzo, the type that reminded me of ancient forts. It had large arched doors which led into a wide courtyard with a fountain as the central feature. Around the courtyard were covered cloisters; little stone benches set into the wall at various points were the only ornaments. A grand staircase led up to the gallery levels. This was the kind of building I'd been dying to see inside since I came to Florence. It was easy to imagine that the austere frontages hid exciting worlds within.

The art movers were struggling to get the enormous sculptures up the stairs without damaging them. The lift was too small, so they were busy rigging up a hoist to lift them. The arches on the first floor, that the sculptures would have to be swung through, looked very small. I had been anxious that some of the statues might get damaged during transport, but now it was clear that it was their journey inside the gallery that would be the most precarious.

I sat in the wide courtyard on a stone bench and watched the statues rise in the air. My heart was in my mouth every time one swayed towards an archway. I was sure it would either knock out the supporting column, sending masonry crashing to the floor, or annihilate one side of the statue, which would mean I would be feverishly touching in enormous gashes later that night.

Each time I was proved wrong. The two men in charge of the transport were gifted at getting awkward shapes through other awkward shapes. They turned and twisted the statues with such precision that I had nothing to do that night except wander around with a polishing cloth. This gave me time to appreciate the statues properly in their finished state.

The space they were in was enormous. It must have been a ballroom originally with a fine frescoed ceiling showing Venus attended by nymphs in one corner and Diana the Huntress in chase across the centre. The long windows were heavily curtained. The curator and her assistant were fussing with the electric lighting, raising and dimming it for maximum impact on each statue.

They looked magnificent. Many of the pieces were monumental and needed distance to be fully appreciated. Despite Sergio's studio being world class, it had been too small to do them justice.

As I moved around them, I silently said my goodbyes to each piece. I felt their futures running away from me like children who have grown up and must move on. I would be unlikely to see them ever again once they were sold.

Usually sculptures were made in batches. A mould was made, and there may be ten or twenty castings taken at any one time from the original mould. In this case, each sculpture was absolutely unique, because of the patination. While it was possible to cast more of the sculptures, the vibrant dream coats that I had spun around each surface made them individual.

Authenticity was what made the difference between a painting selling for a million or a thousand pounds at an auction. The artist's own handiwork was what made the article valuable. I wondered if, in the future, patination might gain its own ranking as an art medium alongside oils and acrylics, and then some acknowledgment of the patineur would arise.

Tomorrow night would be very interesting. Most people had no understanding of the colouring of sculpture and probably thought that the sculptor patinated his own works. If the exhibition was a success, I wondered if Sergio would take credit for the colouring.

I stood at the entrance of the huge hall and looked along it at all of the pieces together, feeling choked with pride.

MY PARENTS HAD FLOWN into Venice and were travelling up with Terry and Thérèse. I was desperate to see them all and got to the gallery an hour before we were due to meet just in case they came early. Leaning up against the rough stone walls at the entrance of the building, I scanned every car that passed.

The courtyard had been styled. Flickering lanterns were set on the craggy stone sills of each archway. The fountain ran pink water, and garlands of pink roses had been wrapped around the cloister columns and up the staircase. Petals were strewn across the floor. I could see Sergio prowling the perimeter of the candlelit courtyard. He caught my eye warily and immediately ascended the stairs at a pace.

Some young men in a car slowed down as they drove past. They hung their heads out of the window, tossed me kisses and yelled for my attention. The car behind hooted loudly.

I was glad I'd made an effort with my wardrobe. I wore a dress the colour of wild poppies in a delicate fabric that swished when I moved. My hair was piled up, letting some rogue tendrils fall about my face, and kohl shaded my eyes. I wore a flashy eye shadow and finished the look with a heavy dark red lipstick. Last of all was a new pair of black satin gloves which ran the length of my forearms, with my spectacular diamond ring topping them off.

I pressed my palms together and massaged the itchy surfaces while I waited. Pierro Ricco appeared from inside the gallery carrying two glasses of pink champagne. He offered one to me and lingered to chat at my look-out point. As he passed the glass, he held on to it for a second longer than necessary and let his eyes run over me slowly. The look was very predatory and I felt the colour rise in my cheeks.

'You look very beautiful tonight,' he said in his soft, growly voice.

I was saved from making some trite comment by Luca, Sergio's partner, pulling up in a cab and hopping out. He embraced Pierro. Luca was shaking with nerves, which I thought was quite endearing; he must really care for Sergio. He fiddled with his heavy framed glasses as he spoke to Pierro in Italian. Next to Pierro, he looked slight, like a whippet next to a Doberman.

Pierro handed Luca his empty glass to take inside and returned his attention to me.

'I have arranged curators from all over the world to come and see this exhibition. I'm positive it will make Sergio world famous,' he said.

'Well, he is very talented,' I said awkwardly.

I hated making small talk and felt completely distracted by my hands. Nerves were making them moist so they were stinging, and the fabric of the gloves was making it worse. I felt Pierro's attention being drawn to my hands.

'Sergio has left a bonus for you in the studio. I hope you will accept it. We were discussing his next project this afternoon. He particularly wants you around, as you make such a great partnership.'

I didn't deliberate for a second.

'Thank you for the offer,' I said as politely as possible, 'but I'm afraid I can't accept. I need to take care of some personal business, and I'm unlikely to stay in Italy.'

He seemed to be searching my eyes for something, but what it could have been was lost upon me. He held my eye contact and took hold of my wrist. Turning the arm over slowly, he traced the vein at my elbow and gently began to pull the glove down from my arm.

The second I realised his intent, I tried to wrench my arm back, but he held his grip and his stare and continued to peel the fabric downward.

'Shh, *cara,* it is far too hot for these gloves. Let me relieve you of them.'

His face was completely blank. My heart was beating so madly, I felt breathless. He had nearly reached my wrists.

At that moment, I saw Terry and managed to squeak his name. Pierro dropped my arm and I pulled up my glove. He stayed to kiss Thérèse and shake Terry's hand.

Before moving away, he said, 'Come to my summer party next week. I did promise I would show you my little collection of treasures – the ones I told you about in Venice.' He gave me a charming smile, one I'd never been graced with before, which totally confused me.

What had just happened?

I didn't get a chance to reply as I was swept up in a wave of hugs and kisses from my family.

THÉRÈSE LOOKED VERY beautiful in a black satin dress, though if it was possible, she looked even thinner than usual. I noticed that she wore a white Spanish wrap, as delicate as cobwebs, around her shoulders, despite the heat. I wondered if it were to prevent anyone noticing her diminished figure.

Marco, his mother Barbara and Cattrine arrived on the back of my parents' entrance, causing even greater booms of excitement. Barbara and my mother were eeking with glee over Cattrine, who was now beginning to show.

'Cattrine, congratulations, darling!' My mum kissed her. 'You're looking so lovely. Have you met Thérèse?'

Cattrine shook her head.

'Do you know what sex it is yet?' Thérèse asked.

'No, we've chosen not to know,' said Cattrine.

'May I?' asked Thérèse and put her hand on Cattrine's small bulge, looking thoughtful.

We all fired questioning looks back and forth at each other.

'My grandmother used to be able to tell the sex of a baby just by laying her hands on the bump. She was spot on every time, too,' said Thérèse, smiling at us.

'Can you tell?' Cattrine asked, her eyes wide. Thérèse paused dramatically, and then laughed at our awestruck faces.

'Not at all!' she said, making us laugh too. 'Terry and I both come from large families so we always imagined we'd have a whole bunch of brats ourselves.' Thérèse shrugged.

'You've still got plenty of time,' my mum said, patting Thérèse's arm with affection.

'Yes, of course,' replied Thérèse, but a slight sadness stained her voice.

Marco joined us, draping his arms over his wife's shoulders.

'It's a good job I brought some friends along, Abi. You're a disgrace not having a date.'

'Of course, she has a date.'

These words came from behind our group. We turned and there stood David. He was beyond handsome. He wore a dark suit and his hair had been cut short, revealing the strong angles of his face. He had a little stubble beginning to darken his skin.

I couldn't even speak.

My champagne glass was almost empty. He exchanged it for his own, and stepped back to enjoy the surprise which his appearance had caused. Terry and Thérèse gave me time to recover by hugging him, and ribbing him for his deviousness. Then he met my parents, in an exchange that was charged with embarrassment. I introduced him haltingly as my *boyfriend* and blushed furiously at his reaction to those words. Lifting my eyes, I saw he was grinning at my discomfort, which made me blush even more.

'Could we take a moment?' he asked my parents in a very formal manner, and we gratefully escaped the group.

We sat on a little stone bench outside the gallery which was nestled into the wall. Leaning into him, I kissed him with everything that I'd previously held back.

'I can't believe you came back,' I whispered. He held me close and brushed my hair with his lips.

'I wouldn't have done, but your letter changed my mind,' he said, then looked into my eyes earnestly. 'How could you think it would matter?'

I shook my head. 'It has frightened people all of my life: the lady in the shop who has known me since I was a baby and won't touch my money, or the kids in school who shouted "Leper" and wouldn't sit next to me, and so many others.'

He put his arm around my shoulders. 'Well, it doesn't scare me,' he said, stroking my hair away from my face and kissing me again.

16

My father came outside to get us.

'Come on, are we never to see this exhibition? Stop gossiping; we can go for dinner after and talk all night.'

We both stood up abruptly, and followed my father up to the gallery. I could tell from the hubbub of the enormous crowd that the exhibition was a hit. I kept looking over at David, trying to read his reaction, but Thérèse was questioning him keenly about something.

The dreamed-up sculptures and the people in all shades and hues made it difficult to discern where the crowd stopped and art began. Euphoric voices shuttled back and forth; photographers' flashes blazed unceasingly. I breathed in the excited vibes of the room as my father put his arm around my shoulder.

'Inspired,' he whispered to me. 'Larry would hate it.'

I smiled to myself. He was right; it couldn't be further from tradition.

The size of our party grew as we were carried along by the momentum of the other groups. We picked up acquaintances, merged with journalists, and generally got tangled up in each other. David and I were becoming further and further separated. Everyone felt that the serious issue of the exhibition had to be addressed before their judgement was too much impaired by the champagne.

I listened mostly, trying not to interfere unless I was specifically asked a question. Thankfully, they were friends first and critics second. They were lavish with praise and cautious with finding fault. They talked of what the sculptures reminded them of and which other artists might have inspired us. Both Sergio and I were attributed with far more lofty thoughts than either of us ever intended. There were many toasts and a good deal of genuine sentiment before the exhibition became just a backdrop for another Florentine party.

At last, David's hand found my own. He was smiling down at me and drew me nearer.

'It's a brilliant exhibition.'

Sergio came sweeping past us and spotted me. He was very drunk, and following him was Pierro Ricco.

'Success.' Sergio grabbed me. Putting one arm around me and the other around David, he gave us both a squeeze simultaneously. His styled hair fell forward damply on his forehead and the buttons on his shirt had come undone and been done up again wrong.

'What have you been up to?' I laughed at him.

'Success. Success,' he roared.

I could see Pierro looking slightly annoyed by him, but I liked Sergio much better this way. He spent too much time taking himself seriously.

'I want that drink.' He launched himself forward at a passing waitress. Tapping his glass, he yelled in Italian, 'A toast. A toast to Abigail Argent: a master of metals.'

There was much clapping and shouting. I was surprised and touched by Sergio's acknowledgment.

Pierro had moved so that he was standing next to me. He was wearing a soft grey suit and his smile was warm.

'You see, I'm not the only one that thinks so,' he said, clapping politely.

Davɪᴅ ʀᴇᴛᴜʀɴᴇᴅ with me to the flat that night. I was euphoric, partly from the success, and partly from the free-flowing champagne. We went straight to the bedroom; there was no hesitation. He undressed me slowly, one garment at a time, admiring each new part of my figure that had been revealed before moving on. Occasionally, he kissed some part of me: my hip; my thigh; my neck.

At last, I stood naked before him, apart from my gloves. The curtains were only partly closed, and the moonlight gave my skin a silver tint. I waited for him to continue, but instead he sat down on the elegant Edwardian chair adjacent to the window.

'It's your turn now,' he said. 'It's up to you whether you want to take them off.'

Just for a second, I quaked at revealing everything, but his next kiss, at my midriff, was so gentle and enticing it brought my hands to his hair. Though the satin couldn't have been more delicate, it felt like a barrier between us. It was easier to let him slide my knickers to the floor than it was for me to slide my gloves over my hands, but the feeling of no return was the same.

I moved forward so that he was looking up at me. As each kiss and caress became more urgent, so the conscious-

ness of my imperfect hands fell away, and I became lost in
the intoxicating love that I felt for this man.

DAVID SPENT A WEEK IN FLORENCE. Most of that time, we
were wrapped around each other, talking about small
things. I can't say that all embarrassment about my hands
was gone, but I could tell that in time, that would change.
This man was the remedy I had needed.

Having no work meant we never had to look at a clock.
We drifted through Florence arm in arm, drunk on each
other, and enjoying glasses of Prosecco to heighten our
already ecstatic mood. We hired a Vespa and flew up and
down the side of the Arno, visiting some of my favourite
places like the ancient town of Fiesole. It was on these trips
that I told him more about the alchemy and what I had
pieced together in Florence. Sometimes I caught him
staring at me; I could see him trying to understand. Was I
eccentric? Did I really believe in what I was saying?

Strangely, he did make me feel better about my fears by
dismissing them out of hand. He laughed long and loud
when I told him about the note in the museum library.

'It's probably some standing joke that the staff dole out
to gullible readers. Ooh, the book police are after you,' he
chuckled. 'We were always doing stuff like that at the bar I
used to work in; it's just pranking. I bet they had a really
good laugh.'

I found myself laughing along with him, feeling like I
was gaining the perspective I'd lost.

We planned out the next few months in the warm
evenings, looking over Florence on the roof terrace at my
flat. David was enjoying some unexpected luck which had

impacted on his plans in the US. A couple of years previously, he had given a Swedish friend several songs he had written. His Swedish friend had a brother in a band called Century which had already had two quite successful singles. The band members were interested in David's songs and had decided to record at least one of them. This meant that David needed to spend the next couple of months in LA.

When he was telling me about this, he began to look a little guilty and kept running his hand through his hair.

'Before I came out here, I spoke to an art agent. Ellen put me in contact with him. He looked at the website for this exhibition and was incredibly excited about you. He said there would be a hundred sculptors who would pay anything for you to work with them. I know you might be annoyed that I'm so keen to drag you away from Italy, but I really want you to come with me.'

He leaned forward and stroked my cheek. I looked into his eyes and said with complete honesty that I was done here. We booked my flights that night. I couldn't get on the same plane as David, but just over twenty-four hours later, there would be another flight.

ON OUR LAST DAY TOGETHER, I slipped out of the flat early, leaving David sleeping, and headed over to Sergio's studio to collect the bonus he'd left me. I spent a few minutes in the space saying goodbye. It was completely clean and empty; it looked more like a dance studio than a sculptor's workplace.

Though Florence is home to wondrous places like the Medici Chapel and Piazza della Signoria, this modern space was what I'd remember most of the city. I loved the ceiling, which reminded me of looking through a kaleidoscope. This morning, the sun shone through with peachy hues, but on other days they were yellow, blue or icy white.

I popped to the market on the way back, buying fresh fruit and bread for our breakfast. I was in the flat's communal area waiting for the lift when my neighbour, Gloria Cianti, entered.

Gloria had been very sweet during my stay. She was an ex-pat from Dagenham with Italian parents. A small lady with immaculately-styled dark hair and eyes, she had a full figure and was always impeccably dressed. Whenever I met her or her husband on the stairs, they gushed with genuine affection. They were very sociable and had invited me in for dinner and drinks a couple of times. I'd been glad to accept as I knew so few people in Florence.

Gloria and John Cianti were in the marble business: import/export. They enjoyed the irony that their parents had left Italy for a better life in London and they had returned back for exactly the same reason.

Gloria smiled knowingly at me as soon as she spotted me.

'Saw you with your boyfriend the other evening; very handsome.'

I couldn't help beaming.

'I'm a little relieved that you're not one of his girlfriends, though John and I didn't think you were his type. We didn't like to ask before.'

I must have looked completely blank because she galloped onward to fill the awkward pause.

'Not to say that he's not gentlemanly. He is very gentlemanly indeed – especially to the ladies, if you know what I mean.'

She winked and the pitch of her voice went up a little.

She licked her lips as if she had a taste for the gossip I could see she was dying to spill.

'I'm sorry, Gloria. I haven't got a clue what you are talking about,' I said, shaking my head.

Gloria almost squeaked with glee, and she moved her plump feet up and down with excitement.

'You know...your landlord. Well, apparently he has had many liaisons with Mafia daughters.' She slowed her pronunciation and nodded over certain words; "Mafia daughters" was made to sound dirty, salacious and absolutely forbidden. 'Oh yes, his family are very well connected. We've seen some of the most notorious villains in Italy come to meet him here. There are always late night comings and goings.'

She stopped momentarily to draw breath.

'He has violent arguments with his girlfriends, though they sound like they do give as good as they get. Most leave with dark glasses – put it like that.'

Gloria stood back to enjoy my reaction. My brain suddenly started to engage.

'I'm sorry, but if there's anything I'm sure about, it's that my landlord is gay. In fact, I know his partner.'

Now, it was Gloria's turn to look mystified. She spoke slowly, almost to herself.

'Mr Ricco is gay? No.'

'Mr Ricco? Mr Ricco's flat?' I said in disbelief. Gloria looked disturbed at the turn our conversation had taken. She nodded and offered an exaggerated frown.

I left her without furthering the conversation and got into the lift. I banged the apartment door more loudly than I had meant to when I entered the flat. David raised his head and called out.

I stormed into the bedroom. He looked warm and

comforting. I slipped off my jeans, letting them fall to the floor, and climbed in next to him.

'What's bitten you?' he said sleepily. He was lying on his front and draped an arm over me, pulling me closer.

I sighed. 'This is Pierro's flat, not Sergio's. I just found out from my neighbour.'

'So?' He closed his eyes again.

'So, he lied to me. He told me it was Sergio's.' I was rigid with annoyance. 'Mind you, I should have known Sergio would never have such good taste.'

David was strumming along the length of my collarbone. I could tell he was hoping to distract me.

'There could be any number of explanations. Maybe Pierro does own it but he rents it to Sergio, or he thought you might think he was coming on to you if he offered you his flat.'

'Hmm, maybe,' I murmured, still feeling cross.

I thought back over what had happened outside the gallery. I couldn't decide whether he had been flirtatious, trying to undress my hands, or whether he suspected there was something wrong with them. Either way, he hadn't handled it well.

'I'm just not mad on him. I don't want to have been his guest. Now he's done me a huge favour. He's like aluminium.'

'What?' David laughed.

'I hate aluminium, but there's no good reason for it at all. In fact, it's a really useful metal, but when I touch it, I want to shudder. If you try to weld it, it's completely awkward, and its colours are really murky when you anodise it.'

For a minute, David was silent. Then he moved like lightning. Suddenly, he was on top of me, and I was pinned below with him looking down on me. His smile shone through his eyes. He kissed me on the lips.

'You know you are completely mad, don't you? Whatever the reason he didn't tell you, it doesn't matter now because we are leaving. Plus, I think you're paranoid: first the book police are after you, now the art police.'

'But what about Thérèse and the cards?' I persisted.

He started to kiss my neck very softly and insistently, then broke off for a moment.

'Mm, because drunken predictions by amateur fortune-tellers are always right,' he said, sarcasm lacing his voice. 'Besides, I don't think you're Pierro's type.'

'You're the second person that has said that to me in the last quarter of an hour,' I huffed. 'Not that I want to be, but why wouldn't I be a rich, handsome man's type?'

'You're my type, though,' he said between kisses.

17

A fter seeing David off at the airport the next morning, I spent the remainder of Saturday in a very loved-up mood. I had decided not to go to Pierro's party, which was on that night.

At around lunchtime, I was cleaning the flat when Marco called me.

'What do you mean you're not going? Why? It's the party of the year,' he barked down the phone at me.

'How come you're going?' I asked a bit lamely.

'I always go. This isn't some tin-pot party. An invite is like a letter of recommendation here. Every door will be open to you after tonight.'

'I don't need doors opening. I'm going to America.'

Marco made a snorting noise.

'You'll be back soon enough. Burning your bridges with Pierro is not a good career move. Besides, my uncle Domenico Milliardo is coming tonight. You remember Dad's stories about him being the black sheep of the family? You have to come to meet the family legend.'

I felt my resolve slipping. Marco and I always had fun

when we went out. It was my last night in Florence after all. Only the tiniest bit more pressure and I was agreeing to meet him there.

I LEFT my flat that night feeling ultra-cool in a tight-fitting black designer dress that David had chosen for me while we wandered around Florence together. My special ring was the only thing to add a spectrum of colour.

It was immediately obvious which house was having the party. Bright lights radiated across the river, and noise spilled out from its open windows. The house glowed in the dark from the huge lanterns that had been hung out on every balcony.

Marco and I had arranged to meet outside. I waited for him for half an hour, but he wasn't answering his phone. Eventually, I went inside to see if I could see him. I was wrapped up in the heady smell of perfume and body heat as soon as I entered.

The hall had been styled especially for the party: a garden with small trees, tiny lights threading through the leaves. Guests stood and peered at fish in a rectangular pond that had been installed in the centre of the space, a cerise beam diffusing through the water.

I moved from the hallway into a much larger room. I could see Marco talking to a small group. He was leaning towards the girl with long blonde hair I'd seen in his office. His hand was beneath her hair, slowly strumming her backbone. The hand remained there, relaxed, comfortable.

A warm hand settled on my own back, grabbing my attention instantly. Pierro was standing to my left, looking amazingly handsome and holding out a glass of champagne. He kissed me on both cheeks, then he bent down and whispered, his lips almost touching the lobe of my ear.

'I won't tell on him, if you won't.'

My throat dried. I glanced back at Marco, but the group had moved on, and I could no longer see them. I wondered if I should bring up the issue of the ownership of the flat, but somehow it seemed churlish.

Pierro gestured to me to follow him. Damn Marco, I thought. Having to chat with Pierro alone was exactly what I had wanted to avoid.

We passed through rooms full of people. I spotted Sergio surrounded by handsome young men. He looked very drunk. We seemed to go deeper and deeper into the house until I was sure we must have passed right through it and into someone else's. Then Pierro came to a solid door with a key pad. He tapped in the code and, amazingly, it opened into a private gallery.

I hesitated for a moment, but then I saw some sculptures on small plinths which I just had to see. There were also display cases scattered around and a real Titian on one wall.

Pierro guided me over to one display case. 'What do you think?' he asked.

Inside was an ornamental platter. Half of it was lead while the other half was what seemed to be solid gold. I gasped.

'I thought you'd be interested in this one, *cara*. Everyone is.'

The pride was thick in his voice.

'Is it really gold?' I said, moving closer.

'Yes, it has been authenticated by some of the world's leading scientists.'

'Surely it has been joined somehow?' I screwed up my

eyes and got as close to the glass as possible. 'Though I can't see any fixing marks,' I added.

'No, it has been looked at from every angle and with more sophisticated equipment than just your pretty brown eyes. It has not been joined.'

'How did you get this?' I said, moving around it to scrutinise the seam. I tried not to show how interested I was, but my voice shook with excitement.

'It's a family heirloom. The alchemist who made this vanished. He was never seen again after he performed this amazing feat.'

Something about Pierro's expression sent a chill right through me, and I turned away from the display unit towards another. Inside were two preserved fingers, black with decay.

'These are an alchemist's fingers. You shudder, but they are very valuable. It is no different to wanting to own a saint's relics really.'

'Where did you get all this stuff?' I asked, hardly able to drag my eyes away from the grotesque fingers.

'My family have been collecting alchemical memorabilia for a very long time. I have only added one or two things to the collection.' He steered me over to a small painting. 'I bought this recently; it's called *L'Alchimista – The Alchemist*.'

The little painting showed a man standing at a table in a small room. There was a window, and I could just make out the sun in the right hand corner of it. What particularly interested me were his tools. There was a pestle and mortar, something that looked like a pumice stone, several brushes in a heap on his table, and a fire burning in the grate with a rack above it. There were also jars of substances on shelves, but I couldn't tell what they were. There was a cross above the door, and lastly a sickle-shaped knife upon the table.

At the bottom of the painting, written in Latin, was a phrase. My Latin was ropey so I asked Pierro to translate.

'It means the blood of Christ,' he said.

My heart leapt. Nearly every detail of this little painting, which looked as if it might be the least valuable of the collection, confirmed my own theory of how the alchemical process came about. The brushes were those of a patineur; each one was an ancestor of my own brushes. There was also a pumice stone, which was essential to prepare metal and clean it ready for patination. The pestle and mortar, I assumed, must have been for grinding the powders that would be used to colour the metal. In this day and age, the compounds I used were already ground or in solution, but centuries ago this would have been done by the alchemist himself.

The fire must have been used to heat the metal for certain colours, just as I had used gas lamps and blow-torches at Sergio's. However, in the painting, the alchemist seemed to have left a bowl to heat on the rack over the fire. I was unsure what he could have been heating.

The cross – well, that must have been of religious signifi-cance to the alchemist. The sickle-shaped knife stumped me – what could it possibly have been for? I had no idea.

Everything kept coming back to the blood of Christ. It was so frustrating. I had no other ideas apart from the use of the sacramental wine, but my instinct told me this was wrong.

'Pierro, this is incredible,' I breathed, and he laughed at my serious face.

'I hope my little collection can help with your research?' he said, smiling.

There was a lounge-like area at the far end of the gallery. He gestured towards it, and we sat down on low geometric sofas clad in grey velvet. There were several bottles of champagne on the glass coffee table, and he opened one up.

'Tell me about your research, *cara*. I'd be very interested to hear.'

'There's not much to tell,' I said evasively.

He waited for me to continue, and so I told him about the little bits and pieces that interested me. He was not my preferred confidant, but he didn't look at me with mocking disbelief the way Marco or even David did sometimes.

When I told him about how I was stuck on the sickle-shaped knife, he spoke for the first time.

'I've read that the knife is a very important part of the process, although differing texts attribute alternative roles to the tool. One text said that it was used ceremonially as a part of the alchemical ritual. The idea was that the alchemist cut the very fabric of our dimension with it, allowing him to use physics that does not apply to our world.'

'Wow, I wasn't expecting that. It sounds a bit too science fiction for me.' I giggled, feeling light-headed from the champagne.

'The other theory is that a sacrifice must be made and the knife is used during the ritual. Do you like that theory any better?'

I shook my head. 'I haven't come across anything about sacrifice in what I have read so far, but I suppose it is an ancient tradition. Many cultures believed it to be the best way to please God. My hypothesis sounds miserable in comparison to those two. I just thought the knife might have been used as a sort of saw for cutting up the metal.'

'It does all sound rather unlikely. I think the key is to keep in mind that it was thought to be used ceremonially rather than literally. Perhaps, the actual fabric of our dimension remains intact.'

He smiled.

'I really don't think I'd be a good academic. I'm sure it's very bad practice to pick and choose theories according to how much you like the sound of them,' I said.

'Theory and research are all very well, but the question is, do you really think it can be done?' he asked, his face serious.

I paused, then said in as jovial a manner as I dared with Pierro, 'Well, only by me...' I laughed a little too loud at my own joke. 'I should really go and find Marco.'

He nodded and we both stood. As the two of us walked towards the door, I felt the need to fill the silence.

'I'm leaving for New York in the morning so I may not stay long at the party. Thank you so much for showing me the collection.'

He smiled and let me out of the gallery, but remained inside the room himself. 'I will come and say goodbye properly, *cara,*' he said, 'but I need to make a few phone calls first.'

18

I made my way out of the gallery and found Marco in the library. It was a double-height room, and there were books floor-to-ceiling. The floor space had been completely cleared. Marco was standing with an older man who had platinum silver hair. He introduced us, and informed me that his uncle had bought two of Sergio's sculptures.

I was interested to meet Domenico Milliardo, as he had always been spoken about in a disapproving way by the part of Marco's family that I knew. He was not tall, but broad, which made him imposing. He had a large Roman nose, and yet, despite this unfortunate feature, managed to look handsome in a tough, rugged way. He bore some resemblance to Marco through his unusual eyes, but there was a steeliness there which couldn't be seen in his nephew.

From the gossip that constantly ricocheted between Marco's mother and my own, I had heard him spoken about as Italian *mafioso*; a fiendish businessman with a hand in several unlawful areas. I got the impression he controlled the whole family, despite his brother holding the title, and that they were all slightly scared of him. To me, however, he was all charm, and very flattering about my work.

Sergio was close by, still being drooled over by young admirers, but within a minute of Domenico Milliardo catching his eye, he was standing by my side. Domenico now addressed Sergio with questions about his inspiration for the collection, and then proceeded to beckon over Pierro, who had joined the party.

As if to establish hierarchy, Domenico sent Pierro off to claim drinks for us all. When he returned, Domenico addressed him in rapid Italian. In the few months I'd been in Italy, I'd managed to progress to a working knowledge of the language. I could converse on simple subjects and understand some responses if they were delivered slowly. The conversation now batted back and forth between Pierro and Domenico, with Pierro's responses becoming more heated and insistent. Marco just listened.

I had no clear idea what they were discussing so intensely, but I had a strange sense that I was the topic, though they didn't use my name. They moved their eyes towards me and away from me very often, and for just a second, bizarre as it sounds, it felt as if they were discussing how best to eat me.

I made an excuse to slip to the loo. I felt weary; the weeks of hard physical work had my body knotted up tightly. The alcohol had tired me, and I just wanted to get back to the flat and go to bed.

I returned to the library to say my goodbyes only to catch the tail end of a row between Pierro and Marco. The others in the group had drifted away, doubtless embarrassed, leaving only Domenico between them. I stopped and hovered, not wanting to intrude.

Domenico noticed me and lifted his eyes as if to say,

'What will we do with these two?' and then said something to the pair which stopped the argument in its tracks and left Marco looking furious. Domenico steered Pierro out of the library allowing me to step up to a scowling Marco.

'What was all that about?' I asked.

'Nothing,' he snapped, 'just Pierro being high-handed. Shall we go?'

'I didn't know you knew him that well.'

'As well as I ever want to,' he said as he turned away.

I was relieved, but surprised, as Marco wasn't usually one to call it a night so early on. Though he said almost nothing, I could feel his mood plummeting. It didn't seem worth berating him about not meeting me where we'd arranged earlier in the evening, which was what I was itching to do. We walked quickly back through the beautiful Florentine streets, and I mentally said my goodbyes to them.

Marco remained morose, I asked him what all the intense discussion between Domenico and Pierro had been about earlier in the evening. He didn't seem to want to answer.

'Domenico just wanted Sergio to make you an offer you couldn't refuse so that you'd stay in Florence and carry on working with him. He thinks it's foolish to let you go.'

'That's flattering. It all sounded more heated than that.'

'Domenico doesn't like being disagreed with,' said Marco.

He wasn't inclined to carry on the discussion so I let it drop. When we reached the flat, he lingered, seeming in two minds whether to stay or go. I asked him to join me for a coffee; I thought he might want to talk some more. Finally, I made the decision for him, and sent him on his way to Cattrine.

I couldn't have been back in the flat more than five

minutes when there was a knock at the door. I thought it might be Gloria popping in to say goodbye. I had left some flowers for her earlier in the day.

To my surprise, it was Marco again.

'Sorry, I will have a coffee, if you don't mind.'

'I was about to get changed.'

'That's okay -I'll make the brew.'

I changed into some jeans in record time. I couldn't help wondering whether Marco might be about to confess all about his relationship with Serena. He was definitely behaving strangely. When I returned to the kitchen, he kept fiddling with the coffee machine while it was percolating and moving about the kitchen, not settling in one place.

'Are you feeling alright, Marco?' I asked with concern.

'No...yes...actually, I wanted to ask your opinion about something Pierro and I were arguing over. He wants me to involve a colleague of mine with a project of his, but I definitely don't want to get involved. He says if I don't, he'll get my funding pulled at the museum and tell Cattrine about an affair I had a while ago.'

'Serena? An affair you *are* having, you mean,' I said, raising my eyebrows at him.

He gave the briefest of nods.

I breathed out very slowly.

'What do you think I should do?' He looked at me with huge pleading eyes, an expression I'd never seen from the handsome, cocky boy I'd known for so long.

'Does he really have the power to get your funding pulled?'

'Definitely, and I have absolutely no doubt he'd tell Cattrine, too,' he said.

It was easier to scold rather than solve his problem.

'You're such an idiot, what are you doing messing

around with some girl when your wife is pregnant? Who does that?'

Anger rose up in his face, and his jaw tightened.

'I'm not asking for your approval,' he said.

'What kind of project is it that he wants your friend to work on? Is he likely to get hurt?'

'Maybe, I don't really know. I only know a few details.'

'I'd say, tell Cattrine that Pierro is trying to blackmail you about one of your students, but it's a lie. As for the funding, you've got money. It's not the end of the world.'

'He's got photos of me and Serena.'

'Oh,' I mouthed. 'Maybe your friend would be glad of the opportunity?'

Marco laughed in a hollow kind of way. 'Maybe,' he said and poured us both a cup of coffee. He drank his down quickly, and made an excuse to leave, kissing me on both cheeks and giving me a hug. 'Things will be brighter tomorrow,' he added. 'Drink up the coffee; you'll never get anything that good in New York.'

After Marco left, I wondered whether I should call Cattrine to say goodbye, but decided I would do it in the morning as she was probably asleep. I continued to finish my packing, and was about to strip off my elegant gloves and ring, but suddenly my head started to ache. It felt heavy and I pitched to one side. The room was moving the way it does after too many drinks.

I went into the kitchen for water and two well-built blond men were standing there.

The drunken sensation was becoming stronger. Before I even had a chance to think about bolting, one of them took two great strides towards me and grabbed my arm. I started to scream, but he leaned his bulk against me, squashing me against the wall.

The other man, who had been watching calmly, took out a compact looking gun and laid it on the table.

'Now we are just going to wait here for a while, nice and calmly,' he said.

I tried to speak to him, but my mouth was dry. The words didn't form, like there was some barrier building between my brain and my mouth. I watched as the man by the table took out his phone, but I stopped hearing or seeing anything before he began the conversation.

19

I have no idea how long I was out for in total. I had a sense that we were travelling. Every so often, I got the overwhelming feeling that I was paralysed, and even my lungs weren't able to breathe as they should. This made me try to move, but the paralysis overtook me again, and I blacked out for another duration.

This nightmare waking, gasping, drowning sensation occurred three or four more times. Once, when we didn't seem to be moving, I woke to find one of the men kneeling over me. My arms and legs still felt paralysed so I had no way of moving before I felt him pull the top of my jeans down and jab a needle into my thigh. It stung like a bee. A swirling sensation overtook me, and I blacked out again.

I woke in a room with walls built from thick, sturdy stones that were a blend of russet and grey. I sat up too quickly; instantly, I felt sick and my body heavy. The proportions of the room suggested its owner must be a fairy-tale giant. It gave the impression of being in some kind of castle. The sturdy walls were broken up by small windows placed in a staggered sequence that rotated around the room and rose towards the ceiling.

The ceiling was at least 10m above me. Looking up, I could see gilded geometric mouldings bisecting it. Each one surrounded a frescoed panel about a metre square. The room was an odd shape; its ends were rounded off so that it seemed to have no corners. There was an immense fireplace at the furthest end like a gargantuan inglenook. Its mouth was so large, I could have walked right into it without bending my head.

On one wall, there was a colossal bookcase spanning the entire length, and it rose up to the lofty ceiling. Every inch was filled with books, and these didn't look like decorative features that had been bought for the purpose of showing off. The volumes I could see had jackets with scars, leather that had dried out, and many of them were jostling for position, having been stuffed into a smaller space than they required.

The only other decorations were tapestries hung on the stone walls. I had been laid on a divan upholstered in a fine brocade. The rest of the furniture was in dark polished wood, all large pieces and very regal in style.

The air was dry and the temperature cold which suggested that the place wasn't frequently inhabited. I tried to stand and was leaning on the back of the divan when the door opened. Fear rocketed through me, but anger followed when I saw it was Pierro who had entered.

I practically spat with rage.

'What the hell is going on?' I demanded.

'*Calma,*' he purred. 'Would you like some water?' He poured a glass from a jug on the sideboard, opposite the huge bookcase. He looked relaxed and exhilarated as if he had just been to the gym and afterwards partaken of a particularly refreshing shower. I, on the other hand, felt precisely as fresh as someone who had travelled on the floor of a vehicle for several hours.

'*Calma?*' I growled. 'Calm is the last thing I am likely to be until I am returned home.'

He sat down on the upholstered chair opposite the divan and beckoned me to sit.

'You have caught my attention, *cara*. You are an unusual girl, and I am a powerful man.'

I narrowed my eyes. Was this some elaborate seduction? I wondered in confusion.

'I am the head of an ancient society. We are businessmen, aristocrats, politicians and have a particular interest in seventeenth century science, otherwise known as alchemy.'

I was listening carefully now, but still not seeing what he was trying to say.

'Our members all have something in common: our inherited wealth has come from an alchemical source.'

'I'm sorry, were they alchemists?' I interrupted, not understanding him. A flicker of excitement rose in my chest, just for a moment, despite the situation.

He laughed, genuinely amused, as if we were sharing a joke over dinner. I could see why he had had a succession of beautiful girlfriends; today, he looked like a model in *Esquire*. I considered whether I needed to be so scared. Such a relaxed demeanour didn't fit with the fact that he intended to do me harm.

'No. A better analogy would be that alchemists are the tradesmen and we are the clients,' he said.

'I don't understand. If there really have been alchemists in the world, why would they work for you?'

'Because they had to,' he said in a silky-suede voice. Now I knew I really needed help; this man was super-crazy. 'The reason the world we live in believes alchemy is a myth is because our society has made it so. We have systematically erased the true history of alchemy by removing all of the credible physical evidence from the public domain. For four hundred years, our group has taken alchemists and those suspected of the skill and encouraged them to fulfil their potential under our care. We have also identified and removed every object in museums and private collections that could possibly indicate that this ability is real.'

'But there are textual sources. I have read them myself,' I contradicted.

'There is nothing textual that is substantial. There is plenty of prose. Without physical evidence, science has done our work for us. It destroys any credibility that the myth once had.'

I shook my head. 'It can't be done. It goes against basic science,' I said, scathingly.

'Over a thousand unique objects would suggest you are wrong, *cara,*' he shot back. 'Besides, it's a little hypocritical of you to deny the theory on the basis of science, isn't it? Hadn't you a chemistry degree when you began to entertain the possibility?'

'And achieved nothing, which suggests I was wrong.'

Pierro made a noise of irritation.

'It suggests only that you have not been sufficiently focused on the task. Science is so unimaginative. Every time a new discovery is made, suddenly an explanation is figured out which previously would never have occurred to anyone. Without the evidence of alchemy, science has no reason to hypothesise how it might be done, and that suits us just fine. In fact, the unexplained aspect is part of what our group prizes. Alchemy remains within the category of the miraculous. Explanation would sully it, and make it commonplace.'

'So you don't just do this for the money?' I asked.

'Originally, it was a financial enterprise, but not now. Though gold commands such a high price, even a lifetime of gold making would be but a grain of sand in the desert compared to our members' wealth. Many of us have different motivations; for some, our work is a homage to their family's histories. For others, their wealth is so abundant that regular currency ceases to hold value to them. The rare is what they prize, and what could be rarer than alchemist's gold?'

I rubbed my hands against one another. They felt hot under my gloves. I thought of my father telling me to air them more and tears instantly sprang to my eyes at the thought of my family. I could feel Pierro's eyes upon me and I didn't want him to see me cry so I lowered my head, but I couldn't stop the tears dropping onto my knees.

It took me a while to gain control of my voice.

'I can't do it.'

'I know that. I viewed your notebooks many months ago. I could see how raw your ideas were.'

My brain wasn't working at full speed yet. I couldn't quite process how he had seen my notes.

'I just have a feeling about you,' he mused.

I looked up at him, my eyes still holding tears.

'How will it work? You said I will be here under your care. What does that even mean?'

'You will work here without distractions, aiming to make gold.'

'And if I don't?'

Fleetingly, I dared to look defiant.

'I'm sure you don't want to bring your family or friends

into this,' he said, looking away towards the towering bookshelf.

'What are you talking about?' I wanted him to look at me. 'My friends don't know anything about alchemy.'

When he did turn his head, I saw his expression was a mocking sneer.

'You misunderstand my meaning.' Suddenly, I didn't and my heart clenched.

'How many others have there been?' I asked, though I wasn't sure I really wanted to know the answer.

'It is fair to say that very few have succeeded, but we have tried many.'

'What happened to them?' I said quietly.

He looked down at his manicured hands, and then looked away again.

'We don't need to discuss that now,' he said evasively.

'This is madness.' I felt like I was in some kind of psychiatric unit where it was clear my doctors regarded my sanity as dubious, whereas it seemed crystal clear to me that it was their sanity in question. Without thinking, I moved off the divan, and knelt in front of him so that I was close to his eye level. I tried to take his hand.

'Please don't do this to me, Pierro.'

He looked repelled by my proximity and stood up, moving over to the huge fireplace. I had a fleeting image of other would-be alchemists pleading for their lives, without success, in this room. With his hand on the mantelpiece, he shook his head and looked annoyed.

'You will have a month to show us progress. Don't provoke me, *cara*. I have an unpredictable temper.'

I was still kneeling on the floor and felt so breathless, it was like I'd been running.

'You stole my toolbox, didn't you?'

He did not deny it.

'Did you really arrive at your theory about me from reading jottings in a girl's notebooks?'

He stared down at me with an expression of superiority, though I couldn't fathom why.

'No, *cara*, it began much earlier than that. We noticed you in London. Didn't Marco arrange a pass for you to study in *our* library?'

'Your library?' I shook my head, not understanding.

'Marco told us all about you and how you needed a quiet place to study. He told us about your special skills with metal, and after a little research into you, we agreed to indulge his request for you to use our facilities so that we could keep an eye on you. Perhaps nothing else would have come of it, if it hadn't been for the fact that you stole that rather unusual little book.'

'I didn't steal it, or at least, I didn't mean to steal it. I got hounded out of the library by a crazy old man, and my skills are nothing but good training, for God's sake!' But I had a terrible sinking feeling that arguing with logic in this situation would never work. 'So, I was never recommended by Charlotte Taylor?'

Pierro shook his head. 'Sergio was particularly helpful, though. He knows more about patination than you might give him credit for – after all, he's worked with just about every art foundry in Europe. He said he has never seen metal respond to a patineur the way it does to you. He described it as like watching an enchantment.

'We shouldn't overlook the more minor players either: the priest, Father Peter, then there was the librarian at the museum in Florence who tells us about anyone removing books on certain topics. Marco, of course, never held anything back when given the right incentive. Checking your progress from the notes you made at my flat was, obviously, no trouble.'

I was amazed at the web that I had only just become aware I was caught in. It must have been the tetchy librarian who had tried to warn me with a note. I didn't know how to feel about Marco's involvement. He had been so determined to discourage me from pursuing my research further. It couldn't be possible that he had known what was being planned. It seemed much more likely that he had relayed the information innocently when asked leading questions.

Pierro stood up. It seemed he had decided we'd talked enough and he went to the door. The two blond men, who must have been waiting outside, entered the room. One pulled me up, while the other spoke in rapid Italian to Pierro. They escorted me behind a large wall hanging in the room which I had presumed was only decorative.

It hid a stone staircase.

20

The stairs turned as we descended, and halfway down was a large window between the ground and first floor which allowed some light into what must have been a cellar. One of the blond men gave me an unnecessary shove as we reached the bottom of the stairwell; I staggered forward. The room was divided in half by a partition of iron bars set out close together and a door separating the two areas.

I looked into the cage beyond me. I could hardly believe my eyes when I saw a large workbench with my toolbox upended onto it. Ridiculous as it sounds in this awful situation, our reunion made me feel happy momentarily; I had thought it was gone for ever.

There was a single bed in one corner. It was pressed up against the stone wall, and a large fireplace was in the alcove next to it. A sink and toilet were in the far corner with a flimsy screen that didn't hide much. On the other side of the fireplace were some shelves with various objects on them and a box on the floor filled with pieces of metal. More metal was neatly stacked on the floor, large and small sized pieces, one on top of the other.

'Go on then,' said one of the men. 'Or are you waiting for me to hold the door open, Princess?'

The cell was like something from the dark ages. I imagined this portion of the room hadn't changed since the building was made. I walked over to the workbench and sat down. Laying my head on the bench, I placed one hand on my toolbox which was the only comforting thing in the room. Instantly, I felt tears rise in my throat; they began as a perfect blend of self-pity and terror. My heart shook rather than beat.

All at once, differing emotions made a play for the tears. Each one fought the others, causing an almighty squall: stupidity, futility, anger, vulnerability, cowardice.

How could I have been so stupid? The futility of attempting to change lead into gold was for the first time absolutely real to me. I could suddenly see why Terry had laughed so hard when I'd told him about it. It had stopped being a game, and any faith I'd had in my own ability had completely dried up.

My vulnerability almost choked me. I'd never been in danger before, and now all I found in my inner armoury was doubt. There was no bravery or cunning to be proud of.

Footsteps echoed down the stairs as another man descended, which forced me to check my desperate tears a little. He was quite small and balancing a tremendous amount of cables and computer equipment on top of a largish monitor. Fear prickled over my skin again.

He unloaded his arms onto the table before acknowledging me.

'Phew, I nearly dropped that lot. Hello, I'm Roberto.' He offered a wave. 'I'll be looking after you mostly. Any supplies you need, just ask me, though you will have to justify any unusual requests. I'm out here most of the time. Do you know, you are our first woman here, and you are also Pierro's first ever find.' He paused dramatically as if waiting for some excitement on my part. 'I imagine you'll be no trouble. Oo look, here's the food!'

His holiday camp welcome was completely bizarre, another dimension of the insanity that I seemed to be surrounded by. A rhythmic chanting echoed in my head: *I need to get out, get out, get out, get out, get out.*

'Here we go.' Roberto moved halfway up the stairs and took hold of a tray from another man, who I couldn't quite see. As he moved towards my cell door carrying the tray, he inclined his head to all the stuff on his desk.

'Well, I wasn't looking forward to rigging all that up anyway, so lunch will give us a chance to get properly acquainted.' He managed to open the cell door in a very clumsy manner and manoeuvred the tray inside. 'Here, coffee and ham salad with fresh bread. I imagine you won't be very hungry today; a lot of excitement last night.'

He laid the tray on the workbench and sat down beside me. The thunder of tears had stopped by now, and fleetingly it occurred to me that this whole situation could be imaginary. It was so bizarre; I considered whether I was having some kind of psychotic break. That thought calmed me a little. My body felt stiff and achy like I had flu, but I was hungry.

'You'll be alright in a few days. I've read about how others began. Some wouldn't eat a thing; they thought it was poisoned.'

I looked at him with alarm.

'It's not, it's not, I ate the same myself. The chef is a good friend. If I ask him, he will send you down dishes you might prefer. He used to run his own restaurant, now he's retired.'

I picked up the coffee; it was strong. Roberto might be friendly, but he was definitely odd. He seemed highly excitable as if he wasn't used to having someone to talk to. He didn't seem in a hurry to leave.

'Is there anything you'd like to ask me?' he said, giving me a smile which was trying too hard. Roberto had hazel coloured eyes and olive skin. His hair was quite long, dark and slightly wavy. He was not unattractive, but something about his earnestness was.

'The only thing I can think of is, who are you?' My voice sounded bitchy.

He threw a glance over to the stairs and lowered his voice.

'Pierro is my brother. All of our family are involved. Chris and Vic, your escorts, are brothers, but also cousins to Pierro and me.'

I huffed at the description of escorts, kidnappers being more accurate. Roberto repeatedly stroked his forehead from left to right in jerky motions as he continued.

'Pierro is running the project, as I'm sure you realised. My role used to be called scribe. I must document everything. Vic and Chris are guards; their remit does tend to be more violent. These things that we do are part of our family history and we take it very seriously.'

'I suppose Pierro will get one of them to kill me. He wouldn't do the dirty work himself, evil coward,' I said bitterly.

'No, you mistake Pierro. He will do whatever needs to be done, as we all will, but we do not tend to work outside of our remits. Pierro is strong enough to do the distasteful things, but that is not his role. I, on the other hand, am not, and am pleased I do not have to. I respect the importance of what we do here, but I have less appetite for the things we may have to do to bring it about. I am the supporting act.'

Roberto stood up, perhaps feeling our discussion had drifted outside of his remit. I put out my arm to stop him stepping away and looked up directly into his eyes.

'You may as well organise my execution, because what Pierro is asking me to do cannot be done.'

Roberto shook his head.

'You are wrong, it can be done. Although I have never seen it within my lifetime, my grandfather has, and he is still alive. This myth that you do not believe in has empowered our family. Pierro really believes in you. In my grandfather's generation many were brought here and made to try based on much less evidence than Pierro has gathered on you.' He detached himself from my grip. 'I have things to be getting on with,' he said and went back to his desk.

I watched him fiddling with cables, setting up a small security camera with a little red light facing into the cell and his computer. I willed him to leave and give me the smallest degree of privacy. His presence invaded my space, but he seemed in no hurry to go.

MY BAGS WERE STANDING NEATLY in one corner; they should have been in David's flat. He would be wondering why I hadn't arrived. He would be making telephone calls, trying to contact me, thinking I'd shied away again. If he loved me as much as I loved him, then I knew the kind of pain he would be in. It was salt in the wound that he might think my absence was purposeful.

I took off my fancy gloves which I hadn't had an opportunity to change since the party and swapped them for more comfortable ones that were packed away. My ring caught the light in the gloomy cell and sparkled. I took it off and hid it under my clothes at the bottom of my suitcase.

I suddenly felt completely blank. Now that the immediate fear had passed, I had no idea what to do next and sat on the bed, feeling like my thoughts had been glued up.

'It's a beautiful day. If you stand on the stool and look out of the window, you can see the lake from down here,' remarked Roberto.

His words irritated me so much that they pierced through my foggy brain. Behaving as if this was an entirely normal situation was becoming increasingly wearing. Nevertheless, I went over to the window and looked out on to the lake. It was such a peaceful scene, completely incredible that it could have been the backdrop to such horrors.

'Where are we exactly?' I asked.

Roberto, who was sitting at his desk reading some papers, batted away my question.

'You need to start thinking about your work. Is there anything you need?' he pressed.

'Only a key to the door,' I said sarcastically. He smiled.

'Good one.'

I went over to look at my toolbox. It was a comfort to find it here, captured as I was. It had been ransacked, and lay on the bench as if it had vomited everything out. I stroked its wooden surface in sympathy, and cursed the hands that had been so rough with it.

This box was particularly special to me. I had saved for and collected its contents slowly like most women collect trinkets. It told the history of my training, and the breadth of my interest in metals. Considered more carefully, it was evidence of how I had lost myself in an obsession in order to blot out the other part of my life which involved rejection. Disgust, shock and squeamishness were the most common reactions to my hands. There were reminders nearly every day, particularly when people saw their naked state unintentionally, like when I was washing them.

I began to sort through the mess of bottles and tools, pigments and pots, laying each one out on the bench in their various categories. It was a comforting chore, but I still found myself crying on and off during it. However, for a short time, it acted as a balm, just as my foundry work had always done.

I had collected the tools one by one as I was introduced to each skill in the foundry. I had bought myself files of all different shapes and sizes after learning how to make wooden patterns. I had medieval looking tongs for pouring molten liquids, and rasps and chisels for removing imperfections on a metal's surface, known as fettling and metal-finishing. Like an apothecary, I had every remedy and pigment which was beneficial for bronze, from ammonia to various acids to common salt, and dozens of small pots of chemicals for patination. I had a delicatessen of differing waxes, from carnauba to micro-crystalline, and a range of polishing cloths lying together like slices of white bread. These were of varying weight and strength to provide the perfect shine at the end of any job.

Nothing appeared to be missing. There were a few spillages, but nothing dangerous. Fortunately, my blue ink bottle marked 'Pete's Potent Pickle' hadn't broken. It would have had a devastating effect.

I had worked for about a year with the only other patineur in the foundry. Pete's work, unlike my father's, was not artistic. He worked on colouring objects like doorknobs, light switches and furniture frames. The patination process he used was quite different to the one I used daily. It involved preparing the metal with a strong acid mixture known as pickle. Pete claimed his particular pickle was the Muhammad Ali of the pickle world. Though he wouldn't disclose his exact recipe, I suspected it was predominantly sulphuric acid with a dash of hydrochloric, perhaps, for good measure. The pickle would eat away every bit of dirt, grease or corrosion before the bronze was dipped into another chemical, which would colour it. The process was about chemistry and precision rather than artistic licence.

I turned the bottle over. Shame I didn't have a vat of it, then I could do some serious damage. Unfortunately, it was only a small bottle, but it might be worth a try if I was desperate. The label on the back said: *Do Not Drink.* Then underneath, Pete had written: *Duhhhhhhhh...*

I smiled and slipped my hand into the bottom compartment to see if my notebook was still there. Something sharp sliced into the pad of my middle finger. I pulled my hand back, and then carefully removed the offending article. It was the sickle-shaped knife.

I stared at it in disbelief, then looked over at Roberto, who was writing at his desk. This must belong to Pierro. I wondered if he had a full set of his own alchemist's tools that were tucked away with his dead fingers and other treasures.

Laying the tool in front of me on the bench, I pushed it away. I didn't like it mingling with my own possessions. I reached back into the box a second time to retrieve my notebook. The kit had been stolen to secure this worthless notebook. Pierro must have been at a very early stage of evaluating my potential.

Flicking through the pages, I left bloody prints on nearly every one. This tool, shaped like a question mark, made me think about the big question again: could this be done? It answered itself, too: ? – don't know. Theories about rituals didn't sit well with me. As I stared at the knife, all I could see was a weapon which I had no idea how to use effectively. I would be instantly overpowered by the hulking men who seemed determined to contain me.

It was late afternoon now and the stone room felt chilly. In the fireplace was everything I needed to make up a fire so I set about it. Roberto came in to light it. I dragged my bed out of the alcove and pulled it parallel to the fire so that I could turn my back on Roberto and gaze at the flames in peace. I refused dinner, which Roberto pouted at, but eventually he left me with just the red eye of the camera upon me.

21

Worry gnawed at the little sleep that I managed to gain. Questions kept bubbling up to the forefront of my mind; questions that burned with importance at the time and repeated over and over. When morning came, most of those questions teased me by drifting just outside of my recall. All except one.

Once I was awake, the worry morphed into a full-body fidgeting mode. No part of my body wanted to keep still. I patrolled the cell twitchily from dawn until Roberto arrived with breakfast.

As soon as he came through the door, I quizzed him.

'What can you tell me about Domenico? Pierro said he was central to the organisation.'

Roberto put down the tray and looked evasive.

'Signor Milliardo's interest is not really relevant to your success. I have a lot to do this morning.'

He took a few steps backwards towards the cell door. I sprang after him and grabbed his arm. He turned.

'Please, Roberto. You've got me here. It's sunk in now; I'm not getting out. I won't be able to tell anyone. Signor

Milliardo knows my family. His brother's wife is my mother's best friend. I can't understand why he would let this happen to me.'

Roberto studied me.

'He hasn't let this happen to you. There are some in the society who feel that cultivating alchemists, as we call it, should be relegated to the past. They think we should be caretakers of alchemy's secret history, but no more. Domenico is more open-minded. He sees some value in the traditional ways.'

He pulled his arm out of my grasp. Footsteps sounded on the stairs. My heart upped its beats. I shrank back as Roberto relocked the door.

The two blond men, who had taken me, descended.

'No, no, no, another fifteen minutes. She hasn't eaten breakfast yet.'

Roberto's voice quivered as if he was unused to giving orders. His hand sought his temple for reassurance.

'Pierro said first thing,' the taller of the blond men said.

'Quarter of an hour will make no difference.' Roberto frowned in irritation. The lines that formed on his forehead looked well worn.

The blond men ascended the stairs again, talking to one another. Roberto turned to me.

'Eat,' he commanded. 'No more questions.'

I picked up one of the small rolls which were in a wicker basket and spread on some preserve.

'OK,' I said eating nervously and pressing my face between the bars. 'Why are they here?'

Roberto had stationed himself at the desk and was writing.

'They aren't going to hurt you,' he said. His eyes held

mine for a second and I saw something there: sympathy; shame. I took a sip of coffee.

'They speak English to each other, don't they?'

Roberto sighed and put down the pen.

'I hope you will not always be this inquisitive. I don't suppose it will matter if I tell you that their mother was English.'

'Which one is which?' I said, beginning on the second roll which was incredibly light and sweet.

'Vic is taller. Now stop talking.'

The two men descended again only a few minutes later, and this time I looked at them with proper attention. They were very similarly built: tall with thickset bodies, but that was where the similarity stopped. Chris had small eyes and a round face. His hair was short in a military style, spiked with gel. Vic had a rectangular face with large features: big nose, large lips and bulging eyes. Also, Vic's complexion was ruddier.

Despite Roberto's words, I didn't like the idea of going anywhere with them again. I really panicked when they came towards the cell. I grabbed a hammer from the work-bench and ran to the back wall. They opened the door, and I heard Roberto saying something to me, but didn't register the content.

I thrashed at them with the hammer, but one of them grabbed my wrist expertly and squeezed so hard I dropped it. They took an arm each, and although I kicked off the workbench, the grills, and the wall, they lifted me quite easily out of the cell.

My heart leapt around in my chest like it was looking for an escape too. They took me up the stone stairs and into the room I'd woken up in. I noticed the windows were very tiny, and also had fixed clear sheets over them, making them more secure. We went out into the hallway and through an enormous main entrance door.

Once outside, the huge men hemmed me in so that I was as much imprisoned outdoors as I had been in my cell. There was no point in trying to make a break for it. They manoeuvred me into a car parked on the wide gravel drive. I pulled ineffectually at the door handle from the inside as the men took the front seats. Chris turned towards me with an irritated expression and reached around to slap my hand away from the handle.

'Stop it,' he growled.

They sped off up the drive. I looked around madly for anything in the back of the car that might help me: nothing. The awareness of having no options was petrifying. I felt my skin flush and could hear my own breathing rasp with panic.

Vic looked at me through his mirror and smirked.

'*Coniglia*,' he said to Chris. *Rabbit.*

The car halted before pulling out on to a road. I glanced back, and for a second, I saw what my prison looked like from the outside. It was a wide circular stone tower, resembling a castle, though it was not large enough to be classified as such. To one side was a lake and to the other a small wooded area.

We moved quickly into what was obviously an agricultural grey-green landscape. The land may once have been part of the palazzo's grounds. I moved back and forth from one side of the car to the other, scanning the outside. I was hoping to see something that might be useful to me, like another dwelling, but apart from a couple of old barns and a corn storage crib, there was nothing.

I laid my head against the cool glass. Please, there has to be something, I wished fervently.

After about fifteen minutes, we pulled over at a deserted crossroads. There was an old phone box on one side of the road. I could hardly believe my eyes; it was so rare to see one these days. It was particularly unusual as it was completely lopsided. It looked drunk, in the way gravestones can when they are placed on ground with no foundations.

Vic stayed in the car and Chris went with me. He let go of me when we were actually in the booth, but then thought better of it. Bending one arm behind my back, he pressed himself into me. He gently pulled back my hair and held it while he spoke. His lips brushed my ear. I felt salt in my mouth and a lot of saliva. Sure I was about to be sick, I tried not to move at all.

'Call your family, say you are fine. Tell them a friend has invited you to their holiday home in Tuscany, and you are having the most wonderful time. Tell them they can't reach you as there is no phone, but you'll keep in touch. Keep it brief, keep it convincing, and don't try anything stupid, or I'll have to hurt you.'

He forced my arm up my back far enough for me to be sure that a tiny bit further, and it would have snapped. I lifted the receiver and held it between my shoulder and ear while he put some money in. I dialled the number and my mum picked up.

'Hi, Mum!' I started haltingly. 'Sorry I haven't been in touch.'

She scolded me for a couple of seconds. I followed the story line exactly. She seemed convinced and asked me if I'd been swimming and if Marco had gone with me.

'I'll call you soon, Mum. Can you tell David I'm okay, and...' my voice began to crack. I felt the emotion swelling up like a wave and breaking in my throat. Chris increased the pressure on my arm.

I yelped, 'Bye,' and put the phone down.

I immediately started to cry. Outside the telephone box, Chris took a cable tie out of his pocket and bound my hands in front of me. He hustled me back into the car.

'You'll have to do better than that next time,' he barked and slammed the car door.

The tears were uncontrollable; I was in such serious trouble. It was torture to speak to my family but not ask for help. We set off back to the palazzo, but on the way, Vic stopped the car. We were on a narrow road parked partly on the long grass with a tall hedge to one side. I couldn't think of any good reason why we would be stopping.

'Finally, I actually have reception here!' Vic pulled the phone from its cradle and looked delightedly at it. 'I'm going to order in a tonne of stuff: DVD player, films, Xbox, games. I'm not sitting another night up there without anything to do. I'm dying of boredom, and God knows how long this could take.'

He threw a glance in my direction.

'You'd think Pierro with all his connections and money could get some cable laid or a phone mast put up so that we could communicate with the outside world.'

Chris had turned in his seat slightly and his gaze fell upon me. I didn't like the way he was looking at me; the hairs on the back of my neck stood as if I were cold.

'How long is all this ordering going to take?' he asked.

'For God's sake,' Vic snapped. 'What on earth do you want to rush back for? Pierro's in Florence, it's not as if we've got anything to get back to.'

'I think I'll take Abigail for a walk,' Chris said. 'Cooped up all day, I'm sure she would appreciate it.'

Vic looked up at his brother with an irritated expression and then seemed to understand his meaning. He shrugged.

'Pierro wouldn't like it,' he said.

Chris had turned away from me again so I could only see the back of his head and couldn't be entirely sure of his meaning, but I anticipated this was about as bad as it could get.

'Well, as you pointed out, he's not here.'

The moment he said that, my heart sped up to an insane pace. Please, God, don't let this happen, I kept thinking over and over. Chris got out, and I tried to push myself to the furthest point in the car. He opened the door, and I kicked out at him several times. He grabbed my leg, giving the top of my thigh a couple of hard punches, which made it go dead, and pulled me out.

He stayed a couple of paces behind me as we walked along a road. I could feel him, though he wasn't touching me – yet. It was as if his shadow was making the first moves. His steps seemed unnaturally loud in a landscape that had gone mute.

The hedge to my right stopped at the entrance to a field. The gate was wide open as if waiting for a tractor to enter. He turned me into the field and we continued to walk in sync, though our minds were in opposite states of anticipation. There was a large tree that had fallen many years ago parallel to the hedge, and he seemed to be heading towards that. My mind was in overdrive, thinking what I could do. With my hands tied in front of me, the idea of running was ridiculous.

I started to jabber. 'Pierro's told you I'm ill, hasn't he? He's told you about my illness.'

Chris laughed really loudly behind me, then moved in front of me, blocking my way. He stood very close to me so that my chin nearly rested on his chest, but I didn't want to lift my head to meet his gaze.

'I have a disease that I contracted when I was a child and it's catching,' I said, though my voice kept disappearing.

He put his hand to my face and lifted my eyes.

'You look fine to me,' he said in a tone more akin to a hiss than a whisper. There was something gargoyle-like about his expression. It was as if he was smiling and snarling at me at the same time. 'Very fine,' he hissed again.

I held my hands up and forward.

'Take off my gloves. Take them off,' I said in an authoritative voice.

With the cable tie stopping him, he could only push them down to my wrist, but immediately he could see the messy rash on the underside of my forearms. The stress I had been under in the last couple of days had made their surface about as bad as it could get. I had been rubbing the skin constantly.

He jumped back as if electrocuted.

'If you cut the tie, I'll show you my hands: they're worse.'

'What is it?' he asked.

My mind was buzzing. I wasn't sure how far to go with this answer. I needed to say something he'd heard of that was bad enough to scare him, but not something he might know about.

'It's a blood disease. It's related to leprosy, but worse in some ways as it's resistant to antibiotics. It's contagious by contact and it's not just on my arms.'

This was entirely fictional, but it was my best shot. He looked like he wanted to be sick.

'Come on,' he shouted at me and shoved me really hard in front of him. He continued these monumental shoves and kicks to the back of my knees, which made me drop to the floor, until we got back to the car. Each time I went down, I thanked God for what I had always seen as my affliction.

Each time I felt pain at the back of my knees and skin torn by the fall, I felt fortunate.

Vic looked amazed when we arrived back so soon.

'Drive!' Chris ordered.

'But I haven't finished my emails,' Vic complained.

'You can come back when you've dropped us off.' Chris spat out of the window. He was obviously in a black mood, so Vic didn't argue and started up the car. The venomous look that Chris gave me was another thing to worry about. I knew I'd made an enemy, and that he would be the first in line to assist in getting rid of me when the time came. Revenge was written all over him. I prayed that he didn't speak to Pierro about my so-called disease.

I was crying as I made my way down the steps to my cell. Roberto looked sympathetic, assuming it was just the trauma of ringing my family. He disappeared upstairs as Chris and Vic locked me back in.

Chris picked up the stapler from Roberto's desk and ran it childishly along the bars. I stood a few inches inside the cell, staring back at him. Vic was mounting the stairs and speaking to Roberto at the top. Chris lost no time in spitting on me. He just missed my face, and it ran down my neck.

Roberto came down with coffee and shooed Chris away. I couldn't control the shaking, which was coming in violent spasms. Now the crying really took hold, and I dropped to my knees with my hands still tied awkwardly out in front.

22

I spent a lot of time in the first few days staring out of the window. My great hope was that David would contact my parents, and upon hearing the story I'd given, become suspicious. He was the only one who knew I'd been worried about my safety. He may have laughed at my worries at the time, but now the things I'd told him might help to find me.

Vic gave me most to watch. He spent much of his day outdoors, careering around on a quad bike, flying over every dip in the landscape and practising tricks. He often took two huge German shepherds, more like lions than dogs, out with him, and let them chase after the bike. They would try to bite the wheels. He also took cans outside and shot at them from greater and greater distances. This activity made me want to lie down as I couldn't help imagining what target practice was readying him for.

Vic would walk about for what seemed like hours trying to find a place with phone reception. Every few steps, he halted in anticipation, but then his body would sag slightly, and he'd continue on in a counter direction. He was obviously madly bored.

Chris, on the other hand, I rarely saw until one morning when the day began with a lot of shouting upstairs.

Roberto scuttled down and sat at his desk, looking boot-faced. I went over to the bars.

'What's going on?' I whispered to him.

'Pierro's back and not in the best mood. He's shouting at Vic who has had some huge delivery. He doesn't want attention drawn to the palazzo, or anyone focusing on anything but the project.'

As Roberto's words faded, Pierro came downstairs. I raced over to the bed and sat with my back against the wall. I knew he was going to be angry; I hadn't been working at all. I couldn't see the point in even attempting it.

Vic and Chris were at his side. Vic looked surly while Chris radiated daggers at me. Three terrifying men humming with differing pitches of anger; the result was a terror that made me lightheaded and shaky.

Pierro stood directly in front of me, but I wouldn't look at him.

'I've come to see how you are getting on. Roberto says you are not working.'

I didn't bother responding. He bent down to my eye level, reached behind my head and tugged my hair so that I was forced to look into his angry eyes.

'Do you think this is all a joke, Abi? Do you think we are just going to let you go because you can't do it?'

He brought his face very near to mine; his brows were narrowed and skin flushed.

'I am not some fool who goes about plucking random people out of their lives for my own amusement. I have watched you, and I have seen what ability you have.'

Tears were in my eyes before I could control them.

'I can't.' I shook my head.

'You're pathetic,' he said. He dropped my hair and stood upright, walking over to the workbench. I had left some of my toolbox contents on the bench. He picked up a glass pot, and threw it fractionally above my head. It smashed dangerously, spreading glass splinters all over me. Some of the compound splashed my forehead and across my cheek.

It took only seconds for me to realise that the pot had contained dichloromethane, a harsh commercial product that stripped paint and varnish. It immediately began to burn, and the sensation escalated alarmingly. I leapt up on my bed in fear and surprise, trying to wipe the stripper away, which only spread it further.

Another second and he'd thrown my heavy tongs, hitting me squarely on the shin. I cried out in pain, and crouched down just in time as he lifted the entirety of my heavy toolbox up and aimed it straight at me. It crashed against the wall, missing the side of my head by only a few inches. Its many contents clattered to the floor, several of my precious glass pots of chemicals smashing on the stone.

My breath was coming in short, sharp starts as he approached the bed again. I tried to back away. Fury and frustration blazed in his face.

'This doesn't make sense,' I pleaded.

We held each other's eye contact. Every feature of his face was ticking with anger. He reached into his pocket, and I glanced at his hand, expecting to see a gun. Instead, he pulled out a key, turned away, and left the cell without another word. Chris and Vic followed like a pair of pit bulls.

I got down off my bed and ran to the sink to wash away the stripper. An angry red burn mark, in the perfect pattern of the splash, ranged across my face. Thank God it hadn't gone in my eye. Patting my sore skin dry, I went down on to my knees as my legs folded under me, fear draining my strength away.

I PASSED three days in anticipation of Pierro's next move; it was like waiting for a clap of thunder after seeing the lightning strike. Every slight sound made my nerves jangle. I began to sharpen the sickle-shaped knife obsessively by passing it backward and forward over the smooth stone mantelpiece whenever Roberto left his room. The meditative motion of sharpening the knife encouraged my mind to run over my recent encounter with Pierro.

There had been a change in his demeanour. The controlled, self-satisfied state of only a few days ago had been replaced by something more desperate. His rage was definitely tainted with something more than frustration; he had looked like a man under pressure.

Fear had completely penetrated me, and I found myself unable to stop shaking or keep warm. I moved around the cell constantly, trying to stimulate my circulation by rubbing my arms and legs. On the third night, when I lit the fire as had become my custom, I suddenly had the overwhelming urge for a drink.

I got up and walked to the bars.

'Roberto, would you be able to get me some brandy?' I asked.

It was dark on his side of the cellar as well. He had a single desk lamp which threw light on to only one side of his face. I could see he looked unsure, so I pursued it.

'I'm so frightened, Roberto.' My voice broke slightly. 'Next time, I think he's going to kill me.'

'You won't be that lucky,' he said, shaking his head. There was a pause; images of a situation where dying was a good thing flashed in front of me. 'Even if Pierro conceded he'd made a mistake, others wouldn't let it go so soon.'

My stomach clenched at his prediction. 'Can't you sugar-coat it, Roberto?'

'That's not why I'm here.' He sighed and stood up, rubbing his temple with one finger like a violinist playing a note vibrato. 'I wish you were a big, ugly man. I'd feel a lot less sorry for you. Chris has got some brandy, I'll go and see.'

'No. Please don't ask Chris.'

The desperation made my voice high-pitched.

'What happened between you and Chris?' Roberto asked. 'He really loathes you, and you sound as frightened of him as you are of Pierro.'

I shrugged, not wanting to go into it.

'He just doesn't like me.'

'I'll get you some whisky. There's plenty of that as it's what Pierro drinks.'

I watched him disappear upstairs, and thought over his ominous comments until he returned. He poured himself a large glass first, and then passed another glass and the bottle through the bars. I took it over to my workbench and poured one for myself. The whisky was harsh and clawing, but this was probably due to my novice taste buds; I couldn't imagine Pierro drinking cheap whisky. I took a great gulp of it and waited for it to push back the cold.

The room was almost dark apart from a little chiaroscuro from the fire.

'Is it Domenico who won't let it go? I mean, even if Pierro would?' I asked.

Roberto shifted on his seat before lifting the glass in a

toast to me, and then taking a large sip. I could only just make out his features; he was scowling.

'Domenico is a difficult man to predict. I have worked for him for nearly a decade.'

'You work for him?' I nearly choked on the whisky. My assumption had been that Roberto reported to Pierro. Not that this error altered my position at all, but I had a sense that I was missing something. 'I'm disappointed in you. I imagined you as an academic of some sort rather than a lackey for a Mafia-type.'

He raised his eyebrows and looked offended.

'Don't mistake him for a thug. You couldn't count the number of people who would line up to take my place. I would say Domenico has more power than any other man in Italy.'

'How so?'

Roberto pushed his long hair back from his face.

'He's not Mafia per se, though many of his associates are. He's actually a dealer. He makes untold money buying and selling everything from bauxite to oil, fine art to diamonds. He's made himself powerful by dealing in favours. Someone needs a favour, Domenico will make it happen. Payment, however, is always a favour in return. He is known to be 100% trustworthy, discreet and capable. When he has been refused payment, he is known to be brutal, extreme, and some might say insane. There are not many people that understand Domenico as I do.'

He leaned his head back against his headrest and put his feet up on the desk, looking as if he was assessing whether I was impressed. He held his glass by its base and turned it with his fingertips.

'Domenico is the head of The Golden Illuminati, our secret society, but he is only interested in you in the sense that you have been selected by one of his members. All I meant was that Domenico has a long tradition of leadership to uphold within the Society , and so I doubt he would go against tradition and sanction your freedom.'

He knocked back the rest of the whisky.

Suddenly, I didn't want to talk about Domenico any more. I had been drinking steadily as Roberto had been talking, and I felt the whisky working its way through my veins like a SWAT team, shooting out the fear that had been shackling me.

I seemed to have layers of greedy men between myself and David. All had their individual stakes in me: Domenico protecting his traditions; Pierro needing the success of my discovery; Chris's personal desire to avenge himself on me; Vic, I could only assume, wanting to uphold his family's history by doing the job his forefathers had done. This didn't even take into account the incentives of the other members of the society. I felt anger and rage like I'd never felt before. It swirled up inside me tornado-style, and an immense pressure built in my head. My body was hot everywhere, particularly my hands. I tugged off my gloves, dropping them on the floor, and moved over to the wall at the back of the cell.

My hands were dry and the skin was stiff. I dragged my right hand along the wall, feeling the gritty stone bite my skin, then I about-turned and swapped it for the other hand. I moved back and forth, swift and positive, exchanging one hand for another over and over. I had never been one for screaming out loud, but this rage had a sound of its own. In my head, it was something between a sustained scream and a shriek.

I could see Roberto watching me intently, and his knowing look as he tilted back in his chair made me want to storm through the bars and tear at him. Without really thinking what I was doing, I flew at the bars. I cannoned into them and clasped the iron in both hands.

The most unexpected thing happened: instantly, a sensation flooded my body like a cool shower on sunburned skin. The pressure in my head eased and the loud wail of rage quietened. The iron spoke to me soothingly in its own way, giving me advice.

Calm and simplicity was what I sensed, as I always did when I touched this uncomplicated metal. It was one of the reasons that I seldom worked with it; I preferred the complex personality of bronze. But right now, I needed the sage words of those bars.

'I am only iron,' they said to me. 'You know my ways. I would never hold you.'

I closed my eyes and ran my hands up and down them. How had I not considered this before? Perhaps, it had been the fear. This cell was unmodernised; it was a relic from a former time. The hairs stood up on the back of my neck; I could feel the excitement conduct along them. I smiled properly for the first time since I'd been imprisoned. My smile was dense with emotions: relief, excitement and purpose.

I lifted my head and pushed my face between the bars. They touched the areas which had blistered, but I didn't even flinch, though the skin was almost unbearably sore. To hell with letting an army of men murder me gruesomely. If I was going to die, which was extremely likely, then it would be on my own terms in an attempt to escape.

Roberto had been watching me all this time and I could tell from his expression he was perplexed about what he was seeing.

'I need a Calor gas cylinder and blowtorch,' I said. His laugh echoed around the cell.

'I imagine every captive does. We are not going to let you blow us all to heaven.'

'Don't you mean hell?' I smiled back at him. I actually felt giddy. 'I don't think kidnapping is in the Bible. You can ask Pierro. He will let me have it as he knows it's legitimate. I need it to form the five colours which are the first stages in forming the Philosopher's Stone. I have to patinate the metal to achieve these colours. Pierro knows that; he's read my notebook. He watched me work on Sergio's statues so he knows exactly what's involved.'

'I'll call him tomorrow and see what he says.'

Roberto placed the camera on, leaving me alone with the fire and whisky. His face was full of triumph as he left. He obviously thought our talk had achieved what Pierro's intimidation had not.

If I was going to attempt to get out, I would need a diversion to screen my real purpose.

23

The next morning was different. For the first time since I'd entered the cell, the nerves circling my stomach were driven by anticipation rather than fear.

I had passed the night lying on my bed, studying the vertical iron bars running floor-to-ceiling which divided the room. Centrally located was a door made in the same style. This design, much like a 1970s animal enclosure at the zoo, meant that I could be viewed at all times. Apart from the addition of Roberto's desk with its computer and camera in the outer area, it looked to me as if it had changed little since the Guild had begun hundreds of years ago.

I had only one way of getting out as far as I could see. The most obvious way: I needed the key to my door, and I had both the tools and the skill to make it. I had been casting metal since I was a child and had worked with Larry carving patterns from drawings a thousand times.

Although it had only recently occurred to me, escaping suddenly seemed the most obvious thing in the world. A previous inhabitant must have tried such a thing, but not in

Pierro and Roberto's lifetime. I was their first, so as much as I was new to incarceration, they were new to imprisoning. I imagine they had little concern about the threat of a young female when there were several strong men around. I notched up underestimation as another factor in my favour.

Having something to focus on felt really good; I was actually excited. As the morning light brightened my cell, I went to my battered toolbox. I needed to make a blank key without anyone noticing. I had seen Roberto use his key many times; it was a large iron one, but apart from that, I remembered nothing significant.

Roberto should secure me the gas cylinder today. That could be my heat source, but I knew I would have to request more supplies to form a makeshift furnace.

During the night, I had written a list of all the things I could think of that I would need to bring my plan to fruition. I could make a case for requesting the materials to create a furnace; I would say that I needed to make a really pure lead alloy. Although there were all sorts of bits of metal on the shelves, I had no idea what their exact make-up was. Alloys are a mixture of metals and the two main elements are usually discernible, but, as with a mongrel puppy, I couldn't always be sure what their precise heritage was by eye. I could claim I needed a very specific mixture, and that I had to ensure that there were no contaminants.

I decided to use today to prepare a piece of spelter without attempting anything I shouldn't be doing. I assumed Roberto would be particularly attentive until he felt sure that I was doing what I said I would. I spent the day leisurely preparing the metal, working on it for hours, scrubbing and cleaning with my pumice and then the Greek limestone.

Towards the end of the day, I heard a car pull into the

driveway. I climbed up on my chair and watched as Vic tugged a large red Calor gas cylinder out of the car. He lifted it with ease, reminding me how much physical strength there was between me and the outside world; I could hardly even push one of those canisters over. He brought it downstairs to me and into the cell without as much as a glance in my direction.

Roberto hovered around and looked concerned. As he was the one in constant close proximity to me, I could see it from his point of view. Vic was giving me an exceptionally dangerous tool.

I didn't begin the patination that night, instead wrapping my spelter nugget in plastic so that it didn't tarnish too much overnight. The following morning, my first job was to remove any final tarnish using a dab of Pete's Potent Pickle compound. Though this was all being done for show, I allowed myself to enter the pleasurable world of working with a metal that I now understood, and my present reality faded away. Each colour came so willingly that I marvelled I'd ever had trouble with it. Brown faded to red, red to green, green to white, and finally white to royal blue, just as they had been described in my green theology book and in Father Francis's dream.

Roberto watched me closely until he was clearly satisfied that I really was using the torch to colour the metal as I'd promised. By the time darkness fell, I was completely spent. I'd reached the last colour in the Peacock's Tail, and I left the colours to settle down overnight. The spelter rested on a bed of soft lint-free cloth. My impoverished bed, shunted up against the wall with immobile springs and mean blanket, looked far less inviting.

Tomorrow, I planned to request all the additional materials I needed to cast the key, confident that Pierro would allow me what I requested. I would pretend to meditate tomorrow and play around with adding some sacramental wine. When none of this worked, I would say I wanted to try a new tack and needed to cast the base metal myself to ensure its make-up.

I slept shallowly, as I had since arriving. Each night was the same: flutters of sleep interspersed by anxious restlessness. I woke before dawn, ready to continue my play-acting. Just before sunrise, I took hold of my piece of spelter, but couldn't resist climbing on to the stool to view the waking of the beautiful morning over the lake.

A large tree was the nearest thing to my window, and as the light gained strength, it stood in silhouette. My breathing stopped. Something was hanging from the lower branch. I couldn't take my eyes from it. As the sun rose higher and higher, I couldn't deny what it was: Thérèse's slender body was hanging from the neck.

I placed one hand on the bar at my window and pushed my head against it. I didn't trust my eyes. *No, no, no, no,* crescendoed in my head.

The minute my mind accepted the reality, I felt a shiver run down my body, followed by a flush of heat running up it. My head felt clammy, and then I began to retch repeatedly. I fell down the stool and went on to my knees, bending right over so that my chin was touching them. I felt like my very soul had been poisoned, and I had to expel it from my body.

My skin burned, and suddenly I was shaking violently, but without tears. I tried to stand and felt the floor come up to meet me, so I stayed down like a fighter given the count. I clung to the cold surface of the floor, needing to hold on to something.

Then the tears came. Great, bulging, pain-dense tears

that ran one into the other like long spears. They were so prolific, they seemed to be suffocating me by running down the back of my throat and into my mouth. I spat them on to the floor.

I stayed like this until the intensity of the initial swell of pain lessened slightly, then I got up unsteadily to look at Thérèse again. She was wearing blue linen trousers and a fitted shirt with tennis shoes. Her hair was loose, falling across her face. Her relaxed attire concurred perversely with her rag doll pose. I couldn't take my eyes off her neck; it was so grotesque. It was at a shallow acute angle to her shoulders, and looked overly long like a stretched spring.

The shivering and flushing began again, and I came down off the chair. What kind of man could kill someone he'd known since he was a child? What kind of monster could kill someone as beautiful as Thérèse? Not that her beauty made her a better person than anyone else, but it seemed a violation of unwritten laws, like slashing a Monet or a Turner.

I slid down the grey stone wall beneath the window and put my head in my hands. My mind was sprinting over different scenarios. Had Pierro made a move on her and she'd rejected him? Had he imprisoned her too on the off-chance she could be used as leverage?

Then Terry's pain suddenly occurred to me and sucked my breath from my body. It seemed like time was suspended as my lungs burned to take another breath. When it finally came, the tears fell again, dropping on to my clenched hands and spilling over my thighs. I cried like this until my gloves were sodden and the abraded skin beneath them stung.

A thought interrupted my tears: someone might see Thérèse, on display as she was. I fought the heaviness that had taken possession of my body to regain my position at the window. In an instant, I became frantic, wanting to rattle the bars. Surely, someone could see her. I pushed my face between the bars and my eyes flicked from one side to the other desperately. Nothing: I could only see fields. Where was the road?

I wanted to bang my head against the bars, such was my frustration. How could this happen? How could they do this in the name of something so tenuous? How could they take such a risk and not be frightened of being caught? Were they so shielded from the law?

It was a torture all of its own, being so close and not being able to touch her. Though nothing could affect her now, I hated that she was so alone. That's when I started to speak to her through the bars, my voice travelling out towards her. I stretched my arms out as far as I could.

'I'm here, Thérèse! You're not alone...I'm sorry. I'm so sorry I can't help you. It should have been me. It should have been me. I'm sorry.'

Then I shouted louder. 'Murderers, murderers, murderers,' I screamed in the loudest voice I could summon.

24

There was movement in the room above me; I could hear footsteps. Pierro descended and found me still chanting through my tears.

'No need to ask how you're doing, *cara*.'

His voice was full of pride at the dramatic spectacle he had put on. I turned to look at him; loathing pulsed through my eyes. He cocked his head like he was speaking to a child.

'What did you do, *cara?*' He moved towards me, coming very close, and whispered into my ear. 'You know you killed her,' he purred in velvety tones. 'She was your friend, and you practically forced me to execute her. Before she died, she probably cursed you with all her dark magic.'

I couldn't protest.

'You know, I think it was fate. I was so angry with you after our little meeting last time, and suddenly Thérèse called me, enquiring about you.' The pleasure in his voice pained me, and I tried to move away from him, but he moved closer. 'No, *cara*,' he stroked my hair, 'I want you to hear this.'

I tensed. His hand on my hair provoked all manner of bad feelings.

'Anyhow, Thérèse had been called by your boyfriend who was expecting you in New York. Naturally she became concerned. She wondered if I'd heard from you. I told her you were quite safe and staying at my palazzo in the country. You were doing a little bit of research, relaxing. There was no phone.

'She didn't seem quite satisfied, so I insisted she come up to Florence and we take a drive up here together and surprise you...We did surprise you, didn't we?'

He paused for effect.

I could feel my face burning again, and the skin stung where the tears had been running repeatedly in tracks.

'Of course, I told her why you were really here before the end. Strangely, she didn't seem that surprised. She was an incredibly intuitive woman, and I think she knew you were a rare thing.'

I looked up at him, feeling anger radiating through me. I shouted so loudly my voice cracked.

'I imagine it was then she realised the extent of your insanity. This is all your fantasy, Pierro, and like me, she realised the futility of trying to convince someone who is a raving lunatic.'

Nothing I could say would shake his belief. He lowered himself to my level, looking me straight in the eye.

'You are refusing to believe in this just to spite me. Really the problem is that you refuse to believe in yourself. You will never make this happen if you don't recognise your own ability.' He said this in a different tone, almost pleadingly. Just for a second, I caught my own pressurised expression mirrored in his face.

When I shook my head, he reverted to bullying. He hauled me up on to the chair again, and forced me to look out of the window.

'If I see no progress in a week, I will string you up the same as I did to her. I swear it, so get to work,' he said, pulling me down.

Before he left, he threw a brown paper parcel down on the bed.

'It's from your dearest friend, Marco. He is convinced it will help you.'

I couldn't believe what I was hearing.

'Marco knows about this? He would never do that. You're lying,' I said disbelievingly. Marco was like one of my brothers; it was completely impossible that he would conspire to hurt me.

Pierro laughed. 'You are so naïve. I already told you he provided evidence about your research. Why do you think he would stop there when he has so much to gain? His uncle will see him well compensated. He most certainly does know all about this. Who do you think gave you the Rohypnol in your coffee? Such a helpful boy, it would have been much more unpleasant if Chris had forced it down your throat. What a shame for you – that's two great friends gone in one day, isn't it?'

He said this in the most mocking voice imaginable, then turned away. My face flushed, and now the heat burned through my body like a firework. In an instant, I was on my feet as Pierro was walking to the door. I grabbed the sickle-shaped knife, which I had been keeping under my pillow, and ran at him in a hysterical fit of vengeance.

He caught my wrist and struck me hard across the cheek with the other hand. Glaring at me, his eyes full of venom, he began what I can only hope will be the beating of my life. He repeatedly lifted me up and struck me again and again, kicking out on my descent each time. The pain ricocheted around my body from my elbow to my jaw, my stomach to my head. I'm not sure if it was his hand or the floor that gave me the concussion, but I was vaguely aware of my own blood getting in my eyes before I lost consciousness altogether.

∼

I WOKE LATER THAT DAY, still on the floor. My head was heavy, and my jaw was not so much painful, but felt as if it had seized up. I dragged myself over to the wash basin and stood. It hurt to breathe, but I needed some water.

Roberto was away from his desk, perhaps on Pierro's orders. I leaned against the sink, feeling giddy, Thérèse's beautiful face swimming in front of my eyes. I couldn't escape the knowledge that she had seen her own death in the cards.

My tears stung the cuts on my face. I felt my mind pulling towards the haven of unconsciousness, but something was pricking at me. Sharp points penetrated evilly through my numbness.

I looked down at my hands. I was still clasping the nugget of metal I had been preparing when I'd first seen Thérèse's dead body. My allergy had made one hand look as if it was completely on fire, while the other looked like embers glowing in a grate. The surface was alive as if I was being eaten from the inside out – malicious mouths biting beneath my skin, sending my aching head insane. Never in all my life have I seen my skin so angry. I could feel my pulse chiming in every sore, screaming at me for allowing these terrible events to come to pass.

I couldn't bear the affliction any longer. I dropped to the floor and grasped the sickle-shaped knife, which was lying by my foot where I'd dropped it. It was a relief to feel the knife slice into my skin. I used it over and across, again and again in rapid strikes until I couldn't see my own hands through their blood. I'm not sure if it was the mixing of my friend's murder with concussion, or whether it was the result of years of torture from my hands, but whichever it was, the result was the same: a temporary madness.

I pitched over to one side and fell so that my cheek was against the stone floor. Blood spread out slowly along my horizon and darkness began to invade the periphery of my vision. The nugget of bronze lay where I had dropped it, encircled in a lake of my own blood. Even in that diabolical moment, I wanted to die holding my beloved bronze. I needed to touch it. It slid gladly down my fingers to my palm, and I clasped it between my hands, forcing out more blood.

Only then did I close my eyes and let the darkness swarm round me. I expected the seductive peace of unconsciousness to come immediately, but the heat in my hands was keeping me from going under.

'Dear God, please help me,' I whispered. 'I'm bleeding to death.'

As if they were sitting on a see-saw, my thoughts kept tipping from one place to another, and I couldn't decide which I preferred. I wanted to die and to live; to sleep and to be awake. Whenever one thought got too close, I pushed away from it.

Sleep wanted me more now; I felt its tug. Like a

drowning person, I tried to hold my head above the surface of an unconsciousness that I might never wake up from. Seeing so much blood felt strangely familiar, like a déjà vu. It reminded me of the macabre depictions of Christ on the Cross, blood pouring from his hands, in the book Cattrine had found for me in Florence. At the time, I'd thought they were insignificant. Now I understood them – a shame it was too late. It was so glaringly obvious: it was the alchemist's blood that was required. That was the sacrifice.

I closed my eyes. My body felt warm and comfortable. I knew I was going to die because, for once in my life, the insatiable itching in my hands was completely gone. I couldn't even detect the pain that Pierro's beating had caused.

I let my thoughts go. The first place they went was to David. I thought about the way he looked at me with such desire and need. I could feel the way he kissed my throat, and his touch upon my skin. He had looked into my eyes as we made love with a thirst that could only be quenched by me. I saw moments of the life we might have had together, and the desperation with which he had pulled me to him when we'd last parted, as if he'd known I would never return to him.

The love that Pierro and his Guild had denied me surged up inside me and knocked away any acceptance I'd felt about dying.

It felt right to meditate just as Father Christopher had taught me. The images of David fractured and fell away. I concentrated on the metal in my hands. In my head, I created a large empty space and stood in the centre of it. It was completely dark, and I felt as if I was holding out the walls of this space with my mind.

I don't know how long I remained like this, but I knew I was waiting for something or someone. When it came, it was as if the roof had been blown off the space which I had held together with my mind. Golden light flooded in – not sunlight, not daylight, but a divine light which felt like a mixture of every light I'd ever experienced. Simultaneously, a strong wind, almost like the draught from a helicopter's blades, swirled just above me with no sound.

Still in my mind, I turned my face upwards to the blissful light and lifted my hands. I lost any sense of my body – no heartbeat; no breath. It was as if we had merged; I was the light and it was me.

WHEN I WOKE, my body was stiff and cold. I felt completely wrung out, like any strength I usually possessed had been used up. When I finally moved, I was surprised to see that there was no more blood on the ground than had initially spilt when I had cut myself. It was as if the bleeding had been stopped in its tracks.

The sun that entered my cell in a beam through the rectangular window was a shy amber-gold, its rays blurred. I moved a few inches so that my savaged hands were bathed in the morning light. The nugget of metal was smeared with dry blood, but it felt oddly warm. I tilted my palm and saw the surface of the metal had an amber glow. I rubbed some blood away with the tip of my finger and stared hard again at the metal.

I could hear Roberto coming down the stairs to check on me. As I moved my hand to hide the nugget, the pain overtook me and made me retch. He was nearly in the cell; I had to hide it. I curled my body up.

Roberto bent down to look at me.

'Oh God,' I heard him say under his breath. 'I'll get some supplies,' and he retreated.

There was pain in every part of my body, but something miraculous had occurred.

There was gold in my hand.

25

R oberto propped me up and cleaned me as best he could, but he was too squeamish to be a decent nurse and dabbed ineffectually at the bloody encrustations. Thankfully he seemed content to deal with only what he could see and didn't insist on investigating any of Pierro's handiwork below my neck. The idea of undressing in such pain seemed impossible.

He brought me some contraband in the form of bandages, painkillers and ice for my swellings, which were numerous. He wouldn't meet my eyes, so I knew I must look bad. Though my hands were in the worst state and he repeatedly flinched, he didn't pass comment. He obviously assumed that their poor state was all Pierro's work, and therefore necessary.

Roberto brought me hot, sweet chocolate which he insisted I sip through a straw as my lip was split. I was desperate for him to leave so that I could become acquainted with all my injuries. Numbness was beginning to give way to precision pain. My right eye had closed up; it felt as if a large egg was beneath the lid. My right wrist was three times its normal size and a brooding palette of stormy blues and greens. I could only take shallow breaths; anything deeper burned through my chest. Later, I would look at my ribcage and see it speckled with bruises like some Pointillist canvas.

As he moved away from my face and made an attempt to start on my hands, I stopped him, not because of the pain, but because I was completely shocked. Roberto stared at me with concern as I examined every inch of skin. Aside from the deep gashes that scored my hands, the usually volcanic surface was completely calm. I couldn't remember there ever being a time that I wasn't plagued by their itching; now, there was none, and it felt like blissful silence after blaring music. I couldn't remember ever having seen them look like this, either. It was as if something in my blood had been desperate to get out, so much so that its containment had excessively irritated and aggravated the skin.

'They're too sore,' I said. 'I'll do them myself.' I asked Roberto to get me a basin with warm water, soap and disinfectant, which he fetched obediently. I'd cut myself accidentally enough times on bits of metal in the foundry to know the necessary procedure. I needed to soak my hands for at least a quarter of an hour, and I didn't think I'd be able to stand at the sink that long.

After I'd thoroughly cleaned them with soap, which made them bleed again, I applied the disinfectant, which was about as horrible as I'd expected it to be. Roberto bandaged them so that only my fingertips were exposed. It would keep them clean in the short-term at least.

He seemed relieved that this job was done and stood up to go.

'Why did you have to kill her?' I blurted out. 'You have

no idea how lovely she was, and she had nothing to do with any of this.'

Roberto looked at me but his eyes made no apology.

'Don't forget your post on the floor,' he said. 'Shall I unwrap it for you?'

He left the contents on my knees. There was a large hardback book with a covering note. The note said:

Dear Abigail,

This book about the alignment of planets could be fundamental to your success.

Your Marco

THE BETRAYAL ALMOST CHOKED ME. How dare he push the knife in even further by suggesting he was helping me when really he was helping himself. I felt like throwing the book straight in the fire, which I might have done if it had been lit. I wanted to spit on it, but I couldn't do such a thing to a beautiful book.

I turned over a few pages. It was special, illustrated at the turn of the century with coloured plates showing numerous variations on the alignment of stars in the sky. A man at the bottom of each page was looking through a telescope. It was all irrelevant now, but in view of the fact that doing anything other than looking at this book would involve me moving, which would be excruciating in so many ways, I turned to the contents page to see if it had any relevance to alchemy whatsoever. As I ran my eyes down the column of words, I merely registered that they didn't make any sense and had nothing to do with the planets.

CONTENTS:

MY HEAD WAS BEGINNING to throb. I was in a most uncomfortable position, sitting on the floor propped up by the bed. I looked again at the words, then closed my eyes for some time, drifting in and out of a light sleep.

When I woke, neck stiff and seemingly in more pain, if that was possible, my eyes fell on to the words again. My concentration was not strong, but there was something very strange about this page. As I ran my eyes down the list, I took in only the first letter of each word and there I saw the first message:

P O I S O N T H E M

STARING HARDER, I saw the last letter of each word was darker – that's how I saw the second.

i a m s o r r y

MY FEELINGS towards Marco were entirely mixed, as, it was clear, were his feelings for me. I thought back to the night he had drugged me. Now I understood why he had told me the story about his colleague. He wanted me to know why he'd done it; he knew I'd find out it was him, and his loyalty to me could only go so far. I understood his dilemma, but I couldn't forgive him for it.

Grief swept over me again, but this time, the crying was quieter; more accepting; less desperate. I managed to get myself up on to the bed, although it caused considerable pain, and lay looking up at the bars on my window. I was sure I could feel Thérèse still out there.

One thing I noticed was that there was not a shred of fear remaining inside me. Fear is like a poison in many ways. It attaches itself to every thought rather than every cell, and thwarts it working. Marco's note had given me a new train of thought, one that I began to obsess over. It trickled through my mind, neutralising the fear and leaving me with space for new thoughts.

I had created gold. I had actually performed a complete impossibility without even the slightest idea that I could. Pierro had been right. He had known me better than I had known myself. What else could I do that I had never considered? Could I murder someone?

The thought of what I'd done must have sent adrenaline flooding through me, because the fog my mind seemed full of cleared. I considered my situation; I had two big problems: my physical condition and my imprisonment.

For the first time, I considered my resources. This was something I should have done much earlier. I was a chemist; although poisoning people was not on my university's curriculum, I had lots of knowledge about chemicals and their dangers. Within reason, I felt confident Roberto would provide me with items so long as I could justify my need for them. I might be able to cook up something, though how successful it would be, I had no idea.

I had foundry skills. The foundry had been my instrument since I could walk, and as a soloist practises unendingly, so I had worked in the foundry until I could weld, cast, fettle, pattern-make, not to mention patinate like a virtuoso.

The noise of a vehicle distracted my thoughts. Very slowly, I rolled on to my side and managed to stand up. Moving across to the window like a cartoon crone, bent over with hands held in claw-like positions, I stood up on the stool.

Vic was cutting Thérèse's body down from the tree with some tools. He had positioned his tractor and trailer beneath her so she fell directly between a few bales of hay. He threw a tarpaulin over her and drove off fast. Despite my perception of him being more humane than Chris, he showed no humanity in this task. As he drove away, he swerved the tractor in exaggerated S bends so that the trailer bounced behind and went up on to two wheels, depending on which side it was swerving.

Thinking back to the day when I'd phoned home, I remembered Vic had not raised any objection to what his brother had planned to do with me. I had no doubt that he would dump Thérèse's body with equal detachment. Terry would never know what had happened to her. The idea of Terry without her was a bleak picture; like a dog without a master, he would probably pine away.

For a moment, I wondered about the possibility of the police tracking down Thérèse's kidnappers and discovering me imprisoned here. This thought passed as quickly as it came; it was more likely that the Chief of Police was part of this secret alchemical society. Pierro certainly didn't seem in fear of discovery.

I sat back down on the bed. These people Pierro had working for him seemed entirely soulless; even Roberto, though his disposition was milder. Naïve as it sounds, I was suddenly struck by how much money must motivate some people. Pierro's men were a bleak vision of human character, but in my present frame of mind, I was even considering if this could serve me somehow.

26

I kept replaying snippets of the previous day in my head, but not as it had originally occurred. In fact, my post-concussed state was the stuff of surrealist paintings: the branches of the tree holding up Thérèse's body clawed at her as she swung like a pendulum from her neck. Her body was longer and more distorted than the reality had been. There was a circle of iron bars around the tree, guarding her, but all were slumped as if in grief.

I daydreamed about bronze keys hanging on trees in a forest, all different shapes and sizes, and me desperately searching for the right one. I was distracted from the task by a scene of Pierro doling out a beating in slow motion to someone looking suspiciously like myself.

It wasn't easy to force my mind back to reality. My thoughts morphed from euphoria into grief, and then pre-meditated murder. All were coloured by the physical pain I was in.

One thought that kept resurfacing was that the obstacles to my success seemed to be multiplying. Now, overcoming my physical condition was going to be at least as hard as actually escaping. Apart from my damaged wrist, my hands were my biggest problem. In their savaged state, they were targets for infection. Currently, any pressure at all on them would make them bleed. With the workload they would have to handle in order to make an escape possible, this was a problem. I felt able to face the agony that forcing my hands to work in this condition would involve, but it would take more than bravery to enable my escape.

I hobbled up from my bed again, this time to look in the mirror. Although prepared for what I would see to some extent by Roberto's furtive looks, I hardly recognised myself. One eye was closed over and red, fading out to dark blue around the periphery. My split lip was large, and the jawbone on the right hand side was swollen and dappled a muted blue-grey with yellow. The blistered skin from the chemical stripper that had splashed my face a few days before threaded its way through the bruising, adding texture to the overall effect.

I felt tired again, but suddenly heard Pierro's voice shouting at someone above my head, and my heart leapt. I tried to control it and not let myself be frightened of him. It was his icy blue eyes with such belief in them that scared me the most. When talking about alchemy, he had the kind of intensity that I'd only seen in extreme religious leaders when they discussed their faith. He wanted this so badly, it was clear that he felt any means would justify the end.

I lay down again and turned over to try and find a position that didn't make me ache so much. Before I drifted off to sleep, I realised it was his desperation for success that I could use against him. I felt my heart trill with excitement; I would need to get him to believe I'd succeeded, just for a short time. In the long run, making gold would never save my life, whereas faking it offered real possibilities.

WHEN I WOKE A LITTLE LATER, I sat up on the bed and, with great mental effort, swallowed down the sadness I felt within me. I could not afford to let my grief surface; it would sidetrack me. I needed to curl up and convalesce, but that was a luxury, too. I had to focus every ounce of my strength and not allow the pain to master me.

Very gingerly, I reached into my pocket and used my undamaged fingers to hook out the nugget of gold to look at again. It was perfect. I turned it over, looking for a spot of the original alloy, but the metal it had been had vanished completely. Its surface had a velvety lustre like it was an old gold that had somehow been reincarnated.

After a generous breakfast from Roberto, I considered how I could make my hands functional enough to perform the tasks that were needed. I unwrapped them from their bandages and reapplied more disinfectant; I would have to be extremely careful in order to prevent them becoming infected. Along the seams of the cuts, the wounds were sticking together, making the hands stiff. I could see the bond was very superficial, and knew that the slightest pressure would burst this delicate barrier.

The most obvious solution was stitches. I had no idea whether you could stitch the palms of your hands; it seemed like a terrible idea. I wasn't overly taken with having to inflict more pain upon my sorry body, but I was determined to do what needed to be done.

I knew virtually nothing about first aid, but it seemed obvious to me that hands had very little flesh to keep the thread in place. I presumed the skin would tear as the area would be constantly stretching and contracting as I moved my hands. There was also the fact that there were so many cuts, which meant that it was unlikely I would be able to stitch both sides of the wound.

I knew wounds could be glued, but I doubted my box of adhesives would do the trick. My best hope would be to make a request of Roberto to acquire some medical glue for me. Pierro was so desperate to get me working that I might be able to persuade Roberto to help me. The only drawback was how I could prevent Roberto from asking Pierro for approval. Pierro would immediately become suspicious as he was the only one who knew he hadn't cut my hands.

I didn't want to underestimate Pierro. He knew from our discussion at the party that I'd been struggling with how the sickle-shaped knife fitted in. He might see, as clearly as I did now, that the blood of the alchemist was the missing link. My blood must have bonded with the carefully prepared surface of the metal and formed the Philosopher's Stone.

I was hungry to think about how it had all occurred and examine every detail. It was so delicious a subject that it had the potential to distract me endlessly, but it was a pleasure I needed to postpone for the time being. My priority must be getting out, and so I shoved my mind back towards practical matters.

Even if I managed to procure the glue from Roberto, the problem wasn't all solved. The kind of work I needed to do would require a great deal of pushing and pressure on my palms. I might be able to reinforce the seams with tape, but then I needed some kind of shield over the whole area. I had no immediate answer to this, and so I stood up and moved across to the fireplace to reflect on my next difficulty.

I needed to build a small furnace. We'd had to improvise several times at the foundry when our industrial furnaces had broken down. A furnace could actually be made quite simply with a metal container and a special fire-retardant blanket made with ceramic fibres. I knew how I was going to go about making the key, but I wasn't sure how I could do it without Pierro noticing.

I glanced towards Roberto, who was sitting at his desk as usual. Pierro's desperation to see me active was in my favour. I would have to run several projects simultaneously, showing him what he wanted to see, while getting on with my own projects on the sly. Every time I totted up even the tiniest advantage, I felt a prickle of hope.

Painfully slowly, I moved across to retrieve my notebook and a pencil to jot down the list of things I would need. I found I could hold the pencil by placing it on top of my bandage, controlling it between my index and middle fingers, and supporting it from below with the tip of my thumb. In my weak condition, my mind was the only part of me I could properly engage.

It felt good to be doing something positive again. I allowed myself the briefest moment of pleasure in imagining the perfect outcome: a *Shawshank* moment where Pierro and his men searched my empty cell in dumbfounded amazement.

I tried to tug my mind back to furnaces, but was unsuccessful so settled for poisons. The promise of the damage that could be done was tantalising. However, I was a seasoned traveller in the realm of chemical reactions, and one thing I knew for certain was guessing and approximating were most likely to end with botched results. Chemistry worked best with precision and calculation. Any homespun kit that I could potentially cobble together would be unlikely to be fit for purpose. I wouldn't have enough material or opportunity to gain accuracy through trial and error. Therefore, I couldn't rely on the results of my pleasant daydream to save me, but it was worth a try.

What I would be able to request to help me in this area was limited. I doubted Pierro would sign off on a barrel of arsenic. Like running my fingers over the keys of a piano, I ran my mind over the different chemicals I had in my kit, and considered what harm they could do.

There were plenty of poisons. Most obviously in the context of alchemy was mercury, but I needed something that would act swiftly. For some reason, it was cyanide that sang to me. Hydrogen cyanide or HCN, made up of hydrogen, carbon and nitrogen, is very poisonous in gaseous or liquid form.

Of course, it wasn't the type of compound anyone carried around with them, but completely legitimately, I did happen to have the mother of this dangerous material in my kit. Very few artists' palettes are complete without the pigment Prussian blue. This is a harmless pigment, discovered in the early 1700s: For artists, Prussian blue had been a miraculous discovery. a lustrous shade of blue that meant that artists did not have to rely on the expensive alternative derived from lapis lazuli.

The story goes that Prussian blue had been made by chance, or fate. It's easy to think of chemistry as a dry science, a subject of laws and equations, but this story is one of my favourite examples of why chemistry is the James Bond of the sciences – the one that has the style and the danger.

A little tinkering with a few common chemicals by a German paint-maker, aiming to produce a salacious red pigment, went completely awry when one of his ingredients became contaminated. The result of this mistake led to the most regal blue that had ever been seen. Beneath its beauty, however, was a physical structure that would lead to the discovery of hydrogen cyanide.

Prussian blue is described in chemistry as a metal complex, meaning that the cyanide ions are clustered around a central metal component, like dandelion down around the central stamen. In this form, it is a placid chemical. Anger it by adding dilute sulphuric acid and heat, though, and an entirely different face is presented. The viper comes out: hydrogen cyanide gas, which in the 20th century was used as a chemical weapon in warfare and to commit murder in gas chambers.

I had one pot of Prussian blue, but much of it had spilled when Pierro had thrown my kit at me. Though I knew more than most about chemistry, did I really have the bravery to attempt to form cyanide in these conditions? Even a minor error could kill me. Would it kill me more or less painfully than Pierro would? I didn't like the face of death whichever way I looked at it, but at least this way I had a shot at a different outcome.

My aim was to get out of the cell, but leave something to tempt Pierro to enter it. I would release the poison immediately prior to my escape. If I could convince him I had left a piece of real gold on my bench, I was sure he'd enter the cell. Depending on my resources, I might even be able to form liquid hydrogen cyanide and coat the nugget of metal. Skin contact and inhalation would be my best chance.

Of course, I wouldn't want to leave behind any real evidence of my gift. The piece of gold that Pierro would be drawn to and touch would be a fake, but he would discover this seconds after he had handled it, and then it would be too late.

27

I got up off my bed and made my way over to the
shelves. There were various bowls and pots and
containers. I began to take them down one by one, but
my bandaged hands were clumsy and two earthenware pots
fell to the floor, smashing.

Roberto looked up and came across to the bars.

'Do you need help?'

I shook my head.

'I'm just seeing what containers there are here. I'm going
to start working again.'

Roberto breathed out heavily as if he had been holding
the same breath for hours.

'Good. You must.'

I went across to where he stood.

'Pierro said he wanted to see progress in a week. Do you
think if he knows I'm working, he will give me longer?'

Roberto sucked the air in this time.

'I imagine he will.'

I looked him straight in the eye.

'Truthfully, Roberto, I think I can do this thing he wants

me to do. I was working on it before he...murdered Thérèse, but I need some time and help to recuperate. I'm in a pretty poor state. I can't work like this.'

'You think you can do it?' he said. I nodded.

'If I asked for some medical supplies, would you be able to get them for me? It would help me get working quicker, but Pierro is so angry with me that I'm afraid anything personal I ask for, he may refuse. I'll never be able to show him progress in a week in this state.'

I tried to look as helpless and appealing as possible. I knew my battered face was troubling Roberto; he couldn't hold my gaze.

'What do you need?' he murmured.

'I need medical glue for sealing cuts, butterfly tapes to keep the cuts together, disinfectant, gauze, cotton wool, painkillers and antibiotics.'

'You don't want much,' he huffed and turned away.

'Please, don't tell Pierro,' I said. I didn't want him to hear my desperation, but I heard the vibrato in my voice.

'I'll think about it,' he said and resumed his seat.

I felt buoyed up for the remainder of the day, working on my list of materials to give to Roberto with mounting anticipation. My heart fluttered in my chest whenever I considered that he might ask Pierro about the supplies I had already requested, so I distracted myself by writing an inventory of everything I had on the shelves and in the scrap locker. I considered carefully whether each piece had a role in my escape.

The formation of the cyanide solution had many difficulties. Making it safely was one, but there were some precautions I could take. I had mixed up all our own patination chemicals at the foundry, though none were quite as lethal. I did have my industrial-style mask, and due to my skin condition, I always had a supply of thick vinyl gloves in my kit.

Another issue was whether I really had what I needed to make the reaction happen. Although I had Pete's Pickle in my kit, which previously I had felt sure was mainly sulphuric acid, I had never had to stake my life on it as I would be doing now. In truth, I didn't know the specifics of its make-up.

In order to make the cyanide solution, I would need to distil some of the gas. This would boil at close to room temperature, around 26°C, so it should be easy to condense it to a liquid below this temperature. The salient point here was that I certainly didn't have the right equipment for this.

While itemising everything, I particularly sought some means of adapting the objects I had to enable me to condense the cyanide gas and form the liquid cyanide. I searched among the scrap, but didn't find much apart from an old galvanised watering can. I set it upon my work table, and went to rest again on my bed. Too much moving around exhausted me.

The watering can was quite an elegant piece for such a mundane object. I wondered by what path it had found itself here. It had a calligraphic handle and long, tapering neck. The aperture where the water exited was small. Initially, I shook away the possibility of adapting it, but as I continued to lie pathetically on my bed, the thought began to grow.

If I could find or make something to extend the length of the spout; if I could seal the hole where the water was usually put in; if I could make it air tight, maybe then it would work. If, if, if – my world was full of them.

I looked again through my inventory. Unfortunately, there was nothing directly applicable, but I did have a roll of shim. Shim is thin brass sheet metal which is placed between sections of a mould to divide two areas when casting. It prevents the two areas sticking together, and so when the mould is completely set, you can divide them without breaking the mould. Shim is not designed to be bent much under usual circumstances, but it is so thin that it is easily manipulated.

I got up again and went to my kit. Taking out the roll of shim, I measured its height, which was 12 cm. Its length when I rolled it out fully was one and a half metres. In my head, I rolled the shim into a long, thin tube. The possibility that it could work as a condensing tube was about 10% at maximum. This seemed like reasonably high odds in my situation. I doubted they'd be as high for a successful escape.

I gave Roberto my list of all the things I would need, justifying everything, and he even took notes of what I said. Among the various small items, I asked for more Prussian blue, saying the pigment was to assist in forming the last colour in the Peacock's Tail stage. I asked for an extension on the week Pierro had given me, basing this request on the fact that the book Marco had sent detailed the necessity for a particularly favourable phase of the moon for the transformation. I tried to sound sure when I said that this would be in three weeks. I imagined Pierro's wrath when this request was put to him, but even if he gave me half this time, it was still more than a week. I needed more days to recuperate, but not so many that I would arouse suspicion.

ROBERTO BROUGHT me my medical requirements the

following morning in a large carrier bag, which he handed to me with my breakfast. I couldn't believe my luck.

'Thank you, thank you,' I gushed.

'I didn't get it because you asked me. Don't assume there's any loyalty between us. I will do whatever it takes to achieve our aim, and if this will enable it, so be it.'

His face looked sour. I had put him in a bad position which he resented, and I knew I wouldn't get any further favours.

I didn't want to let a second go to waste, so immediately got to work on my hands. I soaked them again in disinfectant, and carefully allowed them to air dry. This was followed by my attempts to glue my own hands back together, in the course of which I made a pretty big mess. Under any other circumstances, it would have been a funny scenario.

One hand at a time, I forced the wounds open and ran as much of the glue into the cuts as possible. When the glue dried, I reinforced the seams with butterfly tapes. I covered my palms in dressings, followed by wads of cotton wool secured with black insulation tape that I had in my kit. I wrapped the whole of each palm a couple of times round with a bandage, and then placed my hands inside vinyl gloves. This was as much protection as I could give them.

Fleetingly, I considered whether taking the antibiotics before the wounds showed any sign of infection would be bad for my health. Then I reminded myself how bad my current situation was for my mortality, let alone my health, which put the premature use of antibiotics into perspective. With the kind of work that was coming up, the chances of my hands not getting infected were tiny. Metalworking of any description is dirty work, and my hands would be getting very moist in their gloves, creating a heavenly environment for bacteria.

I had another piece of luck that day: Pierro approved the other materials I had requested, though they would take a couple of days to come. This news made me almost giddy. According to Roberto, Pierro had called Marco and asked if my request about the moon's phase was legitimate. As it had been approved, Marco clearly hadn't failed me again.

With both hands as safe as I could make them, I set to work on my first project: my poison-coated decoy. What Roberto saw was me working at my table with my toolbox strategically placed in front of me while I used a small hacksaw from my kit to cut lengths of thin aluminium wire, which had been in the scrap box. When Roberto asked me what I was doing, I willingly explained that the piece of spelter would sit upon this wire when it was ready to be lowered into the bath of oxalic acid, a metal finishing compound. I felt a particularly fearful thrill at his seemingly total acceptance of my explanation.

As soon as he had watched me work for a while and was settled, I took out my grandmother's diamond ring from my case. Holding the diamond in the grip of some pliers, I used the hacksaw again, this time on the shank of the ring. From Roberto's perspective, I hadn't changed my activity.

It would have been a hundred times quicker if I'd had a vice to clamp the ring into and a sharp blade. Then again, a vice might have got me caught. If Roberto had decided to double check, I may not have been able to push the ring into my glove in a heartbeat as was my plan.

I continued to cut until I had decapitated the ring. The stone I hid inside one of my pigment pots, while the gold I returned to my case, ready to melt down. When the materials arrived, I planned to use the furnace for two escape projects: making the key, and covering a piece of spelter in a gold jacket using the shank of my ring and my gold fountain pen. Visually, it would look like a gold nugget, but any testing would reveal its humble heart.

Over the next couple of days, the only other thing I could do before the rest of my items came was to form the shim into a Heath Robinson-style condensing tube. My hands were already aching from the cutting. I took several painkillers, but didn't want to lose too much time by stopping.

I had no idea how to camouflage my work on making the condensing tube, so for a while, outwardly at least, I rested. This was actually a more useful activity than I'd planned it to be. Roberto strayed from his desk several times that afternoon, and during these short intervals, he didn't bother putting the camera on. When all I'd been doing was waiting, this habit had had little significance. Now, it gave me precious minutes to work unnoticed. I would spring to the bench and roll out the shim, turning it lengthways as if I was forming a long cigarette.

The metal did not roll like paper. It was more rigid, and the resulting tube had a triangular aspect to it. I rolled it out several times, trying to achieve the best possible shape. Then, I needed to secure it. I had an abundance of tough rubber bands which I located at intervals along the length of the tube. Numerous times, I I heard Roberto descend, and had to rush back to my bed, slipping the partially formed tube inside the covers. My heart beat so hard each time this happened that I was worried my blood pressure would burst the wounds on my hands.

It was only when Roberto went to dinner that I could use my blowtorch at certain points to make the metal more pliable and shaped the crude tube so that it undulated. By the second night, I was on the final stage of running lengths of insulating tape along the seam of the shim to seal it. I had to make sure I hadn't blocked the tube when working it, but by this stage, I was feeling woozy. I leaned my head against the cool sink mirror as I let water trickle down the tube. There must have been some kinks because the water dripped rather than ran, but enough found its way through to satisfy me that it would work.

Leaving the water running, I quickly hid the tube under my mattress before returning to the tap. Kneeling, I pushed my face under the water, letting it run into my eyes, over my skin and down to my mouth.

28

W heels turned on the gravel outside, and I heard doors slamming. Almost simultaneously, I felt unwell. It began as a prickling, like pins and needles in my hands, and then I became very hot and disorientated. I dropped to my knees and sat on the floor below the sink. I could hear voices getting louder and people coming down the stairs, but it felt impossible to get up. My vision was blurry.

Roberto came in first. He bent down close to me, and I noticed the worry lines were pronounced on his forehead.

'Handcuffs,' he said, holding up a set to my eye level and shaking them.

'Hurry up, Roberto,' barked Vic. 'These boxes are heavy.'

'They are just a precaution,' Roberto assured me as he clicked one cuff on to my good wrist and hauled me up to secure me to the cell's bars. He then opened the door and moved towards the stairs. I swayed and leant against the bars for support.

Chris came through the door first. He kicked the cell door so hard that it banged back against the bars, missing my hand by millimetres. The noise was tremendous and made me cower back as far as I could. Roberto shouted at him in Italian. I looked away, not wanting to engage with Chris at all, though I'd caught a glimpse of his delight at my response. He made some comment to Roberto, which I was glad from its tone that I couldn't understand.

When they'd brought everything down, Roberto released me, but Chris remained behind. I sat back down on the floor close to the bars, still feeling unsteady.

'I'll be down to check on your progress.' Chris spoke from above me. His words spilled down my neck and I shivered. I shook my head, not because of his intimidation, but because little flickers of light were dancing across my vision.

'Don't shake your head at me, bitch! I will be down to check on you.'

The lights were multiplying and gathering into gangs. I lifted my chin up, tilting my head back. I intended my eye contact to acknowledge his threat, but I couldn't even see his features as the flickering had become so intense.

'*Che cazzo!*' I heard him say.

Roberto seemed to be with him in a trice. I could tell they were staring at me, but I could only make out the bulk of their bodies.

'Leave her,' Roberto said in a quiet but forceful tone.

'What's wrong with her eyes?' Chris sounded amazed.

'I don't know. She's an alchemist, isn't she? They aren't supposed to be like other people.'

I heard a beat of excitement in Roberto's voice.

'Freak, rather than alchemist, I'd say,' Chris said scathingly.

He moved away from the bars. I negotiated the obstacles in the room and got back to my bed. What on earth was happening to me? I was starting to feel less unsteady, but my eyesight was still affected. My head and my hands felt really hot. My escape plan had been based on the assumption that somehow I could just push through my injuries.

I wasn't quite sure whether this episode was to do with my injuries or not, but I couldn't afford to acquire anything new to slow me down. I also didn't need any weirdness like this to suggest to my captives that I was a bona fide alchemist. I rested on the bed, waiting for the dazzling to stop. Tentatively, I allowed myself to let go of the tight rein I'd been holding on my injuries. I opened myself up and felt the force of the orchestra of pain in my body.

It was a discordant piece of music. My aching hands were the horns braying; my throbbing wrist was the bass drum being slammed; the tender areas of my face were the violins repeatedly playing on their squeakiest note; my bruised ribs were the cellos playing long, low notes, all flat.

I ALLOWED myself to sleep for a while. When I came round, my eyesight was clear again. Now, I knew I didn't have three weeks. I didn't want to be here when Chris came to check on me. I didn't relish his interview techniques, and knew that physically, I couldn't take any more damage.

I had to get around the problem of having no welding equipment, which I needed to secure the condensing tube to the spout of the watering can properly. I could insert the tube a short way and let the wall of the spout prop it up, but this meant that the condensing tube wouldn't be physically joined to the watering can. I would have to make a seal where the two met to stop any fumes escaping.

My idea was to use the watering can as a beaker, dropping the cyanide compounds and acid into the mouth of the can before sealing it up. I would gently heat the contraption, the components in the can would join forces, and rise up the spout into my rubber-band-bound condensing tube. Twisting and turning up and down the shim, the gas would cool and drip into my waiting container.

My last task would be to make the entire contraption as airtight as I could.

I would only need the tiniest amount of liquid cyanide, and I planned to attempt this lethal trick one evening when Roberto went to his evening meal. This was always the longest period he left me alone without switching on the camera. I needed daylight to observe how much, if any, poison had formed. Part of reducing the risk to myself would involve not forming a drop more than necessary.

I decided to check my hands and clean the cuts with disinfectant. They looked much better than I'd anticipated which cheered me. Tending to them gave me the chance to marvel again at what my hands had performed. The fact the skin was still clear was almost as exciting to me as the alchemy. It didn't seem possible that it was happening so quickly, but the outer edges did seem to be healing.

That night, I made up my most critical tool, which was my furnace, so that the next morning I could begin to work on several fronts in earnest. For the purposes of inspections by Roberto and reports to Pierro, I formed the small ingots of very pure alloy which I had told them I needed. I did this as slowly as possible. Whenever I felt they weren't paying much attention to me, I worked on my gold decoy. I melted down the gold shank from my family's ring and the casing of the beautiful gold fountain pen David had given me in Venice.

I had decided to fire-gild one of the bronze nuggets. It made sense as the main ingredient, other than gold, that was required for this type of gilding was mercury. This was one material I did have readily available which wouldn't arouse suspicion. I was also on familiar territory; about three years before, our foundry had had an unusual commission. A client required a set of contemporary armour. Its design was striking: a series of rectangles interlinked with diminishing rectangles within each one. The design had required us to colour it with a contrasting pattern of blueing the steel and gilding which ran throughout the suit. One of the gold leaf specialist I had worked with in the past had taught me the technique of fire-gilding, which I particularly enjoyed because there was so much scope for imagination. It reminded me of spell-making, and gave me the central role as witch.

First, I would make a mixture of gold and mercury, called an amalgam, with a butter-like consistency. The bronze's surface would be prepared by painting on the ethereal-looking mercury before coating it with the creamy gold amalgam. Once I stroked a flame across the object several times, I would see a change begin. The mercury would leave the gold like a ghost leaving a body. What would remain on the object was an ochre skin, seemingly devoid of any life, but a little stimulation of the surface would bring about a stunning resurrection: burnishing would rapidly reveal the noble glow of the gold.

I knew how impressive it would look. I was sure it would convince Pierro long enough to make him touch it, and that was all I needed.

There was one drawback to this method: the gaseous mercury that would swirl around my head was poisonous. It was a malicious gas, but my mask should protect me. Unfortunately, it wasn't quite deadly enough to save me the trouble of having to make its even more evil associate: cyanide.

$$\sim$$

I HAD FINISHED the gilding by the end of that first day, and hid it carefully in one of my pots of pigment. That evening, I began to make a rudimentary key out of the emerald-coloured casting wax that I had in my kit. This was the same wax I'd used when making Terry's Christmas present.

Though only a fleeting thought, the wonderful things that had happened at Christmas burst into my head and tears dropped down my cheeks unchecked. This unexpected moment of sadness actually did me a favour: when I directed my attention to repositioning my bed so that it was in front of the fireplace, and Roberto asked what I was doing, he saw my glittering eyes and seemed satisfied that I was rearranging the furniture to avoid being seen crying.

By moving my workbench marginally, I blocked the camera's view of me while I was in bed. With my back to the camera just in case, I assumed the position of a sleeper with the fire stoked and burning vigorously. This gave me as much light as I needed, and I was able to form a long rod in wax with a T-shape at one end and a plain rectangle at the other. This would be my skeleton key.

I laid the sickle-shaped knife beneath the fire, allowing it to warm. Then, I pressed its surface against the cold wax, and it wasn't long before the wax became supple enough to shape. To the wax key, I attached a sprue.

I could do no more that night and allowed myself to sleep the few hours until morning.

$$\sim$$

I WOKE AS SOON as the sunlight touched my eyelids. Pausing only to change my clothes, I carried on with my work before Roberto arrived. For viewing purposes, I was continuing to cast small pure nuggets of spelter with my back turned to the camera.

I made up the grog, which had been one of my requests, and began to cast the key exactly as I had the knuckle-dusters at Christmas. Roberto arrived downstairs before the metal had melted. I had used a few small off-cuts of metal, which took quite a few hours to melt as the furnace was so primitive. When the time came, I nervously kept an eye on Roberto as I poured the bronze liquid into the key's mould.

I began to feel odd again as I did this, and decided it was not my injuries affecting me, but my nerves. With shaky hands, I pushed the mould to the back of the fireplace and left it to cool. I went to get a drink of water, making a show of getting my bench ready for the next stage. While I was doing this simple task, my mind played another unwanted trick: my perspective danced around. It grew in very short increments; just for a few seconds, I was viewing myself organising my table rather than being the person organising it. Another few seconds, I was viewing myself from behind, then from above, then back to normal.

Without the strain of the close observation I'd had last time, I was able to think more clearly. This changing of perspective felt familiar; it felt like the exercise I'd done to strengthen my meditation when I could stop the scene and move around it. It stopped soon after it had started and didn't derail my progress that day, but it was not helpful.

When my mould was completely cool, I cracked away the grog shell, revealing a bronze blank of a key. I could only give myself the luxury of looking at it for a few minutes before I had to hide it away. Seeing an object born that had the potential to save my life was so thrilling, it made the fine hairs stand up on my body.

In order to make it work, I would have to take an impression of the mechanism inside the lock. On such an old lock, this was not as hard as it sounded. Coating the rectangular end in a thin layer of casting wax and placing the key in the lock would make an impression in the wax. The hard work would be accurately shaping the metal to follow the profile in the wax. It would be a relentless process with the tools I had, re-coating the key in wax, retrying it in the lock to gain the impression, and once again working to refine the shape. I had never done a lock per se before, but I had assisted Larry with hundreds of patternmaking projects, which was a similar process. I felt confident in my methodology, but a little less confident in how long this task might take.

I taped the key to the underside of the bench for safe keeping until my first opportunity to test it arose. When Roberto popped out for his breaks, these would be my chances to push the key coated with wax into the lock and take the impression. Then at night, as soon as Roberto left his desk and put the camera on, I could pretend to go to bed and shape the metal as best I could.

THE CONDITION of my hands was a huge problem and shaping the metal proved to be incredibly difficult. I did have some good rasps, but many of the ones I needed were oversized, which made them awkward to work with. At least I had books of emery papers, which I would need in the final stage for refining details. It was not only a painful process, but slow.

I usually fell asleep exhausted in the early hours. I had

settled into a comforting ritual of sending up a few prayers for help and whispering a little to Thérèse. In the transient state just before sleep, I felt very close to her, and it comforted me to tell her my plans.

Sometimes, if I had been working particularly late, I didn't wake until Roberto returned in the morning around 7.30am. While appearing to be preparing and patinating my spelter ingots, I used every opportunity to offer up the key to the lock and retry it. I became progressively more tired, and in line with my fatigue, the rate at which I experienced odd symptoms picked up too. By the third day, I was regularly experiencing flashes of colour. I could still see perfectly well, but it was like a brown filter had been put over my eyes, then it was red, then it was green, then it was white, and finally blue – the colours of the Peacock's Tail.

By the fifth day, my hands ached like each one had a migraine, and I still hadn't managed to get the key to turn in the lock. This was beginning to panic me. I knew that any second, Chris might decide to visit. I was living on borrowed time, and I couldn't get away from the horrible creeping feeling that something cold was spreading down the back of my neck.

29

My plan had been to make the key work before forming the liquid cyanide. That way, even if my captors discovered my primitive brewing apparatus, I could still make an attempt at escaping by using the key. However, the delay in getting the key to work meant I felt the need to alter my plan and form the cyanide before Chris got to me. It was possible that I might be able to use it against him if things got out of hand.

That evening, the minute Roberto went to dinner, I quickly fitted my key into the lock to get the impression I needed. Then I hid it and got to work on the watering can.

Sealing the watering can's mouth, where the water was usually put in, had presented a real difficulty. In the end, I had used my pliers to bend up the edges of the hole to make a rim. Having carefully considered every material I had, I decided the only one that seemed vaguely suitable was leather. I needed something that could withstand heat and the chemicals within the can's chamber to some extent. I had a very specialist polishing cloth made of the finest leather. In my work, I only ever used it to polish mirror finished surfaces. It had cost me over £100 to buy several years ago and I had always treated it like the royalty that its pedigree deserved. Leather may seem a ridiculous material to pin my hopes upon. The plethora of plastics that our world is awash with has made us forget leather's usefulness. I needed something that could withstand some heat, was impermeable and would stand to some extent the chemicals within the can's chamber.

It was also important that the material could easily and quickly seal the can. I needed access to the can's mouth to drop the chemicals in, and I needed to seal that opening as rapidly as possible to prevent any fumes escaping. Leather had many of the qualities I needed: it was a good heat insulator; it could easily be attached to the can with rubber bands; and it was likely to be fairly robust when in contact with the chemicals.

Modern leathers are often tanned and dressed to resist pollutants, but I was unsure how my cloth had been treated. What I did know was that leather was absorbent and handled contact with chemicals well. The tanning process was, after all, a chemical process. I didn't know much about how it was done now, but certainly in Victorian times, sulphuric acid was one of the main constituents.

Leather's main drawback was that, although it was stable in contact with chemical fumes, it was permeable. I would need to cover the leather with the only plastic items I had in the cell, which were the carrier bags that some of my new materials had arrived in. The leather was a necessary barrier. Plastic bags alone would be unlikely to stand up to the heat and chemicals within the can. Only very specific plastics could do this, and as I was unsure of the nature of Italian carrier bags, I couldn't risk it.

Donning my mask and placing the watering can in the

fireplace, I suppressed my nerves by concentrating fully on my deadly experiment. I poured in the Prussian blue. Then, without allowing myself to reconsider even for a second, I dashed in a diluted form of Pete's Pickle. I sealed the watering can deftly and triple bagged it in the plastic. Securing it with rubber bands and insulating tape, I stood back for a second to look at the freakish contraption. It looked like a mummified object with bits of insulating tape and carrier bags wrapped over it.

I uttered a brief prayer before lighting a low flame underneath it. If any fumes did escape, they should go up the chimney rather than float around me. I bit at my lip; having no thermometer was a huge problem. As the container was not transparent, I couldn't see what was going on inside. All I could do was watch the little aperture at the end of the tube to see what might exit, and listen as closely as possible, altering the heat by ear.

I was so busy concentrating, I didn't hear him descend into the basement. Chris obviously wanted to take me by surprise. As I heard the key bite into the lock, I spun round with my back to the fireplace, but I was too late to hide my project.

He came in and locked the door behind him. I bent down to extinguish the blowtorch which I was using to heat the bottom of the watering can.

'Ah-ah.' He shook his head. 'Don't touch a thing. Will it spoil if it overcooks?' I nodded. I couldn't speak with the mask on. 'Good. Let's leave it then.'

He moved towards me, and I had an awful moment of desperation. Should I retreat? Or stand my ground? In the time it took me to think which option was better, he had grabbed my damaged wrist and hauled me by it over to the bars at the window. He attached me to the bars with my wrist higher than my head, using a cable tie that squeezed my wrist mercilessly, then he dragged off the mask. Now we would both die if the pressure of the heat became too much for my weak seals.

He sat down on my stool only a few feet away from my lethal experiment, looking at the mask.

'Funny thing to wear. Is it poisonous?'

My wrist felt like it was breaking slowly. I could hear a whirring noise in my head. Panic was choking me. 'How does he know? How does he know? How does he know?' ran through my head. He dropped the mask. It clattered, and he kicked it so that it rolled across the floor like a football.

'It's not poisonous.' My voice was hoarse. 'It's just that the fumes irritate my throat, particularly if I've been working with them for hours.'

My fear had been that Roberto would see the adapted watering can and become suspicious as it was such an odd contraption. Chris seemed to have no idea what I was doing down here so didn't question its presence.

I turned my head to the window which I had purposely opened to maximise the ventilation before I'd started. Chris turned his body around to face the items on my workbench. The pain in my wrist was making me dizzy – or was it the lethal gas beginning to escape and take effect?

I had several pots and jars from my kit laid out on the table. These were the things I'd been using to provide Roberto with enough of a show to report back to Pierro on my progress.

'Is this important?' Chris asked about one of the patination chemicals.

'Yes.' I nodded breathlessly.

He pushed it off the bench so that it smashed on the

floor and the liquid ran into and out of the cracks in the stone paving.

'Anything to report?' he asked, sitting back with his arms crossed like a sales manager waiting for his monthly figures.

'Roberto is here all the time. He watches and checks constantly. I know he has told Pierro every detail about what I'm doing. I don't know what more you think I can tell you.'

My breathing felt laboured and the dizziness was becoming a spin. He got up and walked across to me. Reaching above me, he squeezed my wrist. The pain I was already in soared higher.

'Let's just say, I'm here to double-check,' he said into my ear, squeezing again.

I began to see the dazzling lights on the periphery of my vision again. Darting on and off, they grew wilder and multiplied. Suddenly their frenzy peaked, and darkness swooped in and drowned out the lights. I lost consciousness.

IT COULDN'T HAVE BEEN MORE than a few seconds that I was out, because Chris was only a step away from where he had been, but now I was no longer inside my body. Instead, I was an onlooker of the scene.

I saw my body slumped against the wall with one arm held up at an odd vertical angle. I watched as the slumped figure lifted her head and looked directly into the face of Chris.

His reaction was unexpected. He leapt back from me, stumbling into the chair. I couldn't believe this face was my own. Apart from the swelling and bruises, the expression was enraged, and the irises were completely unnatural. Instead of a warm brown, they were lit up like rings of fire. I didn't recognise myself. These fiery eyes and the fearless anger which was radiating from my body couldn't hail from me.

'Well, report this,' I spat the words rather than spoke them, 'if you don't turn that blowtorch off, you will kill everyone in this building.'

Intensity blazed from my body. I saw the heat of it burn Chris's cool control of the situation and a flicker of doubt cut across his face. He threw a wary glance at the fireplace.

'Why? What is it?'

I watched, completely shocked at what I was seeing play out. My tethered body lunged forward against my restraint, almost barking like an angered dog.

'I'm making the Philosopher's Stone, for God's sake. You come down here asking me what I'm doing like I'm making a bloody cake. You can report to Pierro that I'm killing myself trying to make a mythical substance in a dungeon rather than a laboratory.'

He looked shocked and unsure at the turn the interview was taking. My body stood shaking with rage, but my eyes looked powerful and dangerously insane.

'If the seals go on my container from the pressure of that heat, the gas that will leak out is flammable. It will blow us all to high heaven – that I can assure you of.'

Then I watched as my figure slumped back against the wall, chin on my chest.

Chris looked around a bit desperately. He stepped over to the fireplace and extinguished the blowtorch. He moved away from me and the fireplace, as far as he could, and stood for a moment, obviously considering how to proceed.

Apart from the pain I had anticipated that this interview would bring, I had been worried he may have had time to look into my illness and realised it was bogus. One thing was now clear, though: whatever he might decide to do next, his body language showed no inclination to touch me.

Roberto's footsteps interrupted Chris's thoughts. He was back much earlier than usual from his meal.

'Vic said you were down here meddling.' He sounded very annoyed. 'I don't interfere with your role, so I would appreciate it if you didn't interfere in mine.'

Chris walked to the cell door, looking more casual than he probably felt, and let himself out. Roberto had taken his usual place, sitting at his desk.

'You couldn't do my role,' Chris said scornfully.

'Yet you have done an excellent job as far as I can see. I left her working purposefully, and now she's unconscious. Brilliant strategy. Her already damaged arm will be even worse, which will really enable her to get on with what we need her to do.'

Chris continued past the desk and up the stairs. 'Yada, yada, yada, you're like an old woman,' he muttered.

Roberto was in the cell within seconds, cutting my hand down from its noose. My body fell to the floor, and he part lifted, part hauled me to my bed. He stood over me for a minute, and then went to check my pulse. Satisfied, he returned to his desk and left me to recover.

30

W hen I came round, it was morning. I had lost a whole evening and night of work. Roberto was at his station. My head ached and my wrist burned. I opened my eyes, but stayed still on the bed.

Both my eyes registered a glowing circular halo as if I'd been staring directly at a ring of bright light. It must have been something to do with the way my irises had lit up last night. I blinked and closed my eyes, trying to make it go away, but it was still there even with my eyes closed.

Problems seemed to be piling up. Turning on to my back to stare at the ceiling, I rubbed my aching temples. I had escaped my own body yesterday. Again, fear had driven something impossible to occur in me. Yet, the sensation of my mind stepping away from my body had felt oddly familiar, but I couldn't place why that should be.

Roberto moved his chair a little and coughed. I decided to sit up and stretch my neck. He had left a tray of bread, butter and juice for me on the workbench while I slept. I went through the motions of eating, but the frustration of not knowing the answer to something, and at the same time being certain I did know it, became unbearable. My hands, wrists and head were hurting now, so I got up and rifled through my tool kit where I kept my painkillers, which I noticed were beginning to run low.

As I held the pills, it came to me. The sensation had felt familiar because, like taking these pills, I'd done it many times before. Hadn't I practised Father Christopher's meditations over and over this year until I could fix an image in my mind and then move around it with ease? Last night, it had felt exactly the same as that. Maybe, the alchemy had stretched my mind too far and it had pulled away from its tether.

That was a worrying thought, and to compound the worry, I was reminded of the alchemist I'd originally come to Italy for. The Crowman had written about his mind diverging from his body in the diary I had found in the catacombs. I had thought he had been talking about a dream, but in light of my recent experience, it may be a side effect of being an alchemist.

'What's in the watering can?' Roberto's question brought me to my senses. I'd actually forgotten about what I'd been brewing in the fireplace the night before. I glanced at it uneasily; he'd obviously noticed my contraption last night.

'Nothing. Just trying to distil something, but Chris ruined it. Let it burn. Thankfully, it wasn't important – just tried it on a whim. I'm going to begin practising the meditation today,' I said, trying to change the subject. 'I don't think I can do too much physical work; my wrist is excruciating.'

'Getting late for whims, isn't it?' Roberto raised an eyebrow.

My skin felt clammy.

'Well, I am desperate,' I said in a high, breathy voice. Please don't let my eyes burn, I thought.

He nodded and didn't probe further, thankfully. I unclenched my hands slowly. I'd already talked to him about the role meditation would play in the final transformation; I'd described, in detail, how vital it was that I wasn't disturbed at all when the time came. My plan was to rid myself of Roberto's presence earlier than usual on the night of my escape by pretending to begin the meditation. He had taken this request to Pierro, and it had been accepted.

I walked over to the shelves, purposely moving slowly so that I could take a look at the state of the watering can without apparent care. What I thought I saw made me want to stop and look properly, but I forced myself to move past.

I thought I had seen something in the bottom of the container that I'd placed under my long, wavy tube. As I'd told Roberto I felt too sore to work, I could hardly busy myself with it now. Instead, I ignored it and went to sit on the bed in a mock mediation.

That morning was agonising. I had to stay as still as possible, but what I was desperate to do was run over to the fireplace. I couldn't help fidgeting, and Roberto noticed my unrest, so I made a show of holding my wrist, which was actually throbbing, and looking frustrated before starting over.

At around eleven o'clock, a loud motorised whirring noise could be heard, and eventually Roberto went up to investigate. As soon as he did, I jumped up and went over to the fireplace.

In the bottom of the jar was a clear liquid, and much more than I'd planned to form.

I couldn't believe what I was seeing. I felt exhilaration comb across my skin, lifting every hair to attention. Even if I hadn't been disturbed by Chris, I'd had only the slimmest expectation that any liquid would form. The inaccuracies, the ridiculous equipment, my inexperience, all added up to failure rather than success, and yet I was looking at a liquid which must be the result of fusion of the compounds I had put in place.

I screwed the lid on and placed the jar among several of the solvents within my kit. Roberto returned, bringing with him an early lunch for me. He could see I had moved, and he was in a chatty mood.

'Vic has gone and bought an electric helicopter,' he told me as I ate. 'It's fantastic, but I told him you need quiet so he's going to do it in the other field. Pierro will be so mad if he finds out.'

I needed to get the key finished. If I could actually unlock the door, then a whole wave of other problems would rush to meet me. I assumed it was either Vic or Chris who watched the camera at night when Roberto left. I had noticed from watching from my window that Vic – who preferred to amuse himself outdoors – wasn't out every day, but every other day. This supported the theory that Vic and Chris took the camera watch in turns.

If Vic or Chris were faithfully watching the camera, I would have no chance. I had decided that around 3am would be the safest time to make my break. With any luck, whichever one was supposed to be viewing would be a little less attentive at that time.

I had the layout of upstairs sufficiently clear in my mind from the few times I'd been up there, but I had no way of knowing whether the main door would be locked at that time or not. If it were, my only option would be to get back to my cell as soon as possible. This scenario, which was extremely likely, was a bad one as there was no possible mode by which I could get through such a titanic door.

I prayed that Roberto would have plenty to do upstairs

today so that I might keep working on the key. It did look like the master key by now. I had taken every opportunity to stare at Roberto's key when he brought me my food or my washing.

For show, I ceremonially painted coatings of sacramental wine on to the patinated spelter and made up ridiculous mixtures of mercury and wine. I also passed the time apparently taking notes from the book Marco had given me.

Although I willed Roberto to leave all day, he had very few errands. It was not until late afternoon that he actually went upstairs. I quickly stepped over to the gate and slipped the key into the lock with a shallow breath. I turned the key, and this time it clicked. My heart soared. I turned it back again – click – and forward again – click: an amazing sound.

Footsteps on the stairs surprised me; I hadn't expected Roberto back so soon. I hid the key quickly.

To my surprise, Roberto handcuffed me to himself and led me upstairs to Pierro, who was enthroned on a tall-backed carved chair with tapestried cushions. Vic and Chris were in the room. My heart began to beat really fast in my chest. I didn't want my eyes to change or my viewpoint to alter as had happened yesterday with Chris. Pierro would be euphoric, seeing anything out of the ordinary as confirmation of my ability.

I tried to slow my breathing.

'It seems all you needed was a little encouragement. You have been working very hard, I'm told. Though I must say, you are not looking well.'

Pierro considered me, studying the blush of bruises on my face, pale skin and red-rimmed eyes. I kept my hands behind my back. He stood up and walked across to me. Suddenly, he reached up and stroked the hair away from my cheek. I tried to turn my face away, but he held it, looking me in the eye.

'Roberto has been telling me about your eyes.' I shuddered, but kept my breathing slow.

'I get migraines.'

This was all I offered as explanation.

'*Povera,*' he said, turning his lips down in a frown as if in sympathy.

An idea suddenly came to me.

'Would I be allowed, with escorts, to take a walk outside? I haven't been outside for days. Please.'

Pierro stood up and walked away from me as he considered my request. 'Yes, with escorts. You know, *cara,* if you manage what we require from you, your life will not be as hard as it is now. There will be perks for your achievements.'

I nodded.

'Go ahead then.'

He signalled for Chris and Vic to take me out. I made sure we walked very slowly out of the door so that I could study it as much as possible. I couldn't see any keyhole as such. There were two slide bolts and a large lift latch that was common on garden gates.

We moved around the building and into the garden at the back. Neither Chris nor Vic spoke to me, which was a relief. I had the feeling that they knew Pierro was watching them and me.

We made only one circuit of the garden, and then I requested to go back so that I could look at the door from outside. Again, I saw no keyhole, but its vastness was intimidating. Its design said, '*I am a fortress; you will not enter.*' I just hoped it wasn't such a stickler for not letting people exit.

Pierro greeted us at the door.

'Back so soon?' he questioned.

'I am too weak to walk far, but it was good to be outside,' I said, forcing a slight smile.

He seemed pleased that I was weak, and I was happy to let him think I was more pathetic than I really was.

Vic and Chris took me back to the cell where I sat on my bed and made my final plans. I didn't want Chris to be on guard when I made my escape. I knew Vic had been outside early that morning which suggested he had not been up all night, so it seemed likely to be Vic's turn on duty tonight.

I would try tonight. I squirrelled away some small articles which I felt might help me if I made it out, including my passport which was in the outer pocket of my suitcase in preparation to go to New York. I didn't want to carry too much which would be noisy or slow me down, but I would take a few choice items, including the sickle-shaped knife.

At seven o'clock, I told Roberto that I was going to begin meditation again. Pierro had prevented him from going to dinner at his usual time, and so he told me he would not return downstairs after his meal according to his usual routine. Instead, he switched on the camera and left me alone.

I LAY on my bed and waited for the room to grow darker, staying determinedly still. At first my mind sprinted away from me, running over what I had to do that night, and my heart jogged intermittently with nerves. I knew I had a long time to wait so tried to calm myself and rest.

I hadn't anticipated how hard it would be to stay still for a significant length of time. I wanted to keep looking at my watch and fidget with nerves, but I fought hard to control the impulse. The camera's view of me was slightly obscured, but I didn't want whoever was watching to catch any movement in the cell. I wanted Roberto or Vic to become bored and pay less attention. I spent my time thinking of David: the way he touched my body so that it rippled with desire; the way his eyes creased with laughter; the way he ran his fingertips over my lips before he kissed them to double the sensation.

At 2.45am, the darkness outside was truly profound. I reached under my bed to where I had laid out my pots and poisons in readiness, inching the gilded metal from my pocket. Very slowly, I rolled on to the floor, staying crouched behind the workbench as much as possible. With my vinyl gloves on, I dropped the gilded ball into the cyanide mixture, then using a spoon, lifted it out and up on to the workbench.

I couldn't help holding my breath, both from the danger of the escape I was about to attempt and against the chemicals I was handling. With one of my patination brushes, I dropped more liquid on to the nugget so that the cyanide pooled beneath it. I was in a precarious position on my knees with my hands reaching above the surface. I was shaking so much that I ended up flinging the last drops of the mixture across my tools, which I had carefully laid out.

I crawled over to the periphery of the cell where the shadows were darkest. Following the stone walls, I met the bars of the cell. Two steps and I was over to the door, directly in front of the camera. If anyone was watching, they would see me escape.

I forced the key into the mouth of the lock, but it didn't slot in straight. My hands had little grip in the gloves so I pulled them off, bandages too. Sweat was forming on my head; my hands were shaking and numb. This awkward incompetence felt familiar – straight from nightmares. I tried hard to concentrate, and then the key slotted in and turned.

I stepped out and locked the door behind me. Shooting past the camera, I gained the stairs, stopping on them to breathe for a second. Blood was crashing about in my ears, making echoing noises which made me think, for a second, that someone was running in the room above, coming to stop me.

I continued to move up cautiously. The room above with its beautiful tapestries was dark. As silently as I could, I went through the wooden door and into the hallway where my next adversary stood.

The gargantuan door looked very much like a drawbridge. The slide bolts were open, so I took hold of the simple iron latch in the centre, lifted it and pulled. With the most surprising grace, the colossus swung obediently open. I had envisioned a huge struggle with the door, and its willingness to comply amazed me.

I stepped out into the cool night air at precisely the same moment as Vic walked in. We bounced off each other. He was just throwing a cigarette away and the smoke wafted between us. He looked as shocked as I was, but where my face must have registered fear, his looked confused. He regained his composure quicker than I did. Instantly, he reached out and gripped my left arm.

I dropped to my knees.

'Please,' I begged. 'Please...what he's asking me to do is impossible.'

He stayed in the same position, considering me for a second. With my other hand, I reached into my pocket.

'What are you doing?' he asked with irritation.

'Please, take this.' On the palm of my hand was the

diamond my parents had given me. Severed from its shank, the heart-shaped diamond didn't look as splendid as it had once done, but Vic clearly recognised a quality diamond even without a ring.

'It's very valuable,' I said. 'A 5 carat colourless diamond. Please let me go.'

He might have made a grab for it and taken it anyway, but I could probably have thrown it into the sea of stones around us before he got it. I'd rather lose it than give it to him without some return.

Suddenly, he let go of my wrist and moved to whisper in my ear.

'You are English, is that right?' I nodded. 'You like foxhunting in your country?'

I had no idea where he was going with this.

'I think we will have a game of English foxhunting tonight. Your diamond will buy you a little start, and then we will catch you. It will be fun – don't you think?'

His blond hair fell in front of his eyes, and I closed my hand over the diamond.

'Payment first,' he demanded and held out his hand.

I released the breath I'd been holding for what felt like an age and dropped the diamond into his large hand.

He gave me a push. 'Run, little fox, run. You don't have long,' and he went inside.

31

I sprinted across the pebbles and darted into the woods which were close to the house. I was running frantically, wildly, with the sort of fear that most people only ever know in their dreams. Too quickly, the wood ended, and I looked out over the immense landscape.

I could see why Vic had little fear that I would escape. The fields were wide and bare. There was a pylon in the next field across and, illogical as it may sound, I ran for that only because it was made of metal.

Running as fast as I could across the field, I heard Pierro's dogs barking and looked over my shoulder. Lights were on all over the palazzo. I realised how exposed I was and veered off to a ditch that ran along the periphery of the field. I moved much more slowly along the ditch, but was at least out of plain sight.

I made it to the pylon and stood beneath its enormous legs, pressing myself against it while I took in great gulps of air. People were moving around the house; they weren't that far away. Then I heard the roar of bikes, and two quad bikes jumped up as they accelerated over a little mound and tore across the field before mine.

Where could I go? In my cell, I had thought about making it to the phone box, but that was ridiculous with all these people chasing me. The quad bikes swept to the left of the field, and I broke my cover and ran towards a rockier area a little further ahead of the pylon. The darkness shielded me a bit as I ran up a bank and found an area that dropped down on the other side. I could climb down, but there didn't seem to be any obvious ledges, and I could hear the quad bikes coming nearer.

In panic, I dropped from the bank. It wasn't far down, but I landed awkwardly on my hands. Instead of pain, I felt the most unexpected sense of safety. My fingers were directly in contact with the earth and they felt like they were home.

I ripped off the cotton wadding that was protecting the cuts and touched both my hands to the ground; the feeling intensified. Then I heard the quad bikes again, this time very near me, and scrambled into a fissure between two rocks next to me.

The noise stopped. Someone was talking just above me while obviously looking over the bank. I squatted between the rocks with my hands on each one, feeling oddly calm. I heard swearing above me and the bikes being fired up again. They sounded as if they were being driven along the edge of the bank.

I didn't want to go out again. Behind me was very dark, and it was clear the rocks went back much further than I'd thought. I pressed my hands against the walls again, wondering why they felt so familiar. Then I felt the itch that always came after I'd worked on bronze. There was copper in these rocks.

I went a few steps deeper into the fissure; it was darker than any dark I had ever been in. I had heard of people who explore potholes moving through the veins of caves and had always thought they must be eccentric types, like mad scientists. I knew it was a dangerous activity, but I also felt safer in this pitch darkness with its unknown residents than I did outside.

I went to the front of the rocks again and looked out. I could see a flatter area. Suddenly, Chris and Roberto walked directly on to it. I pulled back between the rocks hastily, but I could still hear them talking. They had with them the two dogs, who were barking madly. I had no idea whether guard dogs were any good at tracking, but I felt the need to move as far away from the cave entrance as I could.

'The cell was closed, and I'm the only one with keys, so no-one could have let her out,' said Roberto.

The dogs were barking really obsessively now.

'Shut up,' Chris shouted at them, and yanked their chains. The dogs took no notice.

'I hope we find her, or Pierro is going to kill us – he hates incompetence. She played some prank on him, gilding a piece of bronze. He's wild. Can't you shut those dogs up?' Roberto snapped.

Chris was quiet for a minute.

'Maybe they're trying to tell us something,' he said.

I suddenly considered making a run for it, and was just about to take my first step when rapid gunfire stopped me moving. I felt sick. One of them had been firing at something below me.

'Just checking she's not in there,' said Chris.

'And potentially killing her if she is,' said Roberto. His voice sounded annoyed as it often did when he spoke to Chris.

'Does it matter? If she's gilding bits of metal, she obviously can't do it,' said Chris.

Though I was frozen with indecision about whether to bolt or hide, I felt an absurd surge of pride. I was an alchemist. In all the plotting and preparation to escape, this incredible fact had taken a back seat.

'I don't know. There's something unusual about her,' I heard Roberto reply.

'I'll say. Have you seen the state of her hands? She's got some disease.'

Chris's voice oozed loathing. Then there was some shouting coming from above.

'Get up here now!' It sounded like Vic. 'Quick, we need you. Come quick!'

The two men moved away from the rocks, and I held my breath while the echoes of the dogs' barks got further away. Without even a trace of remorse, I hoped the poison was working.

I slipped out from the fissure while the distraction was going on above, making my way down to the lowest rocks where Chris and Roberto had been talking. The desire my brain had to move quickly was completely opposed to what my body was capable of doing; fear was impeding every movement.

There was a hole in the rock, but this was no cave. A man couldn't stand fully inside it, but it was too large for any animal. Like the cave I had just been in, it looked very dark.

I moved inside a little way, and pressed my hands against the walls. The sensation of safety and, most of all, familiarity echoed through my senses. I stepped in deeper and spread my fingers apart against rough, pock-marked rocks that I couldn't see, but could only feel. I willed the walls to give me an answer as to why I felt safe when I'd never been in more danger.

My heartbeat slowed slightly; copper was the only thing in the world that made me feel like this. My blood was singing to it in the rocks all around me. This was an ancient copper mine; this was no industrial enterprise.

I could feel a strong breeze pulling through the tunnel. Without an exit at the other end, the air couldn't be drawn through like this. I made my decision in a heartbeat and moved inside. Closing my eyes, because trying to see made it harder somehow, I placed my dirty, shredded hands against the rock walls and walked further into the throat of the mine.

The floor was marsh-like, very wet, and I kept sinking down to my knees. Several times I tripped. There were large webs that I walked into and silken things my face brushed past. Every time I let my fear surface, I felt like I was drowning. At those times, I laid both my hands on the walls, and just thought about the feeling of security they gave me. This was my metal's mother and it was protecting me.

I tried not to think about what I would do if I got to the other end and it was blocked; I just concentrated on the strong breeze. That had to be a good sign.

It was a long, slow progression, and I completely lost the concept of time. At first, I thought the strain had induced the strange glimmering in my eyes to begin again, but then I realised I was seeing glimmers of light from the outside. I rushed forward to meet them.

The exit was sealed with a large steel grill made up of horizontal and vertical wires that bisected each other. I could easily place four fingers inside the squares they made. Though the wires were deceptively slender, I knew they would be immensely strong.

I pushed at the barrier, but it stood firm. I couldn't see any fixings so they must be on the outside. I tried bending the base, but it was rigid. The floor would be softer than the steel. I got out my penknife and dug a little.

Adrenaline had fuelled me so far, but my long, slow trudge through the mine, hunched over, had left me completely exhausted. There was a fringe of grass beyond the exit of the tunnel, and then a road. No car had passed so far, but I didn't want to be seen, so I moved back into the deep darkness of the tunnel to rest. I closed my eyes and longed for water.

It might be that dark places breed dark thoughts, because in a matter of seconds, I felt the guilt I'd been holding on to about Thérèse's death ignite and grow exponentially. Though I was far from safe, the guilt of surviving even this far when she had not threatened to suffocate me, and I had to take great gasping breaths which wouldn't satiate my lungs.

I was smacked by my selfishness which made the tears spring to my eyes. I could have saved her if I'd made different choices; if I'd shown willing and worked. My heart was beating very fast. I knew that this wasn't the time or place to have a breakdown, but I felt dangerously close to that precipice.

As I had done so many times in the cell, I pushed my mind towards solving a problem in order not to have to deal with the present. My mind trickled over the problem of overcoming the grill. I could only think of digging down, but what if the copper ran below as well as around me?

My mind began to settle. I laid out the few items I had brought with me: the sickle-shaped knife, a minuscule quantity of Pete's Potent Pickle, some rubber bands, and a small chisel. Both the knife and the remnants of the pickling solution might come in handy if I was under attack. Though I only had about 10ml of the pickling acid, it might be enough to blind someone.

I had been sharpening the knife before I'd begun my escape plan. Wondering if it would be sharp enough to make a small incision in the steel wire, I tried it at a corner point. It was not a hacksaw, but it did break the surface. Taking the pickling solution, I poured a couple of drops into the cap, and then on to the incision I'd made.

I reckoned if I could break through two points, I might be able to bend back the grill enough to climb out. I worked on another join, cutting into the steel as much as I could, dropping the acid on to the metal, and waiting. Then, I undertook the process again.

I WORKED like this for the remainder of the night and all the next day, until at last, one join gave. This pushed me on to finish the other. The knife was blunt and useless by then, the pickle gone. I threw these items into the tunnel so they might not be seen.

Even with two points cut through, bending back the wires was not easy in my weak state. Eventually, I managed to get one leg, then the other, and finally the rest of my body through. I bent the grill back to its closed position so that only careful observers would notice that it had been cut.

Dashing across the road and into another ditch, I looked over the land in front of me. There was a house a few fields over. I was so exhausted, there was no point in trying to run. I stayed close to the edge of the field and moved slowly up towards the house.

It was quite dark now. When I knocked on the door, an

elderly lady opened it. She looked terrified when she saw me.

'Please, help me,' I said in Italian. 'Please.'

She shouted to her husband, who came quickly. I must have looked terrible: dirty, bruised, bloodied. Cutting the grill had made my hands bleed. He stood firm, blocking the entrance.

'*Aiuto,* help,' I pleaded.

I think it was my desperation that frightened them. I couldn't imagine they wouldn't give someone help, but I was an unusual spectacle at night in that quiet landscape.

Though she had called for her husband, it was the woman who made the decision.

'*Guarda, stigmata, guarda!*' she shouted at her husband. *Look, the stigmata, look!*

She was pointing at my hands, her husband was looking, and suddenly I was inside. This was the first moment in my escape that I dared to think I might be safe. They gave me water and looked at each other concernedly, not knowing what to do with me. I asked to use the telephone and they nodded.

Terry answered within three rings. He began to gabble at me, but I stopped him.

'You need to come and get me now. I'll explain everything,' I said in as controlled a voice as I could manage.

I passed the phone to the lady so she could give him the address. Then the elderly couple showed me to the bathroom to wash, and I could hear them whispering outside. The word stigmata echoed through their talk. My hands, which I had so often cursed, had saved me again. I was happy to leave them to their beliefs if it kept me safe.

The lady made me some food, and kept staring at my hands while I ate. She asked me where I had been. I shook my head as I didn't know the answer, then managed to describe, '*Un palazzo, grand.*' I indicated a circular shape, tall like a castle. She seemed to understand.

Her husband came to sit down. He spoke some English.

'Palazzo Giaembro. Many, many years, many stories of bad things at Palazzo Giaembro. We call *Polizia*?'

He nodded. I couldn't really think clearly. Maybe that was the sensible thing to do, but some country policeman might be on Pierro's payroll and alert him to the call and my destination. I shook my head vigorously. They offered me a chair in front of the fire. Just waiting, I dozed for a while.

Suddenly, there was a knock at the door. I sprang from the seat and went towards it, but the old man pushed me back. He opened the door a little.

It was Chris. He spoke in rapid Italian. The familiar feeling of fear that had been my companion for so long was back in every muscle of my body. I moved back into the room and slid down the wall to hide behind the dresser. I wasn't sure what yarn Chris was telling, but I could tell the old man was becoming unsure. He kept glancing in my direction, and didn't answer straightaway when Chris came to the end of his explanation.

'Where are you from?' the man asked him. I understood that.

'Palazzo Giaembro,' Chris replied.

Then the man was shaking his head, and I could tell he was saying no to the enquiry, but Chris must have had some sense that he was lying. Chris wedged his foot in the door, and then propelled the elderly man back by leaning into it. It happened in an instant, and I wasn't well hidden.

I screamed as he came towards me and tried to avoid him. He grabbed me and lifted me off the floor.

'Please, help me,' I shouted at the people, but they were

completely struck dumb and clearly had no idea how to handle this vast man.

Chris carried me out as I kicked unproductively at him. As soon as we got outside, he spun me around and shook me. I felt the vertebrae in the back of my neck grind together.

'You stupid bitch,' he shouted at me. 'How the hell did you do it? He's dead. Pierro's dead.'

I suddenly took in his appearance. He wasn't just dishevelled from a night and day of searching. There was blood on his shirt and other less specific stains which were bile-like in shade. There were wide wet patches under his arms and his eyes looked unnaturally shiny, like he'd taken something. I stopped kicking and went still.

'What did you say?' I asked to buy myself a second to process the news, but he misinterpreted my response.

I saw a flicker of doubt run across his face. Though everything pointed to me, he clearly couldn't credit me with the capacity for murder. This was a sobering thought coming from such a heinous man.

He turned and shoved me towards the car which was in the driveway. I staggered and dropped on to my knees. He pinched my whole arm between his fingers, and I scrabbled to get away from his grip.

Dumping me in the front seat, which was littered with old newspapers and cigarette boxes, he bound my hands and feet with his favourite accessory: the cable tie. He slapped me a couple of times with his heavy hands when I resisted.

I hoped the elderly couple had called the police and turned my head to see if I could see them. Chris walked around to his side of the car coolly. He sat at the steering wheel and put both hands upon it, speaking to the wheel rather than me.

'You've caused us serious problems. I am in a position to make a decision. Can you do what Pierro believed you could do? Can you change lead into gold?'

I knew whichever answer I gave would result in the same outcome. I didn't want to prolong what was inevitable, so I lied.

'I can't.'

He started up the engine. 'We'll just go for a little drive, I think, maybe take a walk in the woods.'

Tiny shards of splintering glass cascaded through the air. I felt the glass slice my skin in a dozen places and the released blood escape down my face. It felt wonderful, because I had seen the perpetrator before I experienced the sensation. Only one man in the world had bronze knuckle-dusters that were as beautiful as they were lethal.

Chris was momentarily stunned, giving Terry enough time to unlock the door and haul him outside. I didn't see quite how much devastation those knuckledusters caused, but as Terry lifted me gently and carried me to his car, there was a mosaic of blood across his hands.

32

I 've discovered that gold is a sleepy metal. Touching it makes me want to close my eyes and drift off the way I might after a leisurely Sunday lunch. It's quite unlike my good friend bronze, which I would describe as a busy metal. Bronze is always doing something: a statue goes green; a penny tarnishes; a doorknob gains a dappled patina.

I remember only snippets of the days that followed after Terry rescued me. Terry's presence seemed to wrap around me: a cloak of safety, which allowed the weariness of so much work and strain to come to the fore.

When I did wake, it wasn't long before my fingers sought the reassurance of the nugget of gold nestling in my pocket. That's when its sleepy character took effect, leading me back to unconsciousness where I might heal most rapidly.

I wasn't very coherent in the car. I was in bad shape, but one look at Terry's face told me that he had suffered as much as I. He rubbed his eyes constantly, forcing out even the most tenacious of his remaining lashes. His usually

immaculate attire sank on his body like a drunken companion. It was unbearable to see what I'd done to him.

I did manage to tell Terry about what had happened to
Thérèse, but not why. He wanted to know every detail about
her death, and I told him all I was certain of. I could see him
being temporarily released from the grip of despair by the
fury that was gathering within him. Even in my dulled state,
I recognised the similarity between that and the release I
had experienced in my cell the night I had handled the iron
bars and felt them speak to me. At that point, I remember
having a sudden desperate compulsion to make sure I
hadn't lost the fateful piece of gold. Terry must have noticed
my frantic scrabbling, and then instant peace as I made
contact with its surface.

My next recollection was of Terry carrying me like a
child in his arms. My face was pressed against his chest and
he whispered that I had to tuck my bloodied hands beneath
the breast of his coat to prevent them drawing more attention to us. My lacerated hands found a gun and holster to
rest upon.

I was dimly aware of being back in Venice, but not at
Giudecca. There was a small man with fair hair waiting for
us on a doorstep; Terry passed me across to him. My eyes
closed again. I felt Terry brush the hair away from my face.
He bent his head to give me a shaky kiss.

'David is on his way,' he said gruffly. 'She needs a doctor,
Geoffrey,' he told the man, whose body I felt nod in agree-
ment. 'You can trust him, I promise,' Terry whispered to me.
'He's an old friend.'

As he moved to step away, I knew there was something
really important I needed to tell him. It was about Pierro: a
reason Terry didn't have to leave, but my thoughts kept
slamming to a halt like a train running out of tracks. I

became very upset, thrashing around in poor Geoffrey's arms, glimpsing his hazel eyes looking panicked.

I grabbed Terry's shoulder.

'I need to go now, angel,' he said calmly. 'Otherwise they'll scatter.'

Like a child wanting its security blanket, I let my tears run and my hand sought the gold.

THE NEXT THING I remember is being woken by the sound of church bells chiming outside a small gabled window. I was in an attic room clad with wooden panels. My whole body felt in much less pain. My hands had been professionally dressed with only my fingertips and thumbs exposed.

A man was looking out of the window; he had broad shoulders. My intake of breath made him swing round, and my heart bounced with excitement as I realised it was David.

He was by my side in seconds and his eyes were full of tears. He knelt down next to the bed and laid his head on me.

'What a mess, Abi.' He drew me into his arms.

Tears sprang to my throat and I threw my arms around him. 'You thought I hadn't come to New York,' I said.

This had been what had tortured me most when I'd allowed myself to think about David.

'Never. I knew you wouldn't have let me down.' His face was full of guilt. 'I should have listened to you.'

It was then I remembered my gold. The idea I might have dropped it, lost it, been separated from it, was like a thousand needles being jabbed into my skin.

David stroked my hair, trying to quieten whatever had

spooked me, and then I saw it on my bedside table. I grabbed at it, gripped it, and was soothed back to sleep by it.

A FEW DAYS LATER, David and I were driving at some speed along a coastal road, travelling to Lake Como. I felt very weak, but I was as keen as David to get there as it was the rendezvous point that Terry had arranged with him.

Geoffrey had not supported our haste. Although I had returned to longer periods of consciousness, clearly I was far from being well. He had been an extremely fastidious carer. In fact, much to David's annoyance, he had rarely left us alone, unless I was asleep. I had actually appreciated this as it meant I hadn't had to go into all that had happened yet.

As soon as we settled into the drive, the weight of the unexplained began to grow. I didn't want our new beginning to be with me keeping secrets again; I knew that my lack of communication had already tested David.

'I will tell you everything, David. Every last detail, but I want to tell Terry at the same time. I don't want to go through it twice.'

I could see him relax; his shoulders dropped. He laid his hand on the top of my thigh.

'How'd you know Terry isn't dead? He's obviously out for revenge. These people who killed Thérèse and abducted you may have killed him too.' He lifted his hand to his mouth and bit along the cuticle of his nail. 'I don't know what I'll do if Terry dies.'

'I don't think he will,' I said, shaking my head. 'Pierro is already dead. I killed him, and Terry must have done a lot of damage to one of the guards when he rescued me.'

'You killed Pierro?' he asked, in complete disbelief.

I nodded. 'Yes, poisoned him with cyanide.'

David's eyes grew wider and his driving became completely hazardous. I pushed myself into the flesh of the seat and turned my face into the breeze.

DAVID and I took a room in a hotel overlooking Lake Como. David told me Terry used to meet Thérèse here when she was modelling a lot in Europe. It was the most romantic spot possible: an ochre building with vines and clematis sprawling across its walls, and mature trees circling it. It looked directly on to the lake and each room had a stone balcony. The hotel was high up and the view of the surrounding region was epic.

David said that Terry attributed his success with such a stunning girl as Thérèse to this beautiful hotel. He'd apparently said it made even a shortish bullnecked thug like him look handsome.

Terry arrived a couple of days after us. He joined us on the public terrace looking more like his usual self – showered and shaved – and ordered a drink.

'You look a little less ghoulish now, Abi,' he commented. 'I should've stayed and taken care of you myself. It's what Thérèse would have wanted me to do. I'm sorry.'

I took his hand.

'You couldn't have been more attentive than Geoffrey. And David did an okay job too.'

David rolled his eyes and mouthed *thanks* sarcastically.

'It was a waste of time. I found absolutely nothing. The tower was as you described it, Abi, but the entire place had been cleared out. Whatever went on had been airbrushed. I searched the area – didn't find anything that looked like a grave – and hung around for a few days in case one of them came back, but they didn't.'

Terry's voice was emotionless.

In the fading sun, I told them my story, no omissions, no lies. At the end, I laid down in front of them the nugget of gold that had cost so much blood.

JOIN MY READERS' GROUP

WANT TO KNOW MORE ABOUT

THE GOLDEN ILLUMINATI?ALCHEMY
PATINATION
AND
THE ART THAT INSPIRES THE NOVELS?

JOIN MY READER'S GROUP AND RECEIVE EMAILS
FROM ME WITH CONTENT THAT DELVES DEEPER
INTO THE THEMES OF THE SERIES

Visit
www.lucybranch.com

FURTHER BOOKS IN THE SERIES

Want to read more in the Gold Gift Series? Want to know what happens to Abigail next?

RUST UPON MY SOUL

Robert Fitzpatrick is a member of The Golden Illuminati but he has a grudge. Abigail Argent remains their number one person of interest, but guilt and fear over what happened last year, mean she's struggling to know how to move forward with her life. When handsome architect, Robert, offers her a helping hand, she's naturally suspicious, but with very few options open to her, he persuades her to give him a chance.

Characters old and new come together to help her gain control of the gift that flashed into existence last year and form a plan to combat the most formidable secret society in history.

As Abigail's begins to learn more about her strange relationship with metal, and the Underworld she never knew existed. Robert's relationship with Abigail is going in a direction he could never have predicted and he finds himself having to grapples with difficult decisions.

Abigail is not unaware that Robert's intentions don't always stack up, but then again, it seems to be a common theme with all the people around her. Art and Alchemy clash in this thriller-romance where the dark side of the art world meets a classic myth.

'A dark story full of intrigue, conspiracy theory and art. For fans of Dan Brown, Andy McDermott and Kate Mosse.

GIRL IN A GOLDEN CAGE

She has an eye for detail but can she see the truth?

Francesca Milliardo sees something she wasn't meant to see. Her dreams of making a big splash as a contemporary artist are on the line if she's read the situation wrong. Worst still, her father seems to be involved. As Francesca searches for truth, her persistent migraines are beginning to run riot. Some of her symptoms are morphing and she's starting to wonder if there's more to the pain than a pill can cure.

Her father's handsome assistant is a welcome distraction from the confusion of her life, but can he save her from the dangers that lurk? Or, could he, too, be part of them? Francesca doesn't know whom to trust or what to do. It's time for her to make some hard choices. Believe in the people she loves or bet her beloved career on a mystery that's rooted in myth.

'A fast-paced mystery with a hint of supernatural and a dash of romance - Girl in A Golden Cage is a standalone story that introduces a new character into the Gold Gift Series.'

ACKNOWLEDGMENTS

I would like to acknowledge my parents who have had boundless faith in this project from the very start. Without them, I would never have brought it to fruition. I would like to thank my wonderful husband who has been entirely self-less, when I have been absorbed in writing, and encouraging when I really needed it. I would like to thank Catherine Bower who has been a true friend and always inspired me to go for it. Sincere thanks to Alison and Jim McLean who have supported me in every way during the last twenty years, which is when the idea for this book came to me. Finally, I am grateful to Dr Tracey Chaplin, a very helpful colleague, who gave me advice on the history of making hydrogen cyanide.

ABOUT THE AUTHOR

Lucy Branch lives in North London with her husband and three children. She is a restorer of public sculpture and historic features and has worked on some of the UK's most well-known monuments including Eros, Cleopatra's Needle and Nelson's Column. The passion she has for her work inspires her writing.

Lucy loves hearing from her readers so if you would like to drop her a line – please do!

Email lucy@antiquebronze.co.uk or go to Lucy's website www.lucybranch.com where you can become a member of her Readers' Group.

Being part of Lucy's Readers' Group gives you a chance to receive free copies of her new novels, hear about other authors' promotions and have a chance to share your passion for reading.

 facebook.com/lucybranchauthor
twitter.com/lucyBranch11.

Printed in Great Britain
by Amazon